UNDEFEATED

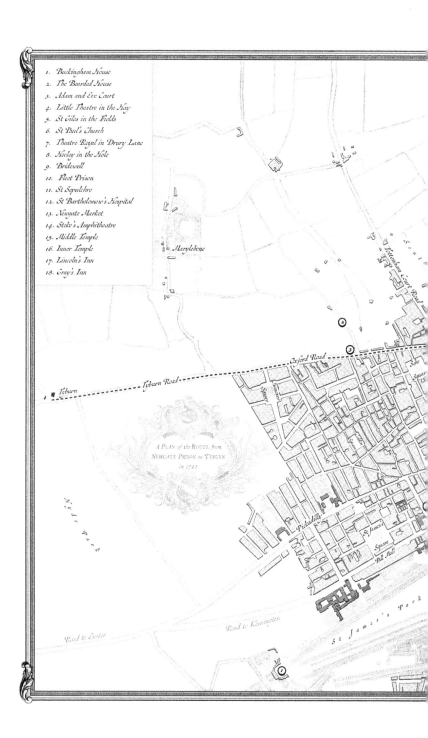

1. Buckingham House
2. The Bearded House
3. Adam and Eve Court
4. Little Theatre in the Hay
5. St Giles in the Fields
6. St Paul's Church
7. Theatre Royal in Drury Lane
8. Hockley in the Hole
9. Bridewell
10. Fleet Prison
11. St Sepulchre
12. St Bartholomew's Hospital
13. Newgate Market
14. Stoke's Amphitheatre
15. Middle Temple
16. Inner Temple
17. Lincoln's Inn
18. Gray's Inn

Marylebone

Tottenham Court Road

Oxford Road

Tyburn Road

Tyburn

A PLAN of the ROUTE from
NEWGATE PRISON to TYBURN
in 1722

Piccadilly

St James's
Square

Pall Mall

Soho
Square

Hyde Park

Road to Exeter

Road to Kensington

St James's Park

First published in 2024 by Gillie Basson,
in partnership with Whitefox Publishing

www.wearewhitefox.com

Copyright © Gillie Basson, 2024

ISBN 978-1-916797-60-4
Also available as an eBook
ISBN 978-1-916797-61-1

Edited by Jenni Davis
Designed and typeset by Karen Lilje
Cover design by Emma Ewbank
Map copyright © 2024 Jamie Whyte
Project management by Whitefox

A NOVEL

UNDEFEATED

Gillie Basson

Gillie Basson is a British-Canadian writer. She's a lawyer by trade (motivated by warm hugs, podcasts and wanderlust), a foodie and a workout junkie who started Thai kickboxing and Brazilian jiu-jitsu as part of her research into what it feels like to be punched, kicked, pinned down and thrown to the ground. *Undefeated* is her first novel.

She lives with her family and fur babies in Aberdeenshire, Scotland. When she's not out bagging munros, she is reading, writing or spending quality time with her girls.

She loves to connect with other creatives and discuss all things book-related. You can follow Gillie on Instagram at @gilliesbookaddiction.

For my family, and especially my girls, Eloise & Mia – be strong enough to forge your own path in this crazy world

Author's note

Very little is known about Elizabeth Wilkinson-Stokes. This novel is a work of fiction but inspired by a real person. It is intended as a story for entertainment rather than a biographical memoir.

The details of Elizabeth's life are obscure, and one can't help but wonder if the records are intentionally vague, given boxing was seen to be a male sport and unbecoming for a woman.

What we do know are dates: dates of some of her recorded fights, which span a six-year period between 1722 and 1728. I have used creative licence with the timing of these bouts for the purposes of the story. In addition, I had Robert Wilkinson's execution at Tyburn take place in the spring rather than autumn of 1722. Known dates are listed in chronological order on the next page.

It is also worth noting that some characters in this novel are real while others are fictitious, as are some of the locations, such as the Tippling House and The Black Hog. Street names are drawn from sources, but there are some conflicting citations when it comes to street names at that time, depending on the map. Similarly, some streets north of the Oxford Road – such as Henrietta Street – were not yet built, as urbanisation of the Marylebone area was still in its infancy. Real persons are listed on the next page. You can assume that all other names are fictitious for the purposes of the story.

Finally, a quick word about the legal system in London at this time. There was as yet no formal police force. In 1720, the Lord

Mayor served as the Chief Magistrate, who dealt with accusations of criminal offences and served as chairman of the criminal court, the Old Bailey.

The City of London was at that time divided into twenty-six city wards and each ward elected an 'Alderman'. An alderman was an administrative leader who sat on the Court of Aldermen, which included and was presided over by the Lord Mayor, who was elected every year, serving a term of twelve months.

Wards in the City of London were divided into precincts. At an annual meeting, all householders of a precinct had the right to choose a constable for the following year. Constables were unpaid, non-experienced ordinary citizens. They were considered ward officers, although they had authority to act anywhere in the City. A constable's general obligation was to preserve peace in his neighbourhood by preventing infractions that might lead to its being breached. They had the power to arrest, imprison and break into houses to carry out their duties. They could be accountable for illegal activity and fined for negligence but not general inactivity. Constables remained at home to be available to respond to requests for help.

As such, constables at this time were often corrupt and lazy.

Patrolling of streets during the day was a duty of city marshals and beadles. Marshals were salaried city officers appointed by the Lord Mayor and aldermen. Beadles also took to lighting the ward lanterns. The night watch were appointed and manned watch-stands, taking turns to patrol their designated area every thirty minutes. The watch house was a point of assembly and where anyone arrested would be held until the morning and taken before a magistrate.

Given the concern about high levels of crime in London in the late seventeenth century, the government adopted the practice of offering substantial rewards for apprehending and convicting individuals guilty of certain crimes. Known as the rewards system, it encouraged the development of more proactive policing, but also turned the practice into a business. Motivated by the prospect of a reward, many constables and ex-constables, and other law enforcement officials, worked hard to help victims find and prosecute the culprits who had wronged them. Some observed that the reward system created conflict between those seeking justice and those seeking financial gain and power. Indeed, dozens of men turned this into a business and became thief-takers, who engaged in multiple prosecutions in order to profit from the rewards, the most notable being Jonathan Wild.

Thief-takers used their knowledge of the criminal underworld to profit from both unofficial and official rewards. Thief-takers negotiated between thieves and the victims of thefts to return stolen goods in exchange for a fee. They also used their insider knowledge to inform on criminals and prosecute them at the Old Bailey. While this second activity facilitated the administration of criminal justice, more corrupt thief-takers went further: they blackmailed criminals with threats of prosecution if they failed to pay protection money. Some even became 'thief-makers' by encouraging gullible men to commit crimes, and then apprehending and prosecuting them in order to collect the reward. Such practices illustrate the point that not all 'crimes' prosecuted at the Old Bailey had actually taken place; some prosecutions were malicious.

Building on the practice of thief-taking, but attempting to control and legitimise the practice, Justice Henry Fielding established the

Bow Street Runners in 1749. Henry, and later his half-brother John, hired thief-takers and ex-constables on a retainer, and sent them out from their Bow Street office to detect and apprehend the culprit when a crime was reported. They became known as the 'Runners'.

With that being said, there were several notable persons who lived in London at the same time as Elizabeth. The following are of particular relevance in the context of this story:

- James Figg: prize fighter, trainer, promoter, known as the Father of Boxing and the first ever boxing champion;
- Jack Sheppard ('Honest Jack'): lovable rogue of a petty thief and prison escapee (hanged at Tyburn on 16 November 1724);
- Jonathan Wild (Thief-Taker General): ran a criminal empire alongside his work as a public-spirited thief-taker (hanged at Tyburn on 24 May 1725);
- William Hogarth: painter, engraver and pictorial satirist; he created his portrayal of the evils of gin-drinking, *Gin Lane*, set in the London parish of St Giles, in support of the Gin Act, passed in 1751;
- Moll King (born Elizabeth Adkins): a shrewd businesswoman who was a prominent figure in London's underworld during the eighteenth century. She owned King's Coffee House in London's Covent Garden with her husband, Tom King. She was, allegedly, a member of the notorious Jonathan Wild's gang of thieves and, while in Newgate, she met Daniel Defoe, who allegedly used her as the inspiration for *Moll Flanders*.

Make no mistake, Elizabeth was real – she fought in a brutal era of London's history and won, defying eighteenth-century gender roles. Courageous and tough, she proved there are no limitations to what a person can do. Remember her name, or don't – but my hope is that after reading this story, you are inspired to conduct your own research and form your own views. I, for one, am in awe of this woman, who forged her own path and made a name for herself at a time when London's underworld was cutthroat and brutal, with an inhumane legal system. It was a time of informers, spies, bullies, gangs and thief-takers ... and of the gin craze. After her last documented fight in 1728, she disappears from historical record as mysteriously as she entered it. When my dad told me about her, I knew I wanted to write a story about her.

Dates

23 June 1722
Elizabeth Wilkinson v Hannah Hyfield

June/July 1722
Elizabeth Wilkinson v Martha Jones

24 September 1722
Robert Wilkinson executed

8 August 1723
Elizabeth Wilkinson v Joanna Hatton/Heyfield

1 September 1725
Joseph Hamilton and Thomas Philips v Ned Sutton and George Bell

1 October 1726
announcement for forthcoming fight between Elizabeth Stokes v Mary Welch (it is not known if this fight ever took place)

17 July 1727
Elizabeth and James Stokes v Mary Welch and Robert Barker

7 October 1728
Elizabeth Stokes v Ann Field

Real people

Elizabeth Wilkinson-Stokes

Robert Wilkinson

James Figg

James Stokes

Tom and Moll King

Hannah Hyfield

Martha Jones

Joanna Hatton/Heyfield

Mary Welch

Robert Barker

Sir Gerard Conyers

Ann Field

CHALLENGE – *Whereas I, Ann Field of Stoke-Newington, ass-driver, well known for my abilities in boxing in my own defence wherever it happened in my way, having been affronted by Mrs Stokes, styled the European Championess, do fairly invite her to a trial of the best skill in boxing, for 10 pounds, fair rise and fall.*

ANSWER – *I, Elizabeth Stokes, of the City of London, have not fought in this way since I fought the famous boxing-woman of Billingsgate 29 minutes, and gained a complete victory, (which is six years ago); but as the famous Stoke-Newington ass-woman dares me to fight her for the 10 pounds, I do assure her I will not fail meeting her for the said sum, and doubt not that the blows which I shall present her with, will be more difficult for her to digest than she ever gave her asses!*

Source: *Daily Post*, 17th July 1728

CHAPTER 1

I REMEMBER THE FIRST time I hit someone.

Mary.

I was six years old. She was seven or eight. A ridiculous girl with silver-blonde hair, sea-blue eyes, strawberry lips and porcelain skin, who resided at the same orphanage as I did, one run by a sour wire of a woman called Mrs Dierdre. Mary was a human doll. The kind of girl who bounced everywhere she went. *Bloody bounced.* Who bounces in an orphanage?

A crow crows through the window, drawing me out of memory lane. To here. St Giles rookery. How many winters have I spent in St Giles now? It's been at least eight or nine. I can't remember: too drunk. Days merge into night, and nights turn into day, and in between I drink, fuck and fight. Not in that order. At least, not all the time.

Nothing but battered timber buildings joined together in the air like birds' nests in the highest tree branches. Air and privacy are as coveted here as bread and clean water. Crumbling tenements surrounded by doss-houses, gin shops and brothels. You're as likely to be robbed or beaten as you are to eat and sleep. I can't recall the last time any parish constable or beadle set foot here. Rubbish and excrement and dead dogs line the alleyways, only ever to be washed away by the rain, which pours down from broken gutters on rooftops. Unlighted and unpaved, the streets are airless due to the overcrowding of seedy bodies. This black hole, where shiftless good-for-nothings come to be entertained – criminals, prostitutes, drunks and immigrants. Bloody immigrants. Irishmen everywhere, piling in on top of each other like a verminous habitation. I hate the Irish. Have done ever since I worked at the Stockton Estate. And St Giles is the worst place to live when you hate the Irish. They're everywhere, just like the rats, drinking, breeding and spouting their holy beliefs while battering their women and children behind closed doors. Damn hypocrites.

I'm not a prostitute or an immigrant, and I wouldn't call myself a criminal (not today anyway), and my appetite for gin isn't something I care to dwell on. And I don't hit children, or women unless they want it. Ask for it. Or deserve it.

I hesitate. Thinking. My mind racing. I can't put my thoughts together. I know there is something there. My brain is trying to tell me something. The hairs on my arms and the back of my neck rise.

Hmph.

I force myself to focus on my surroundings. Yes. This makes sense. The back-alley den, opening onto Church Street, which looks more like a cow house than a room for people. This I know. It's familiar. And familiarity, I find, breeds a sense of comfort, even if it really shouldn't. Light bleeds through rags that have replaced the broken glass in the small square panes of the windows. Lanterns burn, flickering a golden glow. That precarious flicker, akin to life here in the rookery – rebellious, resilient but unreliable. The light no longer wishes to stay on here than the sun in the sky over London, with its forever passing clouds. One moment you feel safe, assured even, with visibility of what's coming next. Then, without warning, you're thrust into darkness, helpless to its wayward ways. The ground beneath my feet smells more like animal muck than soil. My eyes dart around the room.

What a hellhole.

Waiting. I'm used to waiting: for food, for drink, to piss and to fight. I'm not a spectator today. No sitting with the mob, cheering and cursing at whatever enters the pit. No. It is my turn today. The sludge of gravel and mud squelches beneath my boots.

Slish. Slosh.

My feet sink into the sludge as I move my weight. I bounce a few times, to see how far my feet drop – enough to satisfy my curiosity and boredom. The ground is cold, much like the gin bottle in my left hand. I take another drink, priming myself for what is to come. I hear the mob through the wooden planks, stomping their feet on the stalls as they wait impatiently for their next show. It's a private show, of course, not attended by high society – the sort who drink cups of hot tea and dine on venison. No, this show is for the ornery: the throwaways of society.

The air is thick; I can smell the people without seeing them. The stench of stale booze and filth is unavoidable when it's fight night. My mind drifts back to Mrs Dierdre. The woman sold me to Sir Frederick Stockton when I was only nine years old. An Irishman. I press my eyes shut, willing the memories to go away. They don't. They never do. Despite my efforts to drown them at the bottom of a gin bottle … or bottles. My breathing deepens and my palms start to sweat. I begin rubbing my fingers together and crick my neck. Nothing helps remove the images of my old guardian and possessor. So I do what I always do when I can't control my thoughts: I punch something. In this particular instance, the wooden door keeping me penned up like the animal that belongs in this back room bears the brunt of my anger.

It has the desired effect. The tips of my mouth quirk up.

It has to be said, I enjoy fighting. I like punching someone in the face. It's a useful release from everything else. All my life, it seems, all I've known is fighting. But fighting takes its toll on the body, which is a shame, because I'm good at it. I can't help but wonder when will be the last time I walk away from a fight.

'You – it's time,' a man barks at me from the door I just hit. My head automatically turns towards his voice, but I don't look at him. Distracted by my thoughts, I didn't hear the door swing open, but now the waves of noise from the spectators in the next room wash over me. I nod and finish the gin before tossing the empty bottle into the crate next to me.

As usual, I think of Mary. Of the day everything changed for me. That spoiled wretch had taken something of mine. I remember how my rage flapped around my head, like a frantic bird stuck in a cage, trying to find a way out. They rolled into fists, tightening without effort. My teeth clenched. By then, I didn't care if she apologised or not. I remember Mary turning her head to look at me. There was no escaping what happened next.

I hit her. Not in the way Mrs Dierdre hit us, with a stick across our palms. No, I hit her the way I had seen Mrs Dierdre's husband hit her before he abandoned her: with a closed fist. I hit Mary across her perfect cheek with as much force as I could. I heard the crack as my fist connected with bone. I felt the crunch beneath my knuckles as I swiped her perfectly smooth skin. I saw the fear in her eyes as she flew backwards. I had knocked the smile from her pretty face. Her head hit the ground and the other girls screamed, running away from me. I stood over the silver-blonde-haired, sea-blue-eyed girl with porcelain skin and watched as she cried. Bouncing from her sobs.

I got a lashing from Mrs Dierdre after, but it was worth it. Mary and all the other kids avoided me after that day. Pity.

Yes, I remember the first time I hit someone. And it felt fucking good.

Now. In the cold, dark, it's that time again. I don't hesitate. This moment is as ingrained in me as the ability to walk and breathe. I'd already piled my hair as tightly as possible on top of my head, but I hadn't stripped yet. I pull off my blouse. The cold air stings my breasts. The man by the door gawks, even though he's seen them before. Flesh and bone. That's all I am. *Better that than a prostitute*, my mind snaps.

I walk towards the door, leaving my garment on the floor. I push past the man into the next room, ignoring his protruding elbow, which brushes my nipple.

There's no need to look around as I enter the room. I know the set-up: drunkards sitting, standing, hanging from wherever they can to get a glimpse of the event. Drunk prostitutes singing and swaying; one has a baby dangling from her tit. Young boys weave in and out of the crowd, picking pockets as they dance around the unaware adults. The men huddle together in their groups, shouting, either at one another or at no one at all. Gambling is the order of the day, and fighting is the game. For where there is fighting, there's gambling and there's drinking. A wrought-iron basket hangs from the ceiling; in it sits a man – punished for not paying his debts, no doubt – hunched over in an uncomfortable and ignominious way, muttering his apologies. A warning for others. The noise is thunderous as spectators shout bets and roar abuse and encouragement at me, a contestant.

Robert will be in his usual spot, next to the bookkeeper above the entrance. I won't look at him, though, not until after the fight. I know what I have to do. What he wants. What the people expect.

As I approach the round enclosure, I see some men removing the corpse of a bear – something I will never understand. Bear-baiting, bull-baiting and even tiger-baiting! Cock fights, dog fights and prize fights – yes, I can see there is a certain appeal. But what is the appeal of watching a chained animal being torn apart by a pack of rabid dogs? It isn't a sport – it's savagery, but, then again, everyone has their vice. And mine is drinking and fighting other women … or men – I don't discriminate. But I can't dwell on my fellow Londoners and why they enjoy the things they do. There are important tasks at hand. Like survival. *My* survival. I say a silent prayer for the bear and then forget about the beast.

My opponent is already in the centre of the blood-spattered wooden enclosure, pacing and watching as the bear carcass is dragged away. I make it past the crowd, but not before being groped several times by a number of rowdy men. It's not admiration, but impatience.

'Nice teats!' one man shouts.

'Hurry up, wench!' another yells. I can't help it; my lips curl into a smirk. I know exactly what they want.

'Shut your gob, you wretched ass!' I shout back. I reach for the one closest and ram my head against his, knocking him to the floor. The people roar with laughter.

Before jumping the wooden fence that borders the centre circle, I grab another bottle, handed to me by one of the regulars, and take a gulp, tossing it back without thanks – realising too late that it's filled with brandy, not gin. Still, the cold booze trickling down my throat burns my insides, fuelling me. I clear the barricade and drop into the pit. The cheers ring in my ears. The sight of two bare-chested women about to fight sets the spectators off. This scene gets most of them excited. My ears don't register the grunts and heavy breathing any more.

Once inside the pit, I don't let the baying mob distract me from my opponent. While the woman continues to pace around, I stand still, looking her up and down. She isn't as tall as me, but very few women are. I can see the woman has been in battles before. The scars on her torso and arms are as evident as the fear in her eyes. This should be easy.

Should.

A boy standing on the wooden fence, balancing against an elderly man's head – he looks half-dead – shouts to the audience that our fight is about to begin. Most ignore him – too riled up and energised to pay him any heed. I glare at my opponent, a woman I now know is called Sally, thanks to the young tyke. He hops down and that is it. Our fight begins.

There is no waiting. I raise my fists, ready to strike, and launch myself across the several feet of mud between us. Sally reaches out to grab at me but I'm too quick. I feint, side-step and land a quick left-hand punch on the woman's cheek, cracking it immediately.

Sally stumbles back a few paces as I press forward. I hit her another two times across the face: the second blow busts the woman's nose and blood pours down her mouth and chin. A deafening rumble ripples through the audience.

I bob from side to side, focusing on my opponent's movements, then throw a right hook, which connects with her left cheek. I don't stop. I continue my assault as I chase her across the dirt to the other side of the enclosure. In a desperate attempt to defend herself, the woman throws her left fist, catching my jaw. It hurts like hell but not as badly as the bite that follows. The woman sinks her teeth into my right shoulder.

I scream as I feel my flesh being pierced by her jaws. She latches on and doesn't let go. She begins clawing at my skin, scratching my back, neck and arms. I have to get her off me, preferably without her taking a chunk of my shoulder with her.

With all my strength, I wrap my arms around Sally and swing her over my hip; my own body weight throws her off balance to the muddy ground. The landing knocks me free of her bite, as I had hoped. Sally jumps to her feet. It seems she isn't going to be beaten that easily. And she is a biter. Lucky me.

Ignoring the pain, I wipe blood from my shoulder where Sally's teeth punctured my skin, and then turn to face the woman. The people are shouting for more. So I answer them – I lick the blood from my fingers and smile at my opponent.

She yells and runs towards me, but I move out of the way, grab her neck as she passes and, using the momentum, smash her head down on the wooden planks of the pit enclosure. Her head bounces back and she falls to the dirt. Before she has a chance to push herself up I jump on top of her, straddling her stomach and punching her head, ribs and chest – anywhere she isn't protecting. Over and over and over again, I rain punches until I hear the woman's chin crunch. Her arms go limp, no longer defending against my attack.

Confident the fight is over, I stop my assault and spit at the woman. I stand up and take a few paces backwards. I'm livid at the bitch for biting me, but I don't wish her dead. She is here for the exact same reasons as me and, despite what this mob thinks they know, it takes a certain type of woman to enter the pit and fight. Men, sure – it's widely accepted. But women? No.

Not yet, anyway.

But here in St Giles rookery? Well, anything goes. Something as taboo as females fighting adds to the interest. The secrecy of it all. I'm not complaining, as more people coming to watch me fight means more money being thrown in the hat. And I'm going to win. Every time. The alternative is too grim to contemplate. No. I won't go there. No one is beating me.

I will the woman not to move; if she wants to have any chance of recovering, she'll remain firmly on the cold, damp earth.

Just. Stay. Down.

My breathing is heavy, like the weight of my arms. I want the fight to be over. I'm ready to leave and put my blouse back on. I need a drink to ease the pain. But then, to my horror, Sally stirs. She looks up. She looks around and her eyes meet mine.

Damn.

I know that look. It's the look of fear: not fear of me, not of what is happening right now, but of what will happen to her later. This is a brutal sport, but husbands can be crueller. Afterwards. When no one is watching. No one to step in and end things. To call the fight and end the violence. The pain.

Sally realises what is coming as soon as she locks eyes with mine. I press my eyelids shut. The mob is chanting, 'Finish her! Finish her! Finish her!'

I instinctively look up at Robert. He nods. He wants me to please the crowd. And I have to please him. I take a deep breath. I have to do it. There is no choice in the matter. No mercy.

So I do what I have to do, yet again. I trot forward, gathering pace, and begin kicking and stomping on Sally with all my might until I am certain she is unconscious: on her face, her chest, stomach, legs – everywhere.

I kick the last breath out of the woman; I pray not for good. Most of Sally's teeth are gone: either swallowed or lost in the dirt surrounding us. A man suddenly appears, pulling me off, stopping the fight. I step back. The air is stale with the metallic smell of blood and ale.

Before the fight can be called, the shouts change from cheers to confusion. I look around. My body aches, or perhaps it is just my hands and shoulder that hurt, I can't tell. There is only pain.

'Constables!' someone yells. Disoriented, I watch as bodies scramble to get out of the den. My eyes darting in every direction, trying to make sense of the chaos.

Constables? Not here, I think to myself. As whistles pierce the gloom, everyone tries to flee the scene. I see one constable getting attacked by a group of men. I run over and yank the men off him one by one, hitting and kicking them as I peel them away. When I turn to see if the man is hurt, I hear more screams from behind and whip around to find out who they are coming from. I scan the crowd to find the only face I know intimately, but he isn't where he normally stands; the spot is now a blur of people mashed together, scrambling to exit. Stunned, I follow the madness back to the pit. Sally begins to stir. Thank Christ.

Daylight pours in from the opened doors and I am forced to shield my eyes. Distracted, I'm knocked over when somebody runs into me. Everything is foggy as the mob pushes me to the ground, stampeding over me.

I struggle to keep my eyes open. A combination of hunger, pain and exhaustion conquer my body at last.

I blink.

Constables and beadles are wrestling Robert to the ground, his body still writhing beneath their weight. He's eventually shackled.

I blink again.

A man crouches next to me, the man I helped. *A constable?*

Something soft is draped over me.

Then nothing. Darkness.

CHAPTER 2

THE DEEP BOOMS of St Sepulchre's church bells chime. Loud. Distinct. Hurting my head. All of London know what they mean. I know what they mean.

Hanging day.

It is unusually cold for spring. I pull my worn coat tight around me, turning up the collar as I watch the cart halt opposite the church steps. The bell ringer, adorned all in black, lurks on the wall of St Sepulchre's churchyard. I can barely hear his words.

'All good people pray heartily unto God for these poor sinners, who are now going to their death, for whom this great bell doth toll.'

I raise my eyebrows, but not a prayer for the condemned men – each of whom has been cleaned, brushed and wears a suit for their last outing. Twelve men. Twelve men are to meet their fate at the gallows today, but only one interests me. I can see him, but he can't see me. Yet.

It's a three-mile journey from Newgate Prison to Tyburn, and with the number of Londoners crowding the streets I know it is going to be a challenging walk. I don't care, though. I am going to witness every jolt and lurch of the horse-drawn cart, which shouldn't be too difficult as I can see over most people's heads.

I spy nosegays flying towards the prisoners. Flowers, ribbons and bits of coloured paper all drifting through the air. It won't be long before they're replaced with offal and rotten apples. Smiling,

I push my way through the mobs of people to follow the cart as it pulls away from St Sepulchre's. And there are mobs of Londoners out today for the fun – every window and roof full of faces, and the cobbled streets packed with swaying bodies. Long white faces everywhere you look that stand out against the dull grey sky lingering over London. God gives us dark skies to accompany our dark deeds. And London is often overlooked by dark skies.

The procession travels down Snow Hill and will soon cross over the Fleet by a narrow stone bridge up towards Holborn Hill. I have to be quick if I want to keep up with the cart as the bridge acts as a funnel and only the determined will make it across in time. I continue my pursuit, using my solid frame to create space that enables me to squeeze through the masses. I lose sight of the cart, but I can still see the armed guards on horseback. My heart begins to race and my breathing quickens. I need to move faster. Pushing, pulling and stomping, I make it over the bridge and allow the current of bodies to carry me forward.

As I pass St Andrew's church, I notice the roof is packed with more people staring merrily down on to the gathering in the streets. I shift my focus back just in time to side-step a cart stationed in the middle of the street – people jumping down now that the criminals have passed. I could have paid a trifle for such a seat, but I'm not interested in watching the prisoners pass. I want to be much, much closer to the gallows.

I chase after the cart and accidentally stand on someone's foot. 'Watch where you're going, would you!' shouts a lappy woman. I ignore her. This time. Normally, this is the precise opportunity I would use to pick a fight, but not today. Today I am a spectator. I look down at my shoes (which are men's boots – I can't find any women's shoes to fit my feet) and curse them.

I continue to jostle and squeeze through the web of bodies, getting pushed and prodded with every step. This is London: men groping prostitutes; women falling over drunk; children picking pockets; and babies crying from neglect, hunger and sheer raucousness. I blend in well – my blouse and skirt are already stained with dirt and blood. Whose blood, I can't say. I haven't bathed in days – but that is no different to the crowd surrounding me: sour sweat that follows a night of drinking; rotten stumps of teeth that have never been cleaned; and ragged clothes that have been worn too often. A greasy-haired woman catches my eye and my gut clenches. She elbows the equally greasy man next to her and leans into his ear to whisper something. As they both look up at me, I roll my shoulders back and my hands into fists. I wait. However, once they have satisfied their curiosity, they return their attention to their drink and chosen company, and I continue on my way.

I will myself to relax. *Not today, Elizabeth, don't start something today.* Once my heart rate stops racing, my body relaxes and my feet fall in line. It's slow but I finally catch up with the cart as it passes St Giles. Back on home ground. Befitting really, considering the man I am pursuing, Robert Wilkinson. I've known Robert for a long time. Too long. And I can honestly say he is the closest thing to inhuman you can get in human form. Unpredictable and cruel, he has no sympathy for the miseries of others, not least myself. My bones feel heavy from my last fight, but that is nothing compared to the weight on my soul this man has caused. I fought for him for years – and as much as I hated him, he also made me. Saved me in a way. If you can call what I do 'living'. And my body has been in constant recovery from the bouts he arranged and I survived.

But it isn't the underground fights that see him here today. No. He was convicted of highway robbery and murder and sentenced to death. I watched him in court and I watched him receive his sentence. Now I will watch him die.

And there he is. I can see him sitting among the other prisoners in the jolting, open cart. I can also see the two chaplains sitting awkwardly with them. Their lips are moving. I can't hear what they're saying, the crowd is much too loud, but I imagine them chanting something about salvation. I don't think there will be much salvation for the wickedness transported in this cart. Even God must have his limits. I certainly have mine.

The cart rides over cobbled streets along its route from east to west, the Tyburn Tree waiting to fulfil its purpose: the ending of those twelve lives. Some young girls blow kisses, while others throw food and shite. All cheer and jeer, but from a distance. The armed guards on horseback ensure no prisoner escapes, and stop anyone, including myself, from getting too close. As the masses encircle the men, I fight against the current of bodies to keep up with the cart until the end of its journey. I'm relieved to recognise Oxford Road; there is only another mile or so to go. I'm getting closer – closer to the edge of London and life.

Something hits my shoulder. I look down and see an apple. I'm thankful it isn't shite or a dead cat. I'm certain I saw a dog being flung earlier near the whorehouses of Holborn. I can't hear beyond two feet in any direction, my ears muffled by the cacophony of voices, male and female, shouting curses and singing bawdy songs.

It is a queer thing – some people seem to admire the convicts, while others show contempt. I'll admire their execution.

The cart stops; I criss-cross among the people to see why. It is outside a tavern. Hard to miss now that buildings are slowly giving way to open countryside. My eyes never leave Robert as he is taken down from the cart and escorted into the public house. Rain starts to spit down, dampening my hair and clothes. It's fucking cold. The leaves are only beginning to bud, late for this time of year. Much too late. Shivering, I contemplate buying some hot potatoes to shove in my pockets. I wish I had a muffler to wear around my neck too. The air stings my cheeks and the sight of Robert entering the tavern riles my heart.

'What's this?' I yell out. 'What's the meaning of stopping here?' I jump up and down in a poor attempt to warm up, and look around at strange faces. Some laugh. Most ignore me. Most, but not all.

'Calm down, woman.' The husky voice comes from close behind me, accompanied by vinegary-smelling breath. 'They're just getting a final drink before they meet the Tree!'

I whip around to face the man; he is elderly and sways from too much ale. His saggy skin shows the effects of lifelong decay. I take a step back. Sweaty air is better than a drunken man's breath. He looks soaked through, like he's about to melt away into the earth. I retreat away from him and his stench, quickly squeezing past a couple kissing, when I overhear two swill-bellies discussing the convicts. I stop upon hearing Robert's name.

'Robert Wilkinson? Aye! Nasty bastard he is – stopped a coach on the road to Kensington, robbed the nob and then met a Chelsea pensioner and stabbed him in the back!' the younger of the two yells, rocking back and forth on his feet.

'I heard he committed more robberies on the road back to London!' the other adds, shaking his head.

'Evil man! Best rid of him!'

'Nah! Robert Wilkinson? Damn good pugilist! Shame I won't see him on the stage no more, but he'll give the Tree a good fight, that's for sure! Tough bastard he is!' a third, older man interrupts, putting one arm around the younger lad.

'I'll drink to that!' he replies.

'You'll drink to that, I'll drink to that!'

I snort as they clink tankards and finish their cloudy ale. They have no idea how many murders Robert committed, but he only had to get caught once to pay for his sins.

I just manoeuvre my way to the front of the crowd in time to witness the men being loaded back on to the cart. One prisoner jokes, 'I'll buy you a pint on the way back!' Customers cheer at his humour ... or bravery.

Robert still hasn't seen me; he doesn't know I am watching, that I am so close. The hangman slaps the horse and the slow journey continues. I decide to stay as close as I can now to avoid battling my way to the front at the Tree. Easier said than done. People are far more focused on their next drink than on staying with the cart. Can't blame them. I wish I had a drink. I lick my lips at the thought of a gin. Part of me wants to stay and drink at the tavern, but another part of me, a much louder part, wants to stay with the prisoners. I want to see the drop, I remind myself – I need to see him die. To be sure.

'Get out of my bloody way!' I shout at the swaying crowds.

There isn't far to go now. As we leave London and pass the sign for the city of Oxford, to the right I can see the open country of

Marylebone Fields and ahead, just beyond the junction of Oxford Road and Edgware Road, I see the gallows – the Triple Tree, the Tyburn Tree, the Fatal Tree – take your pick. They all mean the same thing for the prisoners approaching. Thank goodness. My patience is dwindling. I've very rarely strayed beyond St Giles since arriving in London; not because I didn't want to, but because Robert didn't like it.

He wouldn't like me being here.

Walking the busy streets of London now, by myself, is not as I remember when I first arrived all those years ago. In truth, it makes me feel small – which is ridiculous, considering how tall I am and how far I can see in any given direction, despite the mob. People in St Giles know me: they know I am a fighter, who I lived with, and they give me a wide berth. Having said that, I didn't relish the thought of staying in St Giles with Robert gone, so I chose to find lodging in the bordering Clerkenwell parish. Yes, the twopence house in Clerkenwell will do for now.

I spot a woman in a dark-blue lace-embroidered dress and a heavy coat, a hand draped over the arm of a man who is clearly wealthy. His clothing, wig and actions say as much. A typical fop. He escorts her around puddles and drunkards, guiding her up the steps of Mother Proctor's Pews beside the gallows. Women who wear fancy dresses are always treated so. On instinct, I glance down at my own attire. My clothes are worn through, barely shielding me from the crisp wind that manages to find its way to me through the crowd of bodies and certainly not protecting me from the rain. I can feel the chill in my bones. My teeth clatter. I need a drink. A drink would help keep me warm. *Later*, I say to myself.

When I look back, the man and woman are gone. Disappeared into the many faces of the well-to-do occupying the tiered seats. A woman bumps into me, forcing me forward and into the man in front of me. I want to hit the woman – old habits – but don't need the attention. So I again ignore the blood simmering beneath my skin and push past the man, leaving the woman behind me. If I look at her, it will only make it worse.

A large roar ripples throughout the mob. The cart must have pulled up under the gallows and I am nowhere near close enough. I need to be at the front. I want Robert to see me. He has to know I am here. The journey has taken hours and now that I am so close I feel a sudden pang of panic at the thought of missing what I came for.

Children dash around playing games and picking pockets; I reach down to make sure I've not been caught off-guard by one of the little vultures. No, my purse is safe. I grip it tight. It holds what is left of the money I managed to find following the arrest. Mostly the proceeds of a stash hidden by Robert, of which only two gold crowns, a few shillings and pennies remain. The stash should have lasted me weeks if I was sensible ... however, sensible I am not. The money is diminishing by the day – gin being the main culprit – and, without Robert, is not being replenished. And so the money I have left I guard and I'd smack anyone who tries to rob me, child or not.

'Oi! I know you!'

I stare down at the young boy, who is playing with a coin between his fingers. He is wearing a flat cap and breeches held up with long strips of rag criss-crossed over his bony shoulders. He has dirt smeared across his cheek, or is it a bruise? I turn away from him, grabbing up my purse, away from his reach.

'You're that giant who fights at St Giles!' he yells. I spin around to face him again. He is smiling now. He knows me, I am sure of it. I don't return his smile.

'You're Elizabeth Wil—' he starts, but I grab his face with my free hand. I am tall, but tall doesn't mean slow.

'Shut your mouth, boy, I'm just here to watch the hangings like everybody else,' I say in a low, serious voice.

The boy tries to pull my hand off his face but he is too weak. Confident he is not going to say anything more, I release him. He steps back from me, nodding. 'It is you.' He smiles again, then turns and disappears into the crowd.

I shake my head, looking around to see if anyone noticed the exchange. Luckily, no one did.

By the time I muscle my way through the masses, Robert is already standing in place with his head through the noose. Fresh straw is on the ground beneath the horse-drawn cart. I missed his last speech. That's if he made one. In any event, I probably wouldn't have heard him. A few men were blindfolded, but not Robert. Typical Robert. He refused the hood.

The hangman jumps off the cart and stands by the horse ready to lead it away, his hands on the reins by the horse's mouth. The noise and cheering die away to a murmur. The heads in Mother Proctor's Pews lean forward. I can feel my eyes growing wider with anticipation, too afraid to blink in case I miss it. I wish I could be the one to lead the cart away. After all the fights, picturing him on the receiving end of my punches, his fate is decided by someone else's hand.

The cart starts moving forward slowly.

Robert appears to be smiling. Even in the face of death he thinks he is invincible. Then, as his eyes sweep over the people, he sees me. I stand still and his expression changes. His smile remains, but his eyes ice over. We don't break eye contact. I would have looked away before, but this time things are different. He can't hurt me any more.

That's right, I think, *I'm still here, you evil bastard.* The corners of my mouth tilt up. I swear I can see his jaw clench right before his feet leave the cart. The roar from the people is deafening as the bodies of the twelve men jerk down, one by one, their legs kicking frantically in the air. Robert is left swinging. The old man was right; Robert gives a convincing fight before death reaches his lungs and heart. Then he moves no more. A stream of piss runs down his leg.

My eyes are dry and burn from holding them open for so long. I feel the strangest feeling of relief sweep through my limbs.

It's over, I tell myself. *It's finally over.*

My husband is dead.

CHAPTER 3

F EET, MOVE.

Nothing. I've seen what I came to see and yet I am frozen in place, my feet firmly planted to the cold, damp earth. *Damn you, Robert: even in death I am unable to shake the invisible shackles chaining me to you.* Motionless, I take a deep breath as I watch the frenzied mob tear each dead man down from the gallows, including my husband – all part of the Tyburn Fair's entertainment. But I don't take part. I'm too tired and thirsty to join in the custom of robbing the executed, nor do I need the supposed luck that comes from touching a dead man's hand. Superstitious fools. I need no more memories of Robert, and the ones I do have ... well, I plan to erase those with the help of my favourite tipple. I close my eyes and imagine a tall tankard of gin in front of me. Even without the bitter taste, the mere thought begins to warm the cockles of my heart. When I open my eyes, I see Robert's lifeless, urine-stained body disappear into the dense, packed mass of people, and then, only then, do I feel the blood in my legs, the strength in my muscles, and will my feet to step away.

I turn to see the City Marshal, escorted by guards, barking orders to recover the corpses and take them back to Newgate. Even in death they are prisoners. I take another deep breath and shove my hands into my pockets. They are sore from the bitter and wet air. My stomach begins to cramp with hunger pains and I remind myself that I wanted this – my freedom. So I turn away from the Tree, from Robert for the last time, and, one foot in front of the other, begin walking away from my past and into the unknown that is to be my future: one of my own making, God willing. Right now, I trust that my feet will carry me where I need to go. As the space between myself and the gallows grows, so does my excitement for what is to come.

During the long walk back towards Clerkenwell through a maze of unfamiliar streets, the stone buildings make the streets seem darker even though the sun won't set for hours. I don't stop to explore; there is no point in lingering on the streets. It's only as I approach the junction between Holborn and Drury Lane that my feet pause. My eyes fix on the dangling wooden sign of The Black Hog, a blistered painting of a plump, black beast. The suspended sign calls to me as I remember my last bout. I really don't want to think about that now. I don't want to think about anything, especially the niggling at the back of my mind. It's been a long day, one that needn't be made longer by unwanted thoughts or, worse, self-doubt. There is plenty of time to consider how I am going to spend my days to earn money and live without Robert's direction. I deserve some time to indulge, to escape, to forget. Yes, forgetting sounds good.

Crossing the street, I notice some children toying with a short-haired, white-and-grey cat. A chubby lad hits the cat with a stick. I quicken my step. A taller, lankier boy gives a second smack to the cat. My fury is so great I almost don't notice the steaming pile of horse shite in my path. I leap over the mound and grab the first boy's ear, throwing him against the wall for the other kids to see. I pick up the stick and hit him on the leg with it.

'Ow!' the boy squeals, his friends retreating.

'Hurts, doesn't it?' I ask.

He runs off with his friends. The cat doesn't linger either. My right eyebrow lifts. Ungrateful animal.

I watch as they disappear around the corner, the kids in one direction and the cat in the opposite. Once they are gone, I approach the corner tavern; a handwritten sign is nailed on to the old red door, paper curling at the edges: *DRINKING ONLY – NO FIGHTING, NO FUCKING, NO EXCEPTIONS!* I laugh and push open the door. It's a step above the drinking houses in St Giles: a solid, scoured sort of place built from brick and poorly stained wood, with a collection of tankards stacked on the wall behind the bar.

Of the thirty-six eyes in the room, only six or eight turn to look at me, for serious drinking is the order of the day here. Those who do turn look just long enough to figure out who I am – or rather, who I'm not – then return to their bitter brown ale.

It is a scruffy-looking crowd resting their elbows and heads on The Black Hog tables, none of them exactly good-for-nothings, but certainly not good for much. Most will have been at the hanging, and work tomorrow will hurt for them; their heads at the very least will pound from the drinking efforts they are putting in. My presence by no means offends or surprises them. In the back, I notice a man with long black hair, dressed in a dark jacket, sitting alone, and on the table next to him a group of working women. *Whores.*

'Oi,' says the innkeeper, raising a hairy hand and rubbing a hairier thumb and forefinger together. 'You got coin?'

'Yes,' I reply, placing my purse on the bar, coins clinking. 'Gin.'

The exchange is a formality, as he's already filling a tankard.

The landlord at the twopence house in Clerkenwell told me I'd have to vacate the room if I couldn't pay for it. He assumed that I had no money. I'd no intention of letting on that I'd found Robert's stash, so instead I paid for a week up front and left without saying a word. The money is beginning to run out, but the landlord doesn't need to worry about that. That worry is my own. My thoughts drift to work. In the weeks since Robert's arrest I have looked for work, and up until now I've had no luck.

I approached dress shops and offered my services as a seamstress. I can stitch: the trade I'd studied at the orphanage, but, of course, I've never had much chance to use the skill since arriving in London, except on my own clothing. Robert never used my winnings to buy me anything new; instead, he gave me clothing taken from his victims, stains and all. My eyes drop to my purple skirt, which should fall to my ankles, but actually only reaches my shins. The fact it's short on me doesn't stop the hem from getting drenched in mud from the streets, which then slaps my legs as I walk. The top of my skirt isn't any better: there are patch repairs in at least four spots (the best I could do with the limited supplies I had at the time) and it's covered in dark-coloured markings. What they are from, I couldn't exactly tell you – food, blood? Probably both. As well as new lodging, I could do with some new clothes. I sigh and press my eyes shut. I might have to consider returning to St Giles to fight again, but without Robert I'm not sure I'd get a fair deal and I won't have any protection from greedy punters. The rookery is not filled with the trustworthy and righteous sort. I trace my finger over my shoulder where the bite mark from my last bout has left a scar. With Robert gone, I've decided to leave the fighting world and try to start afresh. If only a fresh start would present itself. The only thing fresh is the tankard of gin in front of me.

There are the people who work to get by, and then there are the people who get by on the work of others. I fought. Robert stole and fought, and spent my money as well as his.

I have a room (well, it's really a bed – I'm sharing the room with a bunch of other throwaways) for the week, but what I will do after that is another question. Robert always handled money for me – meals, rent, drinks, freak shows. I hadn't bothered with what anything cost. Robert led the way, and I followed. Now, London is an ocean and I fear I might drown unless I find help. *Help*. I clench my hands together at the thought of relying on another for help, but I have to accept the truth, which is: without Robert, or any connections of my own, I am fighting a losing battle – and I don't lose. I just need a way in, an introduction or chance to prove myself. Then I'll be set. I'm a hard worker, when I want to be.

My only vice is drink, and that is a hard habit to give up. Luckily, or perhaps unluckily, the taverns I'd frequented in St Giles didn't cost very much; neither does The Black Hog. You'd think the threat of starvation or the debtors' prison would be enough to put the fear in me to give it up. But no. I pay the man and tie my moneybag back at my hip, under my coat, which I am not removing until the gin has the desired effect – internal warmth and numbness.

The first taste is the hardest, but after a few gulps the fluid goes down ever so easily. It doesn't taste the best, but it's cheaper than beer, which begs the question – what the hell is in it? I daren't ask. I look down at my now empty tankard. It's refreshing drinking at a tavern I haven't been to before.

'Excuse me?' a voice says behind me.

I ignore her, my ass comfortably resting on a stool. Drink is the only thing I want right now. Not company. I peel my hand off the sticky bar top and smell the aroma of days' old alcohol on my skin. It's not just the clientele who could use a wash in this tavern; the whole establishment could do with a proper scrub.

'Oi! I'm talking to you!' the voice continues, but still I don't engage. *Keep calm, Elizabeth*, I think to myself, *remember the sign – there's no fighting and no exceptions.* I order another drink and watch the innkeeper as he carefully studies me, wondering if he is going to have to evict me after only one drink.

'Are you deaf?' the woman shouts, shoving my shoulder, causing me to spill my freshly topped-up drink. The temperature is getting hotter – both in the air and my flesh. I can feel more bodies behind me, encroaching into my space. I take a sip of my gin and slowly turn on the bar stool to face the eager person trying to get my attention and her two escorts. The blonde-haired, flushed-faced woman stares at me.

'Oh, sorry, love, I thought you were someone else!' she cackles and throws her arm around me, patting my stomach with her free hand. 'What are you drinking?'

I don't reply. Instead, I peel her hand off my shoulder and stand up. I tower over the three working women who have decided to join me, uninvited.

'Damn your blood, you're huge!' the black-haired bawd to my left squeals, raising both hands to grab my face, but I jerk away and push her. Not hard, but hard enough to see her stumble backwards to the ground.

'Oi! No fighting! Take it outside!' the innkeeper orders from behind the bar, pointing his hairy fingers my way. I do not want to get kicked out. I'm still thirsty.

'We're friendly!' the blonde one says.

'Yes, real friendly!' the third girl joins in, laughing while pulling her friend up off the floor. All three are chirping merry. They begin dancing around in circles and making faces at the innkeeper. I can't imagine what is so humorous about this situation. I look over to my left at the innkeeper, and shrug.

'Ladies!' a man barks. The lone man appears suddenly, leaning on a cane. 'Leave the poor woman alone. Can't you see she is not interested in your company?'

I can see his face more clearly now – he is older, with piercing grey eyes and thin lips that make a solid line when he smiles. His cheekbones are sharply defined, and his coat looks heavy, warm and of good quality. Despite his good coat, his hair is greasy and the flecks of white on his shoulders remind me of flour dusted on a freshly baked loaf of bread. A dirty beau if ever I saw. And while his presence is a question to me, it is a statement to the other women. They nod and disperse immediately, winking at me as they exit The Black Hog, clearly pleasing the innkeeper who tends to another customer; his intervention no longer needed.

The man with the cane speaks. 'I apologise for their behaviour – some women just cannot be taught—'

'—to stay bloody quiet?' I finish his sentence, grabbing my gin and finishing it in one go, without facing him.

He smiles. 'I was going to say "manners", but yes, I suppose you're right.' His London accent is thick, unlike his long, wispy hair. He begins to retreat, but pauses. 'Forgive me for asking, but you seem a bit lost, my dear. I haven't seen you here before, Miss—?'

I snort. 'Lost? You're the one sitting alone at a table between prostitutes and drunks – not drinking, I hasten to add – and you think I am lost?' I nod in the direction of his bare table at the back and then slam my empty tankard on the bar top.

The man glances down at the floor in front of him and grins. 'You look familiar. Have we met?'

I pause, scouring my memory for his face. Nothing. I shake my head.

'Would you care to join me? I'd be happy to buy your next drink.' He motions at my tankard.

I eye the man up and down. He leans on his cane, but seems sturdy enough – unafraid and assured, like a man who has no cares in the world. Whether that is because he doesn't have any or can afford not to have any, I cannot say. Either way, I feel myself recoiling from him. Something inside me warns me to stay away, the hairs on the back of my neck alerting me. I ignored that same feeling the day I met Robert all those years ago and ended up as his puppet, for him to do with as he wished; I'll be damned if I ignore that feeling now.

'No, I would not,' is all I say, and I return to my stool. I raise my hand to catch the innkeeper's attention. He doesn't see me, too busy nattering to some men at the other end of the bar. My eyes land on the tankards stacked behind the bar and catch the man's dark presence; he hasn't moved. I can't see a clear picture, but the blur is obvious, as is the ominous profile I glimpse from the corner of my eye. I didn't realise how badly lit it is in the tavern; the two stained windows looking out on to the street do their best at keeping out not just a draught, but daylight too. Up at the bar, there are lanterns, thankfully, but step away just a few paces and that light fades to shadows and flickers: a perfect place for demons to lurk. The man leans forward, rests his cane against the bar and places his interlaced hands on top of it, smiling at me. I wait for him to speak but he says nothing.

Minutes go by. I hear the stern voice of my old guardian, Mrs Dierdre, telling me to ignore him, but the thought of the woman puts me on edge even more. My spine lengthens and shoulders begin to tense up. I begin looking around at the paintings hanging on the walls (the ones I can see, anyway) – one of a ship and another a portrait of a gentleman. Next, I focus on the walls themselves – they need repainting, and there's a large water stain on the ceiling above the second window. I'm basically looking around at everything and anything to distract me from the threat hovering to my left. When I return my gaze to the bar, I notice from the corner of my eye that he is still there, quietly staring at me. Waiting.

'What do you want?' I shake my head, finally turning to face him.

'Just your name,' he says, his eyes glued to mine.

I laugh. I can't help it. 'All right, my name is Elizabeth. Now you can leave. Follow the whores out the door,' I bark, pointing to the exit.

'Elizabeth ... ?'

I sigh. 'Just Elizabeth.'

He smiles again and then pushes back off the bar, collecting his cane discreetly. 'Very well, *Elizabeth*,' he says, emphasising my name. 'I'm Vincent. Vincent Love.' My eyebrows draw together at his unusual name. But then again, nothing about this man is usual. 'If you ever need any help with anything ...' – his voice trails off

– 'let's say, money, for instance ...' – he slides a few pennies across the wood towards me – 'then you can always come find me at the Tippling House over in Covent Garden, further down from the theatre. I'd be more than willing to help you.'

I stare down at the coins next to my elbow. I want the money. I need money. But every bone and muscle in my body tells me not to accept it. The hairs still prickled, on high alert, on the back of my neck. There's no such thing as free money. I raise my hand again and finally get the innkeeper's attention and gesture for another drink. I hear Mr Love, the unusual man with a cane, step away. Immediately, I notice there's no limp in his walk – no uneven steps or obvious drag along the wooden floor. The man is still an unanswered question.

'A penny,' the innkeeper shouts, placing the tankard on the bar. I begin rummaging for my moneybag at my hip where it is tied and see the pennies lying on the bar top. I look up at the door where Mr Love is standing, staring at me. He nods his head once and disappears. No, I definitely do not want to accept money from this man with the cane.

I return my eyes to the coins and tell myself not to take them, but my hands, unfortunately, don't always listen to reason.

CHAPTER 4

IT'S A BROTHEL.

No denying it. No flowering it up or trying to convince myself of what I had already concluded the moment I laid eyes on Vincent Love.

The women lounging outside the entrance of the Tippling House, provocatively dressed with ample bosom on display, tell me so. No sign of Vincent, unsurprisingly. My eyes cast over the women and, my breath hitches as one woman in particular catches my eye.

Sophie.

I haven't seen her in years. But the unmistakeable red hair, angelic face and slight frame are as clear as day. I close my eyes, wishing it weren't so. And yet, my eyes can't blink the truth away. Sophie is as beautiful as I remember, with piercing green eyes encased by long eyelashes – eyelashes she is currently fluttering at a young man ambling by the establishment. He stops to speak to her, but I am too far to hear what is being said. Although it doesn't take much to guess at the words being passed between them. But despite her physical beauty, the man isn't tempted. This time. Sophie tilts her chin downwards and gives the man a sly smile as he continues about his day.

I recall the last time I saw her, all those years ago, when I fled the Stockton Estate. Sir Frederick Stockton had bought me from

Mrs Dierdre. He took me to his lavish home in the country, where he put me to work in his household management staff. Sophie had already worked there a few months when I arrived to find myself sharing a room with her in the servants' quarters, as we were the youngest in Sir Frederick's staff. She was a scullery maid assisting the cook in the kitchen. I was taken in as a housemaid and learned very quickly that I had no time to question anything said or instructed by the housekeeper, Mrs Blythe, a stern woman who felt nothing to discipline me if tasks weren't completed to her standards – standards nothing short of perfection. It had been an ... adjustment. Let's leave Mrs Blythe there.

I discovered, too, that my reason for finding myself at the Stockton Estate was not merely as a competent servant maid, but also to participate in Sir Frederick's other passion ... underground fights between servants of various other households. That first year had been the hardest. But hard times build hard souls. And even harder hands. Sophie, it seemed, had also caught the eye of Sir Frederick Stockton, but for not quite the same reasons as me. While I was forced to fight other children for money, Sophie was forced to keep company with the Master ... in his bed. I often heard Sophie sneaking back into our room in the wee hours of the morning. When I questioned her about it, she told me to mind my own business. If Mrs Blythe knew about the scandalous affair, she didn't let on. Which is perhaps why she was so good in her employment.

Despite Sophie's extra night-time duties, she seemed happy through the day. Tending to her chores while humming tunes to herself. That was, until she wasn't. I shudder as the memory overtakes my senses. I was nursing a black eye and busted lip after a tough bout the night prior (a fight I won, I hasten to add – I won all the fights Sir Frederick arranged and quickly earned myself quite the reputation for dishing out blows to end fights rather abruptly, leaving Sir Frederick aggrieved when he struggled to find servants – boys or girls – who could stand opposite me in a fight). Sophie came barrelling into our room and knocked the bowl of water I was using to wash myself on to the floor. She was upset and clinging to her clothes, which were ripped. She curled up on her mattress, gripping her sides while she sobbed. I remember cursing her for being so careless. I was angry and hurting and had absolutely no patience for Sophie's drama or frolics. I never asked her what had caused her to be so upset, but she volunteered the information anyway. She uttered a single name that, together with her torn garments, told me everything that had transpired: *Edward*, Sir Frederick's eldest son. And after that day, Sophie changed. Her eyes lost their sparkle and her smile grew dim. Mrs Blythe didn't notice, but I did; hence, when Edward found me alone one day sweeping soot from the hearth in the main hall and tried to force himself on me, I pummelled his handsome face. I can take most things, but when that young, entitled boy who had never known a hard day's work in his life tried to take advantage of Sophie and then strip away what made me a woman – something I vowed would never be used as currency – I snapped. The whipping I received was ... painful. Excruciating. But necessary. Because it lit a fire in me.

I upped that same night, and halfway to the gate of the grounds I heard a twig snap. Turning, I saw Sophie, bag clutched to her front, eyes wide, holding her breath. When I remained silent, curious as to her intentions, she finally took another step towards me.

She didn't need to ask. I knew she had been broken as well and if escaping with me was what she wanted, who was I to stop her.

Sophie had always been soft, too soft for this world. And as I stand in the alley opposite the Tippling House, leaning my shoulder against the stone building, it strikes me – like a punch to the chest – that life has not been any kinder to Sophie since arriving in London all those years ago. She had gone her way, back to a life between bedlinen, and I had gone mine, straight into the arms of a man who manipulated me to fight for his own gain.

Zounds.

The truth hurts like a cold slap to the face. I frown as I steal one more glance at my past escapee; her head turns in my direction and I pivot to avoid her stare. As cruel as it seems, I don't want her following me a second time.

I have enough to figure out without more of her frolics and antics. London is not a place for sympathetic gestures such as grace.

I wake to a tugging on my skirt. I can't see what it is, but I can feel it. And there is not only a pulling at my hip but a pushing behind my eyes, deep within my skull, blinding my senses. That, or I still hadn't mustered the wherewithal to open my eyes and face the day.

There it is again. Another tug at my side. Someone is grabbing me. *What in all that is holy?* I try to prise an eye open. Zounds, that light is bright. Daylight. So it's day. *Where am I?* My hands rub my eyelids apart and my surroundings start to come into focus, becoming less obscure and fuzzy, as do my thoughts.

I need to stop drinking. I tell myself that every morning after I drink. Today will be different. Today is the day I don't drink. I start giggling at the thought.

The tugging at my hip is rougher, jostling me on to my back. The ground is cold beneath me, startling me. I reach down towards the tugging on my hip – the hip where my purse is tied.

Someone is stealing my money.

Shite. I have to get up. I have to deal with this. Losing my money is not an option after gaining my freedom. I have a room for the week, which I should probably get back to and sleep some more, but what I am going to do after that is another question. A question for later. After I deal with this cunt trying to steal from me.

My nails catch skin as I grab for the thief, and a high-pitched squeal follows. I lose my grip as the thief pulls away. I reach for my purse again, but it isn't there. Bollocks! Bastard's taken my money! And it is a *little* bastard, as my eyes are now wide open and honed in on the boy hobbling away. He turns to look back and the wee shite smiles! Which, for some strange reason, causes me to laugh again. Seems his grin is only fair as I am an easy victim, slumped against the wall of the tavern. Ah, The Black Hog, my new favourite boosing ken. That innkeeper must have thrown my arse out at some point. I doubt I would have had the sense to leave on my own. Knowing when to stop has never been something I have been particularly good at.

I make a mental note of the pickpocket's appearance: his light-brown hair sticks out from under his cap, as do his ears. Bless him. The dandiprat's wearing a blue shirt and brown farting-crackers with matching jacket. I have the vague remembrance of seeing him before. He can't be older than ten years. And he's limping. Not quickly, mind, but as quick as he is able, it seems.

I haul myself up to make chase. Staggering at first, my legs feel unbelievably heavy after my last gin-drinking session and I have to pause to right myself against the tavern's wall. Once steady, I push away and take off after the boy. As I make my way to Hog Lane, the crowd thickens. My steps are falling faster now. *Sorry, boy, but I need that money.*

The hustle and bustle of London continues, oblivious to this cat-and-mouse game between myself and the boy. I follow him through the crowd, weaving in and out of the bodies with purpose. I'll follow him closely and make my attack when he least expects it. He stops, glancing back over his shoulder, so I duck behind a cart – not an easy feat considering there are no goods on it, so I have to crouch down to the floor. My knees moan and my face grimaces at the movement. After a few seconds, I pop back up, but the boy is gone. *Zounds.* Stumbling, I run to close the gap, and reach a junction. Turning in all directions, I frantically search for the boy with the limp and cheeky grin. Finally, I see him limping down Tower Street towards St Martin's Lane. He's heading towards Covent Garden. *Not again.* I'd spent the morning there scoping out the Tippling House and have no desire to venture back and risk bumping into Sophie. No choice, though. The boy turns down an alley and I keep good pace, sticking close to the buildings so I will have nooks to hide in if he turns again.

The boy slows to a relaxed stroll; we are almost at Covent Garden and I need to cut him off before I lose him in the market. I begin rubbing my hands and blowing hot breath on them to waken them for their next task. I feel like a child myself. I am playing a game, whether he wants to or not – he started it, but I will finish it.

The boy stops just before the square. He pulls out my purse, his little fingers moulding the fabric around its contents, trying to figure out how much is in his prize. A horse-drawn carriage drives past him, barely avoiding a collision.

'Watch yourself, boy!' shouts the driver. He doesn't waste any more words on him, his passengers unaware of how close they'd come to hitting a child.

I watch the boy put my purse back into his pocket, check both directions for oncoming traffic and cross the street. Here, he stops. So it's here I make my move. The corners of my mouth are twitching the moment I pounce.

'Gotcha!' I yell, grabbing the boy around his waist, hoisting him in the air. The boy yelps, thrashing as he tries to break loose from my grip. Twisting and turning, his body struggles in my long arms.

'Stop fighting, you little bufflehead!' I order, dropping him on the ground but retaining a firm grip on his collar. 'Calm down!'

'Let me go! Let me go, you big wretch! I haven't done anything!' the boy cries out, still fighting me. He moves around on the ground as if he were dancing. I ease my grip just as he stands and spins, kicking me in the shin.

'Ouch!' I yell, kicking him back, but not hard. The boy steps back, stumbles on the stone edge of the cobblestone street, and falls to the ground again.

'What? What are you wanting?' he growls, looking up at me from the street. I bend over, grumbling as I do, to rub my shin where the boy's good foot had kicked me – not hard, but his aim was perfect. *Feisty little turd.*

I stare at his left foot, which is awkwardly turned outwards, in the wrong direction. I've seen that on grown men – Robert had taken a hammer to a drunkard's ankle once following an exchange of words over a trinket Robert had stolen and was trying to sell. The man had screamed in agony, writhing on the floor. Robert had yelled obscenities at him before he was hauled away by comrades and before any constables appeared at the scene.

I study the boy's left foot, and know that it has similarly been broken, never healing properly.

Sighing, I place my hands on my hips. 'You know what I want. Hand it over,' I instruct, holding out my hand, my body swaying from the gin I'd consumed earlier. The sun is beginning to set, and I need another drink before turning in for the night. And in order to do that, or anything for that matter, I need my money. The money currently resting in the gimp's pocket. It's all I have until I find work. That's tomorrow's problem. Today, this little cripple is giving me another sort of problem, the stopping-me-from-drinking kind.

He tilts his head up. 'I don't know what you're talking about.'

'You know damn well what I mean. Give me back my purse, you little thief, or I'll deliver you to the constables.' I nod in the direction of two men heading our way. I can see two beadles followed by two plain-clothed men – one seems familiar; official-looking, handsome even – wandering along the square towards us.

'Go ahead, I haven't done anything, and I don't have your bloody purse!' the boy shouts, and he tries to flee. I'm ready this time and grab his collar again, pulling him back towards my chest.

'Let me go, would ya!'

'Give me back my money and I will,' I say, standing him upright when he loses his balance on his injured leg. The boy walks on the outside of the maimed foot. I can't help but twist my face in disgust, letting him loose, but not so far from me that he is out of my reach.

'Having a good look, are you? I bet you want to know how it happened too!' he shouts at me, pointing towards his left foot. 'Get a *goooood* look!' He wiggles the foot about for everyone to see. 'I'm not gonna tell you how it happened!'

'Good. Give me back my purse,' I say again, unimpressed. 'Quickly now, the beadles are coming.' They are only a few yards away from us, but have stopped to speak to an elderly couple. Passers-by would likely assume we are mother and child. No one giving us a second glance. The boy looks up at me again. Hurt. I see hurt in his eyes. Hurt and ... what? Despair? Confusion? A sore tummy? *Christ*. What a motherly thing to think. I shake my head.

'I know who you are,' he states.

I blink. Then blink again.

And it clicks, realisation hitting me square between the eyes. He's the young boy who approached me at Tyburn the other day. At Robert's execution. My eyebrows furrow at the same young boy standing in front of me now.

'You!' I gasp, grabbing his shirt again, drawing him close. 'What are you doing? You following me?'

Silence.

'Oi! I'm speaking to you!' I grab his chin with my spare hand, between my long, dirty fingers. 'Answer me! Are you following me?'

He pushes at my hand and stares at the ground. I release him roughly and he kicks a rock away from his feet. It doesn't go far. I hold up my hands, waiting for his response.

'No, I'm not following you, but I have followed you.'

CHAPTER 5

'LIKE I SAID, I know you. You're the woman they call the Amazonian. You fight in St Giles. I've seen you. What does that mean anyway? *Amazonian*,' he asks.

I let out the breath I realise I have been holding and sigh, my body aching from the events of the day.

'You've won almost all of your fights!' he shouts, excited, startling me.

'What do you mean, *almost all*? No one's bloody beat me!'

The boy smiles.

'So you *are* her – the prize fighter?' He winks. I shake my head. The gall on this boy.

'Give me my money. Last chance,' I reply, ignoring his previous remark. I stare. He stares. I stare some more. He looks happy now. Like the silent validation just made his day. I notice his face in more detail – he still has some of his baby features, not quite a child, but not quite a man either. He's around the same age I was when I was sent (or sold) to the Stockton Estate. This boy's life is undoubtedly tough and rough, but far from the hell I'd endured. He has fierce brown eyes and rosy cheeks, with a speckle of fight in him. I like that. A fighting spirit; it serves you more than a hand up or handout.

'Yes, I fight,' I finally acquiesce, giving him a curt nod.

He beams at this verbal confirmation before pulling out my purse and handing it to me. I snatch it before he changes his mind and open it to count the contents.

'It's still all there,' he states, frowning. 'You've just cost me my supper.'

My eyebrows shoot to my hairline. *A lot of fight in him.* I tuck the purse back into my skirt, keeping my gaze on the boy. I'm undecided about him. He doesn't look starved or badly clothed. He should be wearing a coat, though, not that shabby jacket, and as the thought crosses my mind, a chill runs up my spine on a day with no wind.

'So what now?' he asks. 'You going to fight again?'

'No.'

'Why not? I thought you were good. Not as good as you could be, but good enough to watch, for a woman.'

I smirk at his comment, but it disappears as quickly as it forms. I can't believe this boy has seen me fight. Worse, my topless fights. I shake my head, shuddering at the thought of this little boy seeing my bare heavers.

'You like watching the fights?' I ask, still cringing. He shrugs and begins kicking the ground again. 'Your parents let you?' I probe some more.

The boy remains lip-locked. His eyes dimming, the brown darker, as though the very mention of his parents dimmed his soul. I see no fight in those brown eyes now.

An orphan. Another of London's throwaways.

I'm tempted to walk him home – wherever that is – but am interrupted before I get the chance to offer.

'Mrs Elizabeth Wilkinson?'

I turn towards the man addressing me. I mean, the *constable* addressing me, because there's no mistaking who or what he is. Any other time I might be worried about being approached by a constable, but at this head-sore hour of the day the idea of me using unnecessary energy lacks appeal. A second constable stands at a distance, watching me. The one who knows my name is young, but has a worn face, like he's witnessed too much for the years he's lived. Otherwise, he is clean and has the stature of a lawman; a man with purpose. He is tall with dark-brown hair, much like my own, but he has the palest blue eyes I've ever seen on a man. Eyes I've seen before.

'Who's asking?' I say.

'Matthew Boyle, Parish Constable.' He bows to complete the introduction. His tone is warm, like his smile, and when he looks up I feel a tingle in the base of my belly. An uneasiness that forces me to shift on my feet. *I'm still drunk.* I try to steady myself, unsure of what is to come.

'We've met before.'

I nod, remembering the man who covered me with his coat after my last fight in St Giles, whose blue eyes pierced mine then and do so again now. And then I cringe, for the third time this day. *This man has seen my tits.* In the heat of the moment, bare-chested before a fight, with all sorts of panting and gesturing by spectators, I feel nothing but the need to satisfy my own anger. But here, now, in the ordinary light of the day, when everyone is fully clothed and going about their business, that is when I feel it – timidity. Something I am not accustomed to feeling. And I can't say I like it.

I can't hold his gaze any more. I drop my eyes to my feet, then up at the sky, and then around to the boy. But he's gone. He must have slipped away as the ward officers approached. *Sneaky little shite.* I feel a tug on my heartstrings, similar to the tug he gave me on my hip earlier, as if the unknown boy was tugging them from a secret hiding spot somewhere.

'Mrs Wilkinson?' Constable Boyle's voice disturbs my thoughts.

'Yes, sorry,' I reply. 'I remember you. And please don't call me that.' I face the constable; the man may have seen me on the ground, half naked and weak like a wounded animal, but that isn't me. I'm the woman who saved him from having his back broken by an angry mob. I straighten, allowing myself to grow taller as his eyes size me up.

'I just wanted to thank you. You stopped those men. I don't know what would have happened if you hadn't intervened ...' His voice trails off, as if his mind is following the thought to an unwanted place. 'It was—' The constable pauses again. 'It was unexpected, and impressive – heroic even. So thank you.'

And I am speechless. Another thing I am often not – speechless, that is, and certainly not heroic. That is another new description I have yet to hear used when speaking of my character. I had assumed he wanted to question me about Robert or even the wee pickpocket who pulled a disappearing act. Lord knows I'd already given the constables plenty of information when Robert was arrested. I had spoken to a magistrate that day as well; I can't recall his name, just that he was a tall, lean, stiff-necked, middle-sized man, with a full wig that probably cost more than all the money I'd seen in my entire life – *an owl in an ivy bush*, as Robert used to say. That magistrate had orchestrated the raid in the rookery. And I hadn't liked the way he'd looked at me. He'd licked his lips like a dog ravenous for his next meal.

'You're welcome,' I state, not really knowing what else to say. I rub my arms, trying to warm myself. The chill of the air is starting to hit me as the effects of the gin dwindle.

'How are you?' the constable asks. I sense him assessing my clothes, or the condition of them, where it isn't quite spring but not quite summer yet; that horrid in-between.

'I'm fine, just ... not sure what I'm supposed to do now.'

'In what way?'

My shoulders shrug. 'For money. Woman's got to eat. The London I'm seeing now is much bigger and different to the one I've been living in for the past ten years.' I look around at the people walking by. It's almost suppertime and I can feel my stomach shrinking. The scent of fish and potatoes fills the air, causing an involuntary growl from the pit of my stomach, like a bear protecting its young. 'Robert used to take care of the money.'

I finally look back at him. His eyes are downcast, flitting from side to side as if searching his brain for some vital piece of information. He raises his chin and looks up at the clouds and then turns to face the other constable, who approaches.

'Mrs Wilkinson, may I introduce Nicholas Clayton, Parish Constable. He is constable to Covent Garden, while I reside over Clerkenwell.'

'Clerkenwell?' I ask, surprised at this revelation.

Constable Boyle nods. 'Are you much familiar with Clerkenwell?'

'I'm starting to be.'

Constable Clayton bows. 'Pleasure to meet you, Mrs Wilkinson. And thank you for saving Matthew – I dare say he wouldn't have walked away so easily without your intervention. We owe you a debt.' His smile is genuine, filling his eyes.

I ponder this bizarre turn of events for a moment; it might be useful knowing a pair of parish constables. The fact they are out and about speaks a lot about their character, as most constables have a reputation for being lazy at best and corrupt at worst.

'Do you have a trade, Mrs Wilkinson?' Constable Boyle finally asks. 'Other than bare-knuckle fighting and drinking, I mean.' He looks at me intently, his expression difficult to read. *Is he judging me?*

'Needlework,' I blurt, swallowing a couple of times to moisten my mouth and throat, which are becoming drier by the second.

He nods and peruses the streets again. The market stalls are beginning to be closed up by their owners. He puts on the hat he had been carrying, tipping his head at an elderly couple walking past. They return the greeting, but only stare at me. I scowl back.

Constable Boyle takes out some parchment, scribbles something on it, and hands it to me. 'I may know of something. You can read, I presume?' He doesn't wait for my answer. 'Meet me at this address tomorrow morning at eight.'

'Say, what time?' I call after him, unsure I'd heard him right, but he and his friend are already heading towards another civilian, who is clearly disgruntled about something – a pickpocket maybe? I can't stop my lips from smiling this time. My pickpocket, perhaps?

'Try to stay off the gin until then,' Constable Boyle shouts over his shoulder.

Pfft.

I unfold the paper, reading the handwriting: 'Piddington's, King St, Holborn'.

CHAPTER 6

MY EYEBALLS HURT.

The pungent stink of whalebones is enough to clear anyone's head after a night of drinking. Yes, I drank again, despite the constable's warning. No one was going to tell me what to do again. I'm my own woman and my choices are my own – even if they are the wrong ones.

I stand alone in the cold upstairs office of Mr Rupert Piddington, owner of Piddington's Stay-making and Haberdashery shop, a rather ordinary establishment for the ward of Holborn. His wife, a petite, squeezed-up woman with a sour expression, who has been introduced as Mrs Sarah Piddington, does not stay to keep me company. Instead, she chooses to stand at the door leading to the landing that overlooks the shop floor – her shop. She is, naturally, within earshot of her husband and Constable Boyle, who stand at the bottom of the stairs. I can just see them, but can't hear them. I know, of course, from my conversation with Constable Boyle earlier this morning that they are discussing my potential future at the shop, sewing the bone casings for the stays and other female garments. A job I am unsure I even want. It has been a long time since my skills at needlework have been required and my fingers aren't as dextrous as they once were as a young girl. But a job means money, and I need more of it. Fast, given the rate I am making my way through Robert's stash.

I watch as the two men nod some sort of agreement and ascend the stairs to re-enter Mr Piddington's modest office. I get a whiff of the man before he sits, facing me. For a man with poor hygiene, Mr Piddington seems to labour under a blatant sense of his own merits and importance, as well as a flagrant fear of his wife, who has since moved closer to her husband's desk, keeping one eye on me at all times. So she is the boss, not him? *Interesting.* Constable Boyle stands next to me, opposite the shop owners, and makes quick introductions.

I am now towering over Mr Piddington, clearly contrasting against the short, rotund, bald man sporting a bushy black moustache flecked with white – crumbs or old age? I can't tell. Mr Piddington gives one curt bow of his head.

'Rupert, Mrs Wilkinson is well versed in needlework. She is available to start immediately and would be an asset for your successful and growing business,' Constable Boyle offers. His continuous compliments surprise me. He has no idea of my stitching abilities, let alone if I'll be any use here. And given the way this wretch of a woman is glaring at me, I'm starting to think I won't be, no matter how hard I try.

Mr Piddington nods. 'Very well, Mrs Wilkinson, as the constable here has vouched for you, and how well I know his father, I see no reason why we should need to go through any other formalities. I trust employment here at my shop is acceptable to you?'

Unfamiliar with the proper etiquette, I nod.

'Use your voice please, Mrs Wilkinson.'

'Yes.'

Mr Piddington leans forward as if waiting for more. I glance at Constable Boyle, who mouths the words 'Mr Piddington' at me.

'Yes... Mr Piddington,' I repeat, to the satisfaction of what is now my new employer.

'Excellent. Let me show you around.'

Mr Piddington walks past us and out of his office door, avoiding the stern look of his disapproving wife but gesturing for her to show us the way down the stairs to the shop floor. Masses of materials and ribbons are displayed along the walls. There is a curtain separating the front shop from the back room, which hosts a man and a woman, both working diligently; they steal glances at us when we enter their domain. The air is just as cold, if not colder, on the shop floor than it had been in Mr Piddington's office. There are two working boards, two ironing boards and clamps, and a dozen whalebones.

I gawk around my new surroundings and eventually my eyes land on both workers. The woman sits at a table, hidden behind piles of fabric and whalebones. Behind her, garments hang – stunning gowns, robes and coats in every colour and fabric imaginable. They are, quite simply, beautiful. Even in my limited experience, it is clear Piddington's Stay-making and Haberdashery shop caters to the higher end of society. The man is sitting cross-legged on one of the working boards, assembling a stunning bodice. Their skill is apparent, for the woman works steadily and the man precisely. I swallow down my nerves.

'Mrs Wilkinson, you've met my wife, Mrs Piddington. She looks after the front shop and will also assign you your workload each day. You report to her first thing tomorrow.' Mr Piddington sweeps aside the curtain and stands on the shop side, holding the material open for me to follow. But I'm frozen to the floor.

'Why tomorrow? I am here today,' I offer. I catch Constable Boyle suppressing a smile. Mr and Mrs Piddington exchange baffled looks. Conflicted, the owner twists his lip so one end of his moustache touches his chin. He places his hand over his waistcoat pocket and drums his chest with his stubby fingers.

'Certainly, you may start today.' He then spins on one foot to address his wife. 'My dear, would you be so kind as to give Mrs Wilkinson something to do.'

Mrs Piddington speaks through pursed lips. 'Absolutely. Mrs Wilkinson, please follow me.' She bids farewell to Constable Boyle, who smiles in return. The stern, wiry woman softens immediately and holds her hand out, pointing back towards the room behind the curtain, indicating I should follow. She walks briskly without waiting to see if I comply, but I do. When she stops, she is in front of the other female worker, whom I now notice has a fading black eye. Almost healed, the wound must be a few days old. At least. A nasty-looking blow. It would take some force to leave such an injury. I'd know. I've given many of those same bruises to opponents throughout the years. And been on the receiving end of a few myself.

The woman is busily stitching fabric around whalebones and takes no notice of my stares. The man on the working board is cutting some fabric, which would make the component parts of a woman's stay. His hands move swiftly with purpose, exacting each move with utmost precision. It's more than a skill. It's an art.

'Mrs Wilkinson, this is Alice Griffin,' says Mrs Piddington. 'She will get you started. Do as she says and as she does. Please do not distract Benjamin – he is my husband's apprentice.' She gives her best attempt at a smile, but her eyes hold the truth. She is not an admirer of mine, like the pickpocket. Mrs Piddington exudes contempt and, more specifically, contempt for me. That's fine, I am not looking for friends. Just money.

'Alice, once Mrs Wilkinson demonstrates a solid understanding of what is involved, you may return to your remedial work. There's a mountain of garments piling up and the Humphries will be by to collect their clothes tomorrow.'

'Yes, Mrs Piddington,' Alice whispers. Mrs Piddington doesn't linger. She bustles back across the floor, through the curtain, and up the stairs towards her husband's office. The door slams shut, shaking the walls.

'Don't mind her. You'll get used to her.'

My eyes flick back towards Alice, who is concentrating on her work. 'I hope not,' I state, pulling a chair out to sit next to my new co-worker.

Alice smiles and, unlike Mrs Piddington, her smile reaches her eyes, lighting her face despite the terrible bruise she's sporting. 'We cut the fabric first. Faster that way.' Alice takes one of the bones from the pile on the table and passes some pre-cut fabric my way. She takes her needle and begins sewing a new casing for me to copy. It's mundane work, and I stab myself more times than I care to admit with the thin needle, but a job is a job. And I need it. Yes, I need this job and the money. That's all I need to tell myself. I can survive whippings, beatings, lashings, bites and kicks. I can survive Mrs Piddington and her cold shop filled with dead carcass bones.

'I'm Alice,' the battered woman says, without looking up from her needle.

'Yes, that woman mentioned,' I reply. I glance over at the man, who is still focused on the stay, his hands nimble and efficient in the craft. He doesn't acknowledge me. In fact, neither he nor Alice speak again. Heads bob, hands are hectic, but there are no voices. The only sounds are the shuffling of fabric, sporadic coughing, a few sighs and maybe some strong words after I prick myself for the seventh time that day. I groan. Tomorrow will be better. Time practising a skill: that's all that is needed. And time I have now. Too much of it.

I cock my head so I can take in my new surroundings. There's a kitchen off the sewing room and I assume the living quarters would be upstairs, near the office, if not offsite. The workroom has a low ceiling, with a number of candles strategically placed around the walls and on the tables. The only windows I see are the front glazes overlooking the street. There are worse places to work; St Giles is full of them. I'm glad to have found something. I hadn't known where to start when it came to finding employment.

My lodging in Clerkenwell will do for now, although I hope to rent a room to myself soon – sharing with strangers means you never really get a decent night's sleep. At least Clerkenwell is becoming familiar ground. I'd frequented Hockley-in-the-Hole many a time to see Robert fight. And win. Whatever his faults as a husband and human being, he's a talented boxer and skilled with a dagger. Or was, rather. He taught me how to finess my fighting skills. But this needlework provides me with a new life, a second chance – well, a third chance, really – to start over. And I'd rather die than find myself at one of the workhouses – only the poorest, most desperate women go there, ragged, with toothless mouths, sifting the cinder heaps for anything still worth burning – or a brothel. No thank you. I'm far too proud and stubborn to seek refuge at such a place. I'll happily stab myself with this godforsaken needle a dozen more times than stoop to a workhouse or brothel.

I readjust on my seat and look up at Alice, who stops stitching, eyeing me curiously. She's a healthy-looking woman, despite the black eye, but certainly not a happy one. I recognise that unhappiness – the kind of resignation that only comes from a man who seeks to control by any means possible: money, fists, belt or cock. I groan inwardly.

'I'm Elizabeth.'

And just like that, Alice cracks a smile. Not what I am used to cracking, but it may or may not have cracked one from me too.

The woman hates me. And by woman, I mean my new master, because let's face it – it might be Mr Piddington's name above the shop, but it certainly wasn't his trousers he wore. Mrs Piddington runs the shop with stern looks, sharp breaths and even stronger words.

The next few days at Piddington's are much the same. I arrive at daybreak and work tirelessly until late each evening. My body aches in places it shouldn't from sitting all day, like the bone above my arse, or my elbows from having them perched in front of me working my needle. I have taken to standing at random times throughout the day to shake the stiffness from my joints, often to the amusement of my co-workers.

Alice and Benjamin don't speak much. In fact, I haven't heard Benjamin say anything. Makes me wonder if he can. Speak, that is. He doesn't even breathe loudly; I sometimes forget he is there. Their quietness isn't so much a problem, in fact; I'm just not used to it and not entirely sure if we are supposed to speak while working. The bigger, more alarming concern is their general acceptance of the monotonous daily routine without even a notion of rewarding themselves at the end of the working day. I mean, how can you not have a drink after sitting all day! My head shakes at their senselessness and then I sigh a large sigh and my shoulders sag a few inches. Alice glances up at me, smiles and nudges my casing. As in, *here, let me help you by reminding you why you are here* … as if I could forget! All I do now is sit and sew and turn into a statue! Bah. Listen to me, being ungrateful for my new peaceful surroundings. But no, there is no socialising after a hard day's work at Piddington's Stay-making and Haberdashery shop. Sometimes we eat dinner together, but that is purely because of timing and lack of space, rather than want of company. And I am starting to realise that a bit of company might not be so bad every now and then. And I emphasise, *and then*. Because I do not want – strike that – I do not *need* a friend. Friends are like boiling water; they soften you, like a potato.

As for Mrs Piddington, she ignores me for the most part, which suits me just fine. When she does bother to speak to me, it's normally a bark of orders mixed with a handful of sarcasm and a hint of animosity. *Not like that, Elizabeth. Watch Alice, Elizabeth. Not good enough, Elizabeth. Start again, Elizabeth. Stop wasting time, Elizabeth. You, lift that for Alice. You, move the basket to the back. You, get Benjamin his fabric.* All while looking up at me and shaking her bony finger in my face. She seems to have chosen the role of enemy rather than employer. A bossy employer. I don't know why she despises me so, but I have my suspicions. Most women steer clear of me – my crooked nose, dark eyes and pale skin add to my towering stature. Mr Piddington's cavalier attitude towards my gainful employment couldn't have helped. Alice, on the other hand, is another sort of animal – the wounded kind. I see the way Mrs Piddington acts towards her. Complete opposite to me. She isn't kind, I would say, but she isn't cruel either. Patient, maybe even a little protective, would be the best words for Mrs Piddington's attitude towards Alice, always soft tones and gentle gestures. No finger stabbing at Alice; that gesticulation is reserved for me, not my battered co-worker.

And battered she is. On just my second day at the shop, Alice arrived sporting more bruises and cuts on her face; red marks were visible around her throat and left a trail down beneath her dress. London is cruel; husbands can be crueller. Alice didn't speak much but when she did I found myself listening to what she had to say. It only felt right that someone did, even if it was me – someone Alice hardly knew. Yes, I dare say I felt an affinity for Alice from the start. My eyes and my heart took their fill of her that morning. But to be clear, she isn't my friend. I am not a potato.

'Elizabeth,' Mrs Piddington says curtly, 'there's someone here to see you.' The Mistress of Misery, the chosen title I have given my new master, appears out of nowhere. I hadn't heard her approach. I frown at my complacency before following Mrs Piddington from behind the curtain to the front shop, where Constable Boyle is standing with his hands in his trouser pockets. His coat makes his shoulders look broader; a very respectable-looking man. I wipe my hands on my skirt and tuck my hair behind my ears before approaching.

'Something wrong?' I ask, wary of his visit. I am rewarded with a raised eyebrow and a slight grin.

'No, nothing is wrong, Mrs Wilkinson.'

I sigh. 'Elizabeth.'

He looks around the shop before continuing. A few customers are browsing through some ribbons, trying to match them to a jacket strewn across the counter.

'How are you finding the work?' he asks, returning his attention my way.

'Riveting,' I state drily.

'Right, well, I guess it isn't quite the rookery.' Matthew places his hat on his head and turns towards the door, pausing to look out on to the street through the window.

Not quite ready to return to my workbench yet, I blurt, 'Can I expect more of these visits?'

Constable Boyle remains steadfast, observing the pedestrians as they pass.

Unsure if he heard me or not, I try again. 'It's just ... I see you, and I think I'm in trouble.'

'Do you plan on causing trouble?' he asks, finally glancing over his shoulder.

I take a moment to think about this, scratching my neck. The constable laughs at me so I glare at him. 'Why are you laughing?'

'You must think if you're going to cause trouble, Mrs Wilkinson?'

'It's Elizabeth,' I groan. 'And no...'

'Then you should not be nervous to see me. I was merely checking in to see how you have settled into your new surroundings.' He nods once. 'Good day, Mrs Wilkinson.'

Bold bastard.

I march towards him, about to tell him not to call me that, before I see his attention has reverted back across the street. His hand, hovering over the handle, and his head tilt give me pause. His sly smile causes my heart to beat faster, my blood working hard through my hands, which open and close, warming up. For what? I am not quite sure. He pivots to face me. 'It seems... while you may not wish to *cause* trouble, Mrs Wilkinson, that does not mean it won't *find* you.'

With that, he pushes the door open, allowing the damp air to enter the shop floor and my bones. Confused, I follow, watching him fall into line with the other Londoners. He halts at the corner and spins, jutting his chin in the direction of the crowds. I follow his gaze over the heads and my eyes find their mark.

He is trouble.

CHAPTER 7

'**E**LIZABETH! CLOSE THE door! You're letting the cold air in!' Mrs Piddington shouts.

It takes me a minute, but I comply. My pickpocket waves at me, smiling before hobbling off with another boy in the same direction as the constable, and I follow the Mistress of Misery back behind the curtain. I feel Mrs Piddington's eyes on me as I take my seat next to Alice. Once seated, I look up at her, returning her stare. Force of habit. After all the years of Robert drilling into me never to look away first, it's ingrained in me as much as my need to breathe. I was always told it's a sign of weakness. I recall Robert's words: *Always hold your gaze. If your opponent looks away first, you have her.* I can hear his voice as if he were still here, right beside me. I shiver.

Mrs Piddington retreats, allowing me to get back to work.

'She doesn't like disruption,' Alice whispers, not taking her eyes off her needle and thread.

Disruption?

I roll my eyes. *Could Mrs Piddington fight?* I can't help but imagine hitting the Mistress of Misery in the face. Now, *that* would be riveting.

'Elizabeth!'

I turn to see my crippled pickpocket shuffling towards me, away from the wall where his chums are gathered, all watching the streets – looking for their next victim, no doubt. But this boy only has eyes for me, it seems.

He peeks around my hip – because that's about as high as he comes to on me – glancing at the shop, and then returns his sights to me.

'What do you want?' I ask, rather abruptly. I don't mean to sound short, but I'm tired and thirsty.

'What are *you* doing? In there?' he asks, pointing towards the shop, dumbfounded.

'Working,' I reply, cocking my head to one side.

'Working? *There?*' he sniffs, shoving his hands into both pockets. 'That isn't you.'

'It isn't?'

He looks up at me and then back at the ground, shaking his head, trying to kick a stone with his gammy foot. *Missed.*

He looks... lost. Not that he doesn't know where he is in London, everyone knows we're in Holborn, but more confused about something... How he found me again is a mystery. Must have followed me the other day. Regardless, he clearly knows London better than I do, despite his young years. I study him some more; he has a few scrapes – they look fresh – and his skin looks dry from the cold. At least he's wearing a coat today.

'So what am I, then?' I ask, breaking the silence.

'You're a prize fighter,' he states, looking back up at me.

I shake my head. 'Not any more.' I roll my shoulders and stretch my limbs, shaking the tension from my joints after a long day of sitting ... and all the years of fighting. The very thought of it causes my muscles to seize, as if on alert, ready to battle.

'Why not? You're really going to sit and sew for the rest of your life? Making corsets you'll never actually wear?' The boy's face pinches; he looks both disappointed and disgusted. I grunt.

'What's your name, boy?'

He bites his cheek, unsure whether to tell me or not, like it's a secret. He looks around to make sure no one is listening. 'People call me Halfinch,' he finally says.

I laugh. I can't help it. It's too ridiculous.

'Why are you laughing? That's my name, all right? Halfinch, because I *pinch* stuff, get it? Or did all of your fights knock your brains to pudding?'

He's hurt. And just like that, a spark flickers in my chest where my heart should beat. I instantly regret laughing. 'Well, I have to go.' I toss my head in the direction of The Black Hog. It's almost seven and I need a drink. I've been needing a drink since I woke up, except now I have to work through the day. Gone are the days of nocturnal living. Of sleeping all day, only to be woken by Robert or one of his mates telling me whether they need me to fight or not. And through it all, there was always gin. That one constant, the drink to make me forget the pain that comes with breathing.

'See you around, Halfinch,' I say, retreating from the boy. His eyes look up at me in a way that makes me uncomfortable, like he wants to know me. I'm not a good person. And I have nothing to offer the child. So he needs to leave me and go on his way. He can survive his life his way, and I can survive mine my way.

'It's not right,' Halfinch says, stopping me. 'You. In there.'

I don't have to see what he is looking at to know what he is talking about.

I sigh. 'Listen, I need money and I'm not a thief or a whore—'

'No, you're a prize fighter.'

'You're wrong.'

'*You're* wrong!' he shouts, causing a few people to look our way. He has the worst mulligrubs expression I've ever seen.

I glare at the onlookers until they move along before bending down towards Halfinch. 'I only fought because I had to.'

'You were *good* at it, though.' Halfinch straightens himself and hobbles over to my side, looking at Alice as she comes out of Piddington's. I'm surprised to see the Mistress of Misery escorting her, my eyebrows hitting my hairline. It's only Halfinch's gentle voice that lulls me out of my trance.

'I remember, this one time, you beat a woman so badly that it took three men to pull you off her. Then you turned on the men and knocked one of their teeth out! *POW!*' Halfinch mock-punches himself in the face and falls to the ground with great dramatic flair. I snort. I remember the very instance to which he is referring. Halfinch rolls over and looks back towards the shop and the two women, quietly walking away. I don't know where Mrs Piddington is heading; she and her fat husband live above the shop, so I can only assume she is walking Alice home. My head hurts, trying to understand the woman that is my new employer. She appears cold, strict and indifferent, she's a strong woman, exerting her authority over her employees and her husband with hard stares and an even harsher tongue, except ... when she's not. And she's not around Alice. *Hmmm.*

Alice is plump and dishevelled. Mrs Piddington is patting her back. I'm shocked by her sudden – or maybe it isn't so sudden – concern for Alice. Although, now that I think of it, Mrs Piddington always does seem to have more time for Alice, genuine pity and sympathy for the woman. Halfinch and I both watch as the pair stop to talk. Alice nods to Mrs Piddington and then turns to continue on her way. Mrs Piddington stands and watches her employee leave, shoulders hunched, resigned to her fate. Alice works all day to take home money to her husband, who will no doubt spend it on booze and prostitutes. My mouth twitches, and I feel my muscles tighten beneath my clothes as anger begins piercing my thoughts. I shake my head just as Mrs Piddington spots me, raising her chin, her posture and demeanour changing instantly at the sight of me. To my further surprise, Mrs Piddington nods at me. Just once. But it's more acknowledgement than she has given me in the past month I've been working for her. Her eyes then fall down to my side and I follow her stare to the boy huddled next to me, half hiding behind my skirt. I frown.

I start to say farewell to him for the second time that evening, but he looks up at me and I forget my words.

He just stares his sad eyes up at me. 'You don't belong there.'

CHAPTER 8

T HE BOY IS right. This is where I belong, at The Black Hog, drinking my hard-earned money away with the rest of the throwaway citizens of London. I can relax here, disappear, if even just for a while. Let the warm liquid infiltrate my body and senses, numbing me to the world and my so-called life full of responsibilities I never thought I would have.

Drinking. My only vice, and luckily the taverns I haunted in St Giles didn't cost very much; neither does The Black Hog. It's refreshing drinking at a tavern that isn't in St Giles.

'Elizabeth?' a voice says behind me.

Oh God, please no. The voice sounds too familiar. Too feminine and gentle. A voice I'd hoped never to hear again. I just want to drink my gin in peace. Gin is the only thing I want right now. Not company. I only managed to get rid of Halfinch a short while ago; the little pest followed me from the shop to The Black Hog and the innkeeper chucked him out without me having to lift a finger. I mimicked his wave from earlier as the door slammed in his face.

'Elizabeth, is that you?' the voice continues. I slowly turn on my bar stool to face the eager woman trying to get my attention. Her angel face is beaming. *Sophie.*

How can I go for years without seeing this woman and now, in the space of a few weeks, see her twice? I shake my head and rub my hand down over my face; I can't blink her away, though.

'Sophie,' I respond, raising my tankard unsteadily in recognition. Sophie's smile remains.

'May I sit?' she asks, but doesn't bother to wait for my answer; she pulls out the stool next to me and mounts it with great ease, despite the tight stay and dress she wears. Her garment is beautiful. I can't deny her that. And I hate that I like it, especially on her. The intricate pattern, full of green, white and gold. There is a light orange detail stitched through too. It looks expensive. Sophie looks expensive. The gown makes her eyes appear more emerald green than ever, her surprisingly creamy-white teeth even brighter, her smile impossibly radiant.

'I heard about Robert,' she says gently, her eyes glued to mine. I turn on my seat and ignore her comment, taking another sip of my drink, trying to keep my guard up, my face stony.

'How are you, Elizabeth?'

I snort, my smile tight, my eyelids half closed. I shake my head again and continue drinking.

'You look well,' she tries next.

I ignore her remark by asking a question of my own. 'What are you drinking?'

'Me? Oh, I don't drink. Liquor makes me feel horrid and my skin gets all blotchy,' Sophie replies, searching my face. 'I've often thought of you, and heard you've made quite the name for yourself in the fight scene down at St Giles.' She licks her plump lips and looks back at a table of women who are getting loud. They'd clearly had an all-day session; something I no longer get to do, now that

I have to *work*. I follow Sophie's gaze to have a closer look at the group of rambunctious women. They are all pros. I turn when I see Vincent Love sitting a few seats away from the group, a snarl of a smile spreading across his mouth. I hadn't seen him when I came in. But it shouldn't surprise me to see him again. It was here that I first met the brothel owner. I feel Sophie's eyes upon me – she flits between me and the man.

'Well, it was good to see you again, Elizabeth. Take care,' Sophie says, hopping off her stool. She reaches for my shoulder and I automatically flinch at the unexpected touch. 'Oh, I'm sorry, I didn't mean to—'

'Go away, Sophie,' I snap through gritted teeth, straightening up on my stool. Sophie hesitates – she clearly wants to say something to me. She only takes a few steps before coming back and grabbing my shoulder again, turning me so we're face to face.

'Zounds!' I shout, after spilling my drink. The patrons turn their attention to our altercation. I stare right back. 'What are you looking at?'

'You know, it hasn't been easy for me either since Stockton,' Sophie says, tears forming in her eyes.

I don't say anything. There isn't anything to say. I saw where she works.

'You have nothing to say to me?'

I still don't reply. Not even when I see Vincent stand and use his cane to exit the tavern, tipping his head at me before he disappears into the night. I take another long drink of my gin, finishing it and slamming the tankard on the bar top.

'You left me.' Sophie wipes the lone tear falling down her cheek with her hand, forces a smile and nods. 'Not everyone is as strong as you, Elizabeth.'

My eyes snap up to meet hers. Neither of us moves. We just stare at each other, letting our thoughts, words and feelings filter through our eyes. A stare that could be mistaken for love, or hate, both etched with pain. Sophie's friends have clearly become impatient waiting for her to return to their table. Piqued and curious, a couple wander over towards us – still staring, still not speaking.

'So, who are you then?' asks a heavy-set woman, her skin congested with deep lines, well-worn in her expressions. Sophie is in a different class to this harlot. I roll my eyes, and try to catch the innkeeper's attention by lifting my hand. He doesn't see me.

'I know who you are,' announces another in a strong cockney accent; she's taller and less fat than the other one. 'You're that fighting woman. You fight bears and shite ... Yeah, I've seen you before. People call you Elizabeth, don't they?' My eyes fly open, unable to contain my amusement after the whore's ridiculous outburst. My laughter rumbles through my chest and catches the women off-guard and they instinctively take a step backwards. I'm not surprised. I do sound a bit insane.

The same woman says, 'It was your husband who was hanged a few weeks back, wasn't it?' At that, my body tenses. These women know who my husband is, *was*. This is no longer funny. I start rubbing my neck, before rolling my shoulders and extending my fingers in a deep stretch. Sophie must notice the change as she tries to usher the two ladies away from me. I stand up, towering over the three of them.

'My name is Elizabeth,' I state, 'and I have no husband.' I'm not going to talk about Robert. Robert is dead. And any mention of him spoils my attempt to erase him from my memory. Sophie grabs at the women and steers them away again, concern etched in her eyes as they dart between her friends and me.

I notice the innkeeper standing across the bar from me, and it's enough to break the tension. I order another drink and watch as the three women return to the table, where another of the whores is describing one of her client's knot fetishes.

The clatter of their voices gets lost among noise of the other patrons in the bar, filling my ears while gin fills my belly and nothingness clouds my mind. It's liberating. Finally, the stress in my neck begins to subside.

Drinking. That is what I am here for.

Forgetting. That is what is going to help me now.

I wake to find Sophie trying to hoist me off the cobbles and onto my feet. She is such a scrawny little creature compared to me. There is no way she is going to succeed in lifting me up off the floor.

'Don't just stand there, help me!' Sophie shouts at her friends. They all gather around me, each taking a firm grip on my body, dragging me up from the street. It's dark out. Bollocks, I must have passed out when I felt the fresh air. I try to pull away from their grasp, but lose my balance and fall back to the ground. The sound of the women laughing gives me some focus. I try to look around and gather my wits, but my head is heavy. The effects of the gin I drank earlier have worn off a little – my eyes are less hazy now – but not entirely. Sophie crouches next to me and offers me a mug of small beer. I sniff the drink before having a sip, recoiling at the bland taste.

'Gin,' I spit out, pushing away Sophie's hand and with it the beer.

'No more gin for you,' one of the other prostitutes says, giggling, obviously still drunk herself. They are all hanging off one another like a choral troupe from a theatre production.

'Where have you taken me?' I ask no one in particular.

'Taken you? We haven't taken you anywhere, love. You stumbled outside the tavern and this is as far as you got!' someone retorts. They are all laughing now. I can see the wooden sign with The Black Hog carved into it. Sophie is pushing my hair out of my face, tucking the stray pieces behind my ears.

'Stop touching me, Sophie! Just leave me, would you!' I shout at her, slapping her hands away from me.

'Oi, oi! No need to be nasty, we were only trying to help! But if you don't need it, then we'll be on our merry little way. Time for us to be getting back anyway,' the pot-bellied prostitute shouts, grabbing Sophie and pulling her away from me. Sophie tries to protest but is overruled by her gang, who carry her away, all the while looking back at me, slouched on the ground. The cold is beginning to seep through my clothes and hit my body, sending shivers up my spine and down my arms. I instinctively wrap my arms around myself and lean my head back against the wall of the tavern.

After they're gone, I realise the bad smell is the stack of horse dung several yards from me. *Lovely.* I try to get to my feet but the gin hasn't drained from my legs yet. They wobble under my weight, and after only a few paces I stumble back against the wall and slide down again. The lower I get to the ground, the closer my eyes are to shutting again.

'Just leave, Sophie ... Go back to your whores and let me be,' I mutter to the wall. I need to get up. I can't stay here, I'll die from the cold. I laugh to myself at the thought – after Mrs Dierdre, Sir Frederick and Robert, it isn't their wickedness that will be my undoing, but the London elements. I grew, fled and fought through them all and now that I am on my own, I crumple. But maybe that isn't a bad thing, because this is my choice. But then a face flashes in my mind, and then another, and another. Alice, Halfinch and Sophie. They're still here. Surviving. And I'll be damned if I let them win the biggest fight of all, the fight of living. No, I'm not dying tonight.

And with that, I drag myself up off the ground. There is no rest in London. Nowhere to escape. I can't just disappear into the background. I've been doing that too much. Time to step out of the shadows and into the light.

Ha. Listen to me. I actually sound like I believe what I am saying.

CHAPTER 9

'You're late!' Mrs Piddington barks when she notices I am in my seat next to Alice, my head lying flat against the work table. I can't lift it. Not yet. Too painful. I wish I could have stayed in bed. Even if next to a cockalorum who grizzles in his sleep like a slumbering beast. The Black Hog is becoming a regular stop after work. One I need to stop. Soon. My money is quickly evaporating and my wages from the shop aren't filling my purse as quickly as I am spending it.

I'm learning the cost of living in urban London, and it isn't cheap. Tidy clothes are essential – I've been scolded by Mrs Piddington on several occasions because my clothes aren't clean enough. According to the Mistress of Misery, appearing dirty and dishevelled is to be avoided at all costs. If I want my own room to rent, that would cost more money for clean linen, coal, food – and that is after I've consumed my daily fill of gin. I could work every day, all day, at Piddington's and I still won't be able to afford the life I long for.

'Long night?' Alice peeps. I open one eye and study her. She is still focused on her work. The bruising down her neck behind her ear is fading from purple to a greenish-yellow. I cast my opened eye over her quickly and don't notice any new markings on her face at least.

'Something like that,' I grumble, slowly lifting my head to make sure my brain doesn't hit my skull. When I am convinced my brains aren't going to pour out of my ears, I open my other eye and take a deep breath.

'You shouldn't drink so much,' Alice whispers, flicking her eyes to me and then back to her sewing. 'Drinking brings out the worst in people.'

I don't argue. Firstly, because she isn't wrong, and secondly, that would mean engaging with her and I am not ready for that kind of commitment. So instead, I study her hands and how effortlessly she wields her needle – with such graceful finesse it's like she came out of her mother's womb with it attached to her hand. Like it's a part of her. But then I notice the blue bruises on her wrists. Instinctively, I reach out and grab her hands, slowly turning them over to inspect the markings. These are new. God's blood.

I follow the length of Alice's arm up to her face, her eyes facing forward.

'Let go of her, Elizabeth,' a firm voice commands from behind Alice. I wait for Alice to look at me, but she doesn't. After what seems like a few minutes, but is probably only a few seconds, I release her and she continues with her work without missing a beat. I, too, pick up my needle and grab a casing to sew. Mrs Piddington stands for a while, inspecting us – inspecting me – before returning to the front of the shop. As soon as she's gone, I drop my needle and my head back on the table.

It's going to be a long day.

'Good Lord, you chew like an animal,' Mrs Piddington states, tutting and flicking her chin up to exaggerate her annoyance. 'Honestly,' she directs at Alice, 'you'd think the constable had some standards. But I must say, I am beginning to question his integrity if he chooses to bed someone as common as this harlot!'

'Excuse me?' I ask, pushing back my chair, lowering my stale bread and standing to my full height.

'You heard me,' she scowls, rubbing her chin between her bony fingers. 'We all know how you got this job, Elizabeth. No one of your background just walks into an establishment and gets a job as easily as you!'

I roll my head from side to side, stretching my neck, trying to release the tension edging its way through my body. Alice remains seated at the dinner table in the kitchen, silent, quietly eating her food, avoiding eye contact with either of us.

'Poor Constable Boyle! Who knows what disease you've given him!' Mrs Piddington screeches, piercing my ears. I flinch away from the high-pitched sound and squeeze my eyes shut – trying to unsee the red glazing over my senses.

'I didn't bed the constable.' My words spit out through gritted teeth, my eyes still pressed firmly shut. The hatred and anger flow down my neck and shoulders into my arms and fingers, curling into fists. My legs are taut, trying to hold my body in place behind the table.

I can't hit my employer.
I can't punch the Mistress of Misery.
I can't scratch her eyes out of her face.
I can't.
I can't.

I can.

I want to.

I really want to hit Mrs Piddington.

Zounds.

I groan. Willing myself to return to humanity. To the room. Anywhere but the darkness my mind is trying to take me to.

I slowly open my eyes and focus on the jug of beer sitting on the wooden counter that sits under the only window in the kitchen. The daylight peeks through ever so subtly, illuminating the otherwise dark room. My eyes flick to Alice, then to Mrs Piddington.

I really, really want to punch you in the face. Watch your nose bust and bleed all over this floor. Hear the crunch of bone. Feel the bite of pain as my fist connects with your ugly mug.

I could do that.

I could.

But I shouldn't.

I won't, I decide to myself. That would be bad and would end my employment at the shop and guarantee me an escort to Newgate prison. Plus, I am owed wages at the end of this week. I can last until then. Surely.

Mrs Piddington continues her verbal assault, seemingly oblivious to how close she came to a beating. My breath deepens, my mouth no longer twitching, and I focus on releasing the tension from my muscles. Something I learned to do after each fight. You see, you have to be in a certain mindset when you fight another person. You have to strip away your humanity and leave the barest, most basic parts of yourself in order to force yourself to do what you have to do, which is anything you can to survive.

'How many times did you two lie together – once, twice, more?' Mrs Piddington drones on and on, trying to bait me.

'I didn't bed him,' I repeat, slowly returning to my chair. I notice Alice lets out her breath. She must have been holding it.

'You are not fit to work here, Elizabeth,' says Mrs Piddington, leaning forward so I can feel her warm breath. 'You are nothing but a whore—'

It all happens so fast. Crimson with fury, I jump up again, but at the same time Alice knocks over her tea, spilling it all over Mrs Piddington's tablecloth.

'Oh, you clumsy fool, Alice!' she shouts, grabbing at a nearby swatch to soak up the liquid. 'This is coming out of your wages!'

'Yes, Mrs Piddington. I'm sorry, Mrs Piddington,' Alice mutters, grabbing another cloth to help clean. 'Let me, Mrs Piddington, please.' She frantically dabs at the spilt tea, trying to erase its mark and the last few minutes of tension. I step back and shake my head. I almost lost myself to that dangerous part of me I shouldn't allow out again. That dark place inside me, born from depravity, where I unleash everything to destroy anyone in my way – just like Robert taught me. No mercy. Not ever. Oh God, I could have snapped Mrs Piddington like a twig and ended up at the gallows by the next hanging day. I shake my head and glance out the kitchen window. A crow swoops onto a windowsill across the way, watching me closely.

Is this a sign? I've heard of omens before. Maybe this is one. I startle when Mrs Piddington shouts again, roughly brushing Alice off. 'Just leave it, would you! Honestly, just go before I dismiss you! Now! Both of you!'

Alice and I gather what is left of our dinner and head back to the work table in the back room. I chance a look back at the Mistress of Misery, and her tablecloth. She's frozen to the floor; one hand covers her mouth and the other sits atop her chest, which is shaking.

Is she crying?

Alice touches my arm and beckons me to sit with her. I look at her briefly and swallow, nodding once my agreement. I peek over my shoulder again to see if our employer is still there, but the woman has turned to look out of the same window I was just standing in front of. I wonder if the crow is still there. Maybe she'll see it too. I take another bite of bread before I notice that Alice is watching me.

'What?' I snap, pushing away the loose strands of dark-brown hair that have fallen over my face.

'You need this job, as do I.'

I think about this. Do I? What I need is more money. I am almost out of coin and there is no way Mrs Piddington will give me my wages early, it's still a few more days until I am owed money. Maybe I should challenge someone, just for the release of all the stress that's been building. Take out my hatred for Mrs Piddington on someone else. Someone who has no authority over my employment and livelihood. All I have now is a gruelling long day, sore back, sore fingers and lack of sleep from sharing a room with strangers each night. I'm beginning to understand why Robert acted the way he did. Work was for a different type of human. And this place? Well, I'm starting to think this job isn't for me after all. Sure, it is safe and quiet, but God it's boring to Christ. The life with Robert had been hard. Brutal, even. But the money never ran out. And that is new.

Something I am not liking. How am I supposed to cope with this job if I can't drink at my favourite haunt each day?

'And besides, Mrs Piddington isn't as bad as you think,' Alice adds. 'She is a hard woman, unpleasant at times, but ...' Her voice trails off.

I glance up, distracted from my mental ramblings. 'But what?'

Alice pauses, her brow furrowed. 'But she is capable of kindness and has hidden strength not many see.'

'Kindness? She's docking your wages.'

'No, she won't.' Alice smiles a small smile, before it fades just as quickly. 'She just said that because you were there.' Alice then picks up a whalebone to begin stitching.

I look at her for a few more minutes, an idea coming to life.

Alice.

Alice will give me some money. She cares about me. I can tell by the way she is always trying to help me in some way, like I haven't been taking care of myself since I was five. My lips press into a thin smile.

'Alice,' I whisper, clearing my throat, 'I'm a bit short of money for lodging ...' I pause, glancing at her to see if she's listening. She hasn't stopped working that needle and thread, but her eyes flick to me once before dropping down to her task. It's half truth, not a complete lie. 'And I was going to ask Mrs Piddington if she would give me enough to secure my bed for a few more nights to tide me over, but after that' – I jut my chin over my shoulder – 'I doubt she'll be amenable and—'

I'm cut off when Benjamin enters the back room. He doesn't offer any greeting, just hops up on to his usual working board and starts working diligently.

Bad timing, Benjamin. I huff out a breath and grab a piece of pre-cut fabric and whalebone, preparing for another tedious task of stitching. The piles of fabric and bones never seem to diminish in front of me. Alice is fortunate to be able to help with other tasks, especially helping Benjamin when he needs a spare pair of hands to hold items together. He never asks me. Then again, he knows Alice better, I suppose. But as I start to work my needle, I notice Alice sliding her hand over to me. She leaves a half-crown next to my hand and then withdraws her own, and picks up her implements again.

I stare at the coin. I count in my head what that will afford me. Half-a-crown is two and sixpence. I can get a cheap room for a week for around one shilling and four pence if I'm lucky ... My eyes dart up at Alice, my fragile co-worker.

'You're just going to give me this money?' I ask, licking my lips like a dog over a roast bone.

'Yes,' she replies solemnly.

I frown. 'Why?' I ask, not fully understanding why Alice would just give me money. I mean, I know I asked her for it and I hoped she would, but didn't fully believe she would actually do it.

'Because,' she starts, pulling at her thread for tautness, 'you're a good person.'

I swallow hard, not liking the fact that Alice is willing to hand over her money to anyone, especially someone like me. Someone who just took advantage of her meekness for their own gain. I shake my head. 'No, I'm not, Alice.'

Alice's eyes slowly drift up to my face and she drops her hands. 'Yes, you are. You just haven't had the chance to be one yet. And I like you. You talk to me. You …' she begins, and takes a deep breath. 'You see me.'

What?

Alice's focus is back on her task, but her eyes are smiling. I sit here, not sure what to do. But my hands are already reaching for the money. I can't help it. I am imagining the type of room I can get with this – it will cover my accommodation for a few weeks if I am less fussy and stay at one of the two-pence lodgings some more, but I really, really hate sharing a bed with strangers. This woman, who barely knows me, has just given me enough to answer my unspoken wishes.

And then I feel it.

A discomfort.

A tightening in my chest. I rub my hand over my left breast. The thrumming grows stronger. My breath catches.

That squeezing deep within. I squeeze my eyes shut.

It's my heart.

When Mr Piddington returns to the shop at closing time, he isn't alone. I catch a glimpse through the curtain of his companion – I recognise him immediately. He's the same tall, gaunt man I saw at Robert's hanging. The same gent I'd seen meeting with Robert numerous times, when Robert thought I was passed out. The same wig-wearing aristocrat whose last encounter with Robert had not been a pleasant one. He and Robert had a disagreement and Robert had threatened the man. It seems no threatening mattered. This man was capable of far more than vengeful words and flicks of a blade. Seeing him here, not five paces from me, sends a chill down my spine. A powerful man, this fellow standing with my employer, of that I am certain. I frown, wondering why he's here.

Mr Piddington introduces the man to his wife, who is beaming for a change. 'Magistrate Trelawny, may I introduce my wife, Mrs Sarah Piddington. My darling, this is Magistrate Charles Trelawny.'

Magistrate?

Oh no. He can't be here. My heart starts to race and my breathing quickens. Alice pauses and gives me a concerned look, her brow creasing. I force my eyes down to my work, praying the man doesn't come to the back.

But as per usual, God snubs me.

The magistrate bows to kiss Mrs Piddington's hand. My lip curls in disgust as Alice and Benjamin look up, and the three of them enter the back workroom. I keep working, not wanting to draw attention.

'As you can see, my apprentice, Mr Benjamin Halliday, is more than capable of producing high-quality stays. Any design you like for your lovely wife ... I apologise, please remind me what her name is, Magistrate Trelawny?' Mr Piddington is doing his best to sound sophisticated, his tone full of sincerity. I, on the other hand, am frantic, broke and sore from sitting on my arse all day doing nothing but sewing anything and everything Alice tells me to. My spirits had lifted after receiving the half-crown from Alice earlier, but all those joyful feelings fled out of the door when the magistrate arrived. Clearly no space for both in the shop.

'Her name is Dolores, Mr Piddington. You have a wonderful establishment, filled with so many fine things,' Mr Trelawny replies, surveying the various finished garments, loose materials and colourful ribbons, before turning to my male co-worker. 'You produce very fine work, Mr Halliday.'

'Thank you, sir,' Benjamin says, standing when he is addressed only to return quickly to his seated position on top of the working board. I make a mental note that Benjamin can in fact speak, so to be mindful of what I say so he doesn't repeat anything against me later.

The magistrate slithers over to where Alice and I sit, quietly working. I freeze as he positions himself behind me. I can feel my heart drum inside my chest. I glance up at Mr and Mrs Piddington, who are holding their breath. I smile, aware of their apprehension, and close my eyes as I focus on my breathing.

'And how are you finding your new job, Mrs Wilkinson?' the magistrate asks me.

Zounds. He knows who I am. My eyebrows pinch together at the mention of my name. I am seated, so he hovers above me – a dominant position in any game – and I don't like it. Instincts cut in and I push my seat back, forcing him to retreat a few steps, and rise to face the man addressing me personally. He doesn't seem as tall when I unfold myself from my seat. 'It's a far cry from your previous employment in St Giles, wouldn't you agree?'

Well, he definitely remembers me.

'It is, sir,' I say calmly, reminding myself that I am in Holborn and not St Giles rookery.

'And your hands – they are up to this more ... *delicate* line of work?'

'That's a question better directed at Mr and Mrs Piddington, sir,' I state, holding his gaze. He hasn't blinked since I stood to face him. He's testing me, I can tell – for what, I don't know. But this man is looking at me with hungry eyes, and now it seems he wants a taste. By God, I'll give him a taste if he wants one. Never again will I let a man intimidate me.

Just not here. With four witnesses.

'I'm asking you, Mrs Wilkinson,' he says, finally blinking, and exposing stained teeth behind his grimace – stains he undoubtedly wears on his soul too. This man indulges, just like everyone else. He has a vice. A weakness. I see past his façade of nobility; he stinks of a foulness I can't quite grasp.

'They're getting used to the work,' I answer truthfully. No point in lying.

Magistrate Trelawny leans towards me and whispers for only me to hear, 'Pity.'

He then directs his attention back to his hosts. 'Mr Piddington, I believe I have seen what I need to see. Where can we discuss costs?'

They leave my co-workers and me in the back workroom. Magistrate Trelawny is escorted through the curtain and upstairs, where the three speak at great length. Indeed, it isn't until Benjamin has finished his latest stay that they eventually reappear downstairs. It's well past closing time and my stomach grumbles to remind me of the time.

Gin-drinking time.

The curtain opens just enough for me to watch Magistrate Trelawny drape his coat over his shoulders and place his hat on his head. His eyes meet mine once more and he grimaces, causing the hairs on the back of my neck to stand. And then he is gone, into the London night.

Mr and Mrs Piddington stand whispering, conspiring. They both turn towards the curtain and I return to my work. I swallow back the bile rising in my throat, like I used to do whenever Robert announced my next fight. The acidic taste burns through my body.

Well, that definitely isn't how I expected my day to end at Piddington's Stay-making and Haberdashery shop.

CHAPTER 10

SINCE MAGISTRATE TRELAWNY'S visit, Mrs Piddington has become much more agreeable.

She's all 'Good morning, Elizabeth' and 'that's much better, Elizabeth' when it comes to my work.

Good, is all I think. Maybe you'll think about giving me something else to do now instead of picking up whalebones and stitching fabric around them.

And while the sudden change in treatment is welcome, I don't trust the Mistress of Misery one bit. Peculiar as it is, less so is Alice's absence from work yesterday, and again today. It is Mrs Piddington stomping around the kitchen at dinnertime, throwing pots and pans in and out of cupboards without actually cooking anything, that has my eyebrows raised. After about ten minutes of ranting to herself, she stops and spins to see me sitting, alone, at the kitchen table, eating my fill.

Mrs Piddington leans back against the kitchen bench and studies me.

I continue to chew my bread and don't break eye contact.

Habits and all.

'Alice is at St Bartholomew's hospital in Smithfield. She was beaten so badly—' Mrs Piddington's hand flies to cover the sob that escapes with her words. I stop chewing, wanting to hear the news. Needing to hear what happened to my soft-spoken co-worker who gave me enough money to secure a bed for the week and drink my fill in gin the last two nights, and I get my wages at the end of this day. Life was looking good for me. Was.

'Who did it?' I ask, swallowing the bread and taking a sip of table beer. I grimace at the blandness. Again, habits.

Mrs Piddington's eyes meet mine. 'Who do you think, Elizabeth?'

I lean back in my chair and rub the tops of my legs.

'Oh, come on, Elizabeth, you aren't beef-witted! Who do you think beats her every week? You see her injuries just like I do.'

I stare at my employer. She's angry. Beyond angry – she's seething. It finally dawns on me: she cares about Alice. She actually cares about the woman she employs. Maybe there is more to this woman after all. Alice certainly thinks so.

'The husband,' I state, because it isn't a question.

Mrs Piddington nods curtly and then swirls to stare out of the window. Seconds later, she grabs a dish and throws it at the wall. It smashes, and I flinch and throw my arm up to shield myself, but the pieces don't reach the table, or me for that matter. Wide-eyed, I look back to Mrs Piddington, who stands rooted to the same spot. She smoothens her hair and dress, and I stand to fetch the broom from the pantry. I have started sweeping the broken shards together when I feel Mrs Piddington approach me.

'I'll do it,' is all she says as she takes the broom from my hands. I let go and move to rearrange the chairs so she has room to manoeuvre, but she stops me. 'I said I'll do it, Elizabeth. Return to your work.'

For once in my life, I don't put up a fight.

He's the devil.

I'm sure of it. With his brown eyes and matching hair. His gaze is locked on me and I can't shake him, no matter how hard I try. He's taunting me. When I leave the lodging, the shop, sometimes even when I leave The Black Hog.

'Why are you here?' I ask the boy, who continues to follow me around like a lost puppy, including into the tavern. The innkeeper gives him a brief look but once he sees that the boy is with me, he forgets about him. I am annoyed by his assumption that this pickpocket belongs to me, like he's my responsibility.

He isn't.

'Why are you still *there*?' Halfinch asks, and I stop my drink inches from my mouth.

'Where?'

I wait, listening as a look of frustration fills his eyes.

'That swag! It's stupid, you don't belong there—'

'No, I don't belong in St Giles,' I blurt out, then continue to take long gulps of my gin. I clench my jaw as the bitter liquor flows through my throat and burns me from the inside. I feel the warmth spread through my limbs and the effects hit my head quick and fast.

'There are other places you can fight—'

'Not for women—'

'There are!' he shouts, throwing his arms in the air. 'There has to be—'

'Oh yeah, where?'

Halfinch shifts on the stool next to me, pinching his brows together, and looks down at the bar.

'Figg! Speak to James Figg, he'll help you,' Halfinch says, looking up at me.

'James Figg trains *men*,' I snap, between gritted teeth. Of course I know who James Figg is – who doesn't in the prize-fighting world? He's the best prize fighter there is and has a place over on Tottenham Court Road.

Or so Robert once told me.

Robert wanted to fight James. Badly. But it never happened, as far as I am aware.

'What about Hockley?' Halfinch pipes up again. His persistence would be admirable if it weren't so infuriating. I snort as I reach for my drink, and I think about Hockley-in-the-Hole – the infamous bear garden surrounded by ruinous houses on Rag Street. It's frequented by thieves and highwaymen, and not for the fainthearted. I laugh, recalling the story Robert told me of its past owner, a man by the name of Christopher Preston, who was attacked by one of his own bears and almost eaten before people learned of it. I shake my head.

Bastard deserved it.

'Well?' Halfinch asks, propping one arm up on to the bar top, his small fingers running through his hair.

'How old are you?' I ask him, curiosity getting the better of me.

'Why do you want to know?'

I shrug, not forcing the issue. I finish my drink and tap the bar with my tankard, asking the innkeeper (I should ask him his name) for another.

'Why do you drink that gin? It's horrid,' Halfinch says.

'It's cheap.'

I toss my pennies at the innkeeper and he reaches out, catching them. He eyes Halfinch again, but to the boy's credit, he glares back at the much larger man.

'You got money, boy?' the innkeeper barks.

Halfinch rolls his eyes, reaches into his pocket and slams a guinea on to the bar. My eyebrows fly up before I look at the innkeeper. He just quirks a smile and moves back to the end of the bar to continue his conversation with a few of his regular patrons. Halfinch starts grinning and quickly tucks his guinea coin back into his trouser pocket.

'You going to buy me a drink with that?' I ask.

'You have your own money,' he retorts. 'And besides, it isn't mine to spend.'

I eye the boy again, and he dips his head down. I close my eyes, starting to feel dizzy from the effects of the drink. Three gins in and I am already feeling better than I did when I walked in.

'So, how about it?' Halfinch pipes up again, when he realises I'm not going to question him about his loot. I'm no pillock. I know he is supposed to pass that back to someone. He and the other boys I've seen him with. He's part of a battalion, a band of pickpockets, but I've yet to see who leads them. Doesn't matter, though. If he's caught stealing, he'll hang. That's just the way it is here. Stealing is stealing, it makes no difference what age you are. Young, old, male, female. You get caught, you hang. Guilty of coining? You burn. Treason? You get disembowelled and your innards displayed for all of London to see.

This is London, and while humans live here, the inhumane customs that rule our living are enforced by men who have never had to survive the streets. I take another drink. Halfinch is still staring at me.

'Hockley-in-the-Hole?' he chimes again. Ah yes. That wretched place. He has a point. It's distasteful enough to perhaps let a woman fight there. I glance down at the pickpocket sitting next to me.

Little shite may be on to something.

But no, I'm not fighting again.

I look at Halfinch ...

No. Not going back.

Halfinch chuckles before hopping off his stool and pulling me down so my head is next to his.

'Good night, Championess,' he whispers into my ear. I swat him, but he pulls away and laughs some more. I can't stop the smile forming on my face as I watch my pickpocket limp out of The Black Hog, waving at the innkeeper before disappearing through the red doors.

The devil, I tell you.

CHAPTER 11

ALICE RETURNED TO work on the Monday. It was good to see her. I spent the weekend drinking my wages away and trying not to think about Mrs Piddington and Alice. I had to laugh at myself a few times, when I realised I was sitting at The Black Hog moaning about my work. In a matter of weeks, I had become like every other patron at the drinking house. Miserable, drunk and complaining about life. I got to run off Halfinch a couple of times too, which was more fun than I care to admit. The boy thinks I don't see him following me around. He's like a disease, easy to pick up and difficult to shed. When I asked him what he wanted, he just kept asking when my next fight would be, which is annoying considering I left that life behind for a simpler one.

'Boring one' is what he called it. I shrugged. Same thing.

So yes, returning to work on Monday to find Alice at her work place next to mine was a pleasant sight. I felt the strong desire to embrace the woman, but then I realised that would be stupid and probably scare her. I settled for a pat on her shoulder.

'You're back,' I say softly. I scan her face – which is still healing – and her arm, which is bound. She smiles at me, causing the split in her bottom lip to bleed. I frown and quickly grab a cloth from the kitchen for her. She doesn't stop smiling at me, though; she just takes the cloth and gently dabs her lip with her good arm. Alice can't do as much with one arm so she folds fabrics, holds things for Benjamin and brings me items to repair. Now that she can't do them, that is.

I feel like I should say something. Ask her about what happened with her husband, but I am not sure if that's normal or not. Does she expect me to ask her? Am I being nosy if I do? I scratch my head and look at her out of the corner of my eye, unsure of my next move.

'Ask,' she says, picking up another drape and measuring the length she needs. I drop my hand on the table and begin tapping it. Benjamin clears his throat. I shoot him a scowl and shake my head before returning to Alice. She lifts her eyes to mine while continuing her task.

'Why do you stay?' I ask. It's not what I wanted to ask her. But I'm not sure I want to know why she ended up in hospital this time. In her husband's twisted perception, she must have done something really bad for her to end up there. Normally, she just shows up at work with new bruises on different parts of her body, but that night ... it must have been something different that caused his rage to inflict that type of beating.

'Where would I go?' she asks in reply, tilting her head to the side slightly. It's true. Where would she go? The poorhouse? He'd find her. And if he didn't, other men would. Alice is too soft for this city. Like Sophie.

God, Sophie. How could she end up in the exact same position as she was in before? I shake my head. That's why I refuse to fight any more. I won't make the same mistakes. I've learned – especially now that I have this job. A bed each night, thanks to Alice.

I realise Alice is waiting for a response, but I don't have one. The truth is, I didn't leave Robert either for that exact same reason. London is a big city, but not big enough for a woman trying to flee her abusive husband. I swallow and make another attempt at conversation.

'Why did you end up at St Bartholomew's?'

Alice stills. 'What do you mean? I needed a hospital—'

'No, that's not what I meant,' I interrupt, licking my lips. 'I meant, what made him ...' I purse my mouth shut, trying to think of the words to ask the question. 'The other times ...' I try, but fail again. 'I mean, it's just that he doesn't always hurt you so badly.' I look at Alice, seeing myself in her tortured eyes. I know something happened that sent him into a fury. Alice needs to know what it was so she doesn't repeat the mistake. She needs to learn her husband's triggers. It's the only way to survive a marriage built on pain and torment. Alice blinks a few times and takes a long, slow breath, returning her attention to her folding duties. 'My money wasn't enough.'

I squint at her, confused. 'Wasn't enough, how? We weren't paid wages until ...' But the realisation hits me in the face like a swing from an opponent I failed to see coming. My breath catches and I feel nauseous all of a sudden. God, no. This woman ended up in hospital because she gave me money. I caused this. I did this to her – all the bruising, the scratches and the broken limbs are my doing – and I didn't even lay a hand to her. But I may as well have.

I suddenly feel violent. My eyes are hazy and my mind fogs over, devoid of human thought and rationale. All I can feel is tension in my muscles and a fury burning deep within. I'm about to demand where her husband works when Mrs Piddington appears.

'Elizabeth, Alice, I wonder if you both might accompany me to Newgate market today?' Mrs Piddington asks, her eyes in a trance, her mind elsewhere.

I'm still reeling, unable to speak. Alice finally nods and breaks the silence. 'Certainly we can, if that's what you wish.'

Mrs Piddington stands still, her eyes darting from side to side, undecided on where to focus her gaze.

Odd. Is she well?

'Mrs Piddington—' Alice rises from her seat, wincing as she does.

'What? Oh – yes, well, let's go then. Quickly now, grab your things. I want to get there before the dinner crowd. And whale-bones! Don't let me forget that we need more whalebones or Mr Piddington will sulk!' Alice and I exchange glances before following our flustered employer through the curtains, leaving Benjamin to his work.

The last time I walked around Newgate market had been when Robert was still alive, but I still knew what to expect – meat and corn, neither of which I eat much of. I also remember going with Robert to Billingsgate market, best known for its fish – eels, herring, white fish, crabs and other delights of the sea. I recall the scent of the delicacies as if it were yesterday. I haven't ventured back, wary that the aromas could transport me back in time, whether I wish to go there or not.

I'm still thinking about Alice and what she told me earlier. I'm a horrible person. I took the woman's money and didn't think once about what that would mean for her and her vile husband. What she would say if he asked her where the money was. And then I have my second heart-shattering realisation of the day: Alice didn't tell him what she did with the money. Or at least, she didn't tell him she gave it to me. Surely she would have lied and said that it was stolen or I forced her to give it to me. Then again, if I know her husband the way I think I do, it wouldn't have mattered. All that mattered was that she was supposed to have a certain amount of money and she didn't. I've been there. Robert went so far as to tell me that if I told him the truth, my punishment wouldn't be as bad – but it was, if not more so. I learned to lie after that. Come what may.

'I'll pay you back,' I tell Alice as we amble behind Mrs Piddington.

Alice doesn't look at me. 'The past is past. No need for it now.'

I scrunch my brows together, confused by her response. 'That's not the point,' I say.

'It isn't?'

I shake my head. She smiles, flinching when her lip splits again. She runs her fingers over her mouth, smearing the blood onto her chin. I hesitate for a moment but then reach up to help clear the mark away, frowning as she watches me.

'I heard you're working at a haberdashery shop over in Holborn,' a deep, raspy voice says, startling me at the market. Alice and I had been following Mrs Piddington around the stalls, but always a few paces behind her. I hadn't expected to bump into anyone I might know.

Vincent Love stands to one side, leaning against his cane, his stringy hair blowing with the wind. His eyes are dark, even in the day, and sunken into his face, making him more hideous than I gave him credit for.

'You heard right,' I state, turning to see Mrs Piddington still speaking to a stall owner, haggling over the price of beef. I feel Alice standing to my side and I immediately position myself in front of her. As I do, I see Sophie and a few other women laughing together behind Vincent. *Their employer.*

'Such a waste. Why didn't you come to me if you needed money? I could have helped you, Elizabeth,' he says, his lip curling into the semblance of a grin.

I shake my head. 'I'm not a whore.' I can't help but look at Sophie again. It's obvious why men have always liked her – she looks clean and probably smells clean. Out of all the women huddled together, she is the most reserved and unblemished, and has a vulnerability about her. Vulnerability: a beacon for the male gender. The sun seems to have broken through the clouds to shine down upon Sophie just to prove my point. Alice shuffles on her feet behind me and I'm reminded to keep moving.

'The Tippling House – if you change your mind, Elizabeth,' Vincent says, leaning in my path as I pass him. 'My door is always open.' He chuckles as I refuse to indulge him any longer. Alice remains silent as I escort her towards Mrs Piddington, but it seems my punishment for my crime against Alice has commenced because Sophie's angelic voice is next to flow through my ears. I roll my eyes.

'Elizabeth, how nice to see you again.' I turn to face Sophie, still holding Alice's good arm. She smiles at Alice before returning her attention to me. I don't say anything. I don't have anything to say to her. I have one woman I am trying to protect now, and I can't take on another weakling who is unable to fend for herself. Sophie made her bed, she can lie in it. And she does, every night it seems.

'You are working – sewing, I believe. That's wonderful—'

'It's a job and it isn't whoring.' I feel Alice flinch at my harsh words. I close my eyes and wish Sophie to leave before I say anything else that offends my co-worker. She has enough to deal with right now; she doesn't need to be privy to my verbal matches with Sophie, the deity from my sordid past that I am trying really hard to forget.

Sophie's eyes drop to the ground, but she raises her head and recomposes herself. 'I was never good at needlework. My fingers don't do what they're supposed to.'

My eyebrows arch. 'But your cunt does ...' My voice trails off, regretting the words as soon as they leave my mouth. I curse inwardly for being so vicious.

What is wrong with me?

Sophie turns her head as a group of loud men stop near us. They stumble towards a butcher selling fresh meat. She smiles at one of them when he looks our way.

I didn't ask her to come speak to me. I haven't sought her out since that day we parted ways when we arrived in London all those years ago, or rather, when I left her outside Lincoln's Inn. I deliberately walked away from her, thinking she'd be better off on her own – such a pretty face and all. And now, I remember why. I certainly don't want more company from any men being enticed by Sophie's mouth and what she can do with it. To them.

'Alice, go join Mrs Piddington.' Alice doesn't move though. I can feel her looking at me, but I am now focused on the men who are edging their way towards us. I sense Alice's hesitation. For good reason too. I'm on edge, my body tense and my mind spiralling into darkness. I hang on a moment so I can speak to her, reassure her.

'Go on, I'll be there shortly,' I say, feigning a smile. Alice nods and shuffles away towards Mrs Piddington, who is now busy speaking to a woman selling baskets. Sophie and I both watch as Alice rejoins my employer, who gives her a curt nod before looking for me. When she spots me standing next to Sophie, her eyes narrow.

'I don't think the shop-owner's wife likes me,' I say, standing in front of Sophie, breaking her view from the men, who, for now, have suspended their approach.

'That surprises you?' Sophie's question shocks me. I didn't expect such bold words to come out of such a pretty little mouth. I can see sincerity in Sophie's big eyes. She isn't trying to be clever. She is stating a fact. I've never been liked by women. When I think about it, Sophie is the only woman who actually speaks to me and not at me, or about me behind my back. And after everything I've done – or rather, not done – for her. I look up at Alice again, smiling to myself. Guess Sophie isn't the only woman now.

I shake my head. 'No, I suppose it doesn't.' Sophie follows my eyes to Alice again.

'What happened to her?' Sophie asks.

'Husband.' I don't need to say more.

'Of course,' she says, nodding. I look to her.

'What do you mean by that?'

She grins. 'Do you not see it?'

I blink. No, I don't. What is she talking about?

She rolls her eyes at me. 'She's hurt. By her husband. Just like you—'

'Stop.' It's my turn to roll my eyes. 'Just stop. Alice isn't me—'

'Exactly!' Sophie shouts, raising her shoulders and hands, making her look like a stage performer trying for dramatic effect. I look at Alice and then back to Sophie again and sigh. 'She isn't you,' Sophie says. 'She can't fight for herself. But you know you can.'

'Exactly,' I say.

'Exactly,' Sophie whispers, her smile fading. 'You'd help anyone who couldn't fight for themselves. Wouldn't you, Elizabeth? Well, except for ...' Her voice trails off as she looks up at me. She doesn't have to finish. I know what she was going to say.

Except for prostitutes.

'Why don't you cook?' I ask, changing the subject while stretching out all my joints. They're stiff from sitting in place all the time.

Sophie grins. 'Where would I cook?'

I shrug one shoulder. 'I used to ask where would I work? Now look at me, escorting my employer and my battered co-worker to the market, for Christ's sake ...'

This causes a chuckle from Sophie. I find I'm pleased to hear that sound after my earlier remarks. She gazes around. 'I best return to my friends.' She curtsies and bids me farewell like I'm a lady. I sneer at her movements, and the group of men, who are still idling close by, notice Sophie leaving my side. The one who smiled her way earlier blocks her path.

'Hello, where are you off to? Why don't you let me buy you a drink ... and we can get to know one another?' His voice is full of bright cockney wit. My nostrils flare. I'm still sour from Alice's revelation earlier today and this venture to the market has done nothing to subdue my anger, despite defusing the animosity between Sophie and me just now. I find myself irked by the male attention. Sophie is better than this. I push past the man, grabbing Sophie's arm, steering her away from the group. If she won't help

97

herself, then I'll do it for her. I know what she does for a living, but she doesn't need to do it in front of me.

'Whoa, she's huge!' the man shouts, drawing looks from passers-by. I freeze, one hand still gripping Sophie's forearm, the other clenching at my side. I feel my insides twist. Do I stay and fight or walk away? I peek up to see Alice watching me, her eyes wide, as Mrs Piddington stands by her side.

Sophie untangles herself from my grasp, breaking my trance. 'Maybe another time, gentlemen, but we really must be going now.' Sophie directs her words to the man who insulted me. The men stare at each other before losing interest and returning their attention to the butcher. Sophie flattens her palms down her corset and begins walking away from me. I stomp after her.

'What are you doing?' Sophie asks, as I march past her. My legs are longer and my strides wider. It only takes me two steps and I'm beyond her.

'Where are your *friends*?' I ask, emphasising the word through pursed lips, blinking back my anger. My body is wound so tight I feel like the slightest breeze will break me. London is about to know me in all my dark glory if I can't get some semblance of control back. Vincent and Sophie's co-workers are no longer in sight.

'Mmm ... over there,' Sophie says, pointing towards a tall building behind the market. I have no idea where I am heading but I just begin walking. Sophie hastens her pace to match my own.

We begin weaving between the various stalls, not speaking to one another, like friends out for a stroll, albeit a quick one. Reaching one end of the market, we turn, following the buildings in the direction she told me to go.

'I bumped into Robert at Newgate market once, not so long ago,' Sophie says, a bit out of breath. She keeps her eyes on the cobblestones, watching where she places each of her dainty feet. I reel at her words. My mind spins. Robert never mentioned meeting Sophie to me, but then again, it shouldn't surprise me. There was a lot Robert didn't tell me, didn't say. Like whether he cared for me at all, or with whom he'd spent the night ...

Thoughts of Robert cause me to break, that last bit of calm I was clinging to now gone. It's too much. Alice. Sophie. Robert. Halfinch. Mrs Piddington. I grab Sophie's arm and pin her against the wall with one hand wrapping around her slender throat. My fingers can touch, she's that slight.

'Did you bed him?' I ask, wide-eyed.

'What? No, please, Elizabeth, you're hurting me!' she gasps.

'DID you?' I bellow, tightening my grip. Sophie feebly bats her hands against my arm as she struggles to breathe. I hold on until her face turns from pale white to pink, and then from pink to purple. She looks at me with her big green doe eyes. 'Elizabeth, please,' she gasps.

'Stop!' Alice shouts at me, grabbing at my shoulder, pulling me back. I didn't notice her approach, but her voice I heard. I always hear Alice's voice, regardless of the storm I'm facing.

I drop Sophie and she falls to the ground. She bows over and takes big breaths, coughing in between. She rubs her neck as tears prick her eyes. 'You think you are so much better, but you are no different,' she chokes out. 'You sell your body for money too. I may have sex with men for money, but you beat other women because men tell you to. You sell yourself, just like I do.' Sophie regains her breath, but the mark of my grip remains around her neck like a burn. I look away. I did that. I close my eyes, doing my best to keep my arms by my side. I can feel Alice next to me.

'And no, I didn't lie with Robert. He could barely stand straight let alone get his cock hard enough to fuck me!' Sophie hisses. I back away from Sophie and turn to face the crowd. A few have stopped to see what is happening, but most carry on about their business.

'Come on, *we'll* walk you to meet your friends,' Alice volunteers. I shoot my eyes at her, shaking my head. But she ignores me, reaching out to Sophie instead.

What? I know I acted poorly, but Alice doesn't know Sophie. She knows *me*.

It's clear neither woman is going to listen to what I want, though. Alice is going to walk with Sophie and I'm not going to let Alice walk by herself. Truth be told, I don't know why I reacted the way I did. Robert is a cunt. Was. Maybe it's Sophie and everything she is. She's beauty personified and despite her occupation is treated like ... a *woman*. Or maybe it's just Sophie reminding me of everything I'm not and where I came from. I look down at both of the women in front of me, so different, like the sun and the moon, and yet they are the same: they just light the world in a different way.

I sigh. Maybe it is because I'm still angry at the bastard's comment from earlier. Or maybe it's because I just don't like whores and Sophie is a convenient outlet for my hatred and anger.

'You're no better than him,' Sophie says, ignoring Alice's hand. Her words sting. Yes, maybe it was that too. I feel Alice's eyes on me. I should apologise, I know I should, but the words won't come out of my mouth. So instead, when the two women begin to walk, I plod along right behind them, like a sulking child after a scolding. I'd spent so many years locked up as Robert's property, doing his bidding, whatever and whenever he pleased. I don't think twice when confronted with violence or if insulted.

I watch Sophie and Alice walk on without looking back. I follow, but my feet slow and the distance between us grows. I might have hurt Sophie, but for some reason I can't stand the thought of someone else hurting her. She is, after all, the only person in London who really knows me. She knows about my time at the orphanage, she knows about my time at the Stockton Estate, and she definitely knew about Robert. At least Sophie knew the Elizabeth I was before Robert got hold of me. Alice doesn't know any of it. I don't want her to know. I don't want her to change the way she looks at me. I can be good. Better. But, after my assault of Sophie back there, Alice might have a different view now.

A memory comes to my mind, one from our time at the Stockton Estate. I had just been forced to fight my first fight for Sir Frederick and won it, but it had been hard. I was hurt badly during the bout and, when I got back to my room, Sophie woke and tended to me. She was kind even then, sympathetic and beautiful. Much like today. However, I learned that kindness and beauty often had two companions: naivety and attention.

We came to London together, but I left her shortly after arriving. She begged me to stay with her, claiming we would be better off if we stuck together. But I didn't listen. Sophie drew too much attention and I didn't want any of it. I walked away. All those years ago we separated, and it seems neither Sophie nor myself ventured very far from the life we came from. Sophie became a prostitute. And I – well, I became a prize fighter in the bowels of London city.

Children squealing bring my attention back to the two women marching in front of me. I smile at Alice. I'm not that woman any more, I tell myself. I *can* be good. I *can* be better. A seamstress with Alice. Perhaps Mrs Piddington will give me more responsibility in time.

As we turn a corner, I see Sophie's friends and I halt my steps. Sophie's neck still bears the red marks of my hands, and I frown. I wonder if men will look at those marks and get ideas, or be bedazzled by her beauty regardless. People stare at me too, not at my clothes and certainly not my beauty, but my height. I used to hate how tall I am. All the taunts and endless ridicule. But in a fight, my long arms and height certainly give me an advantage. And I've had many fights.

Sophie stops a few feet from her friends and thanks Alice, looking around. When she sees me, she turns up her nose and carries on. I recognise a few of her friends. The fat one – Sophie called her Betty – is there. So is the other one. I don't understand how Sophie can work at the same establishment as them. She is in a different class. They undoubtedly possess talents in the bedroom that assure them return customers. They dress well, but they drink and their faces tell all. I recall Sophie's words: *Liquor makes me feel horrid and my skin gets all blotchy.* I feel my own face. I rub my skin, hoping to erase the blotchiness, and perhaps something else. Alice approaches me and I know Mrs Piddington will be cursing me for disappearing, leaving her alone.

By the time Alice and I return to the spot where we left Mrs Piddington earlier, she has moved on. The basket woman is eyeing me up while Alice and I flick our heads in all directions, trying to locate our employer.

I hear a woman's voice call out behind me.

'Oi! You!'

I turn on the spot, unsure if the voice is addressing me. A ginger-haired woman is loading a cart with fishermen's baskets.

'I've seen you before,' the ginger-haired woman barks with a smug look on her face, hands tossing the baskets behind her. 'I hear you finally found some work.' Mrs Piddington appears at Alice's side.

'Do I know you?' I ask. The woman reaches a stall piled high with more baskets. She must weave them for a living. I'm about to walk away when the woman speaks again.

'Does your employer know you're a whore? I'm sure he wouldn't be interested in hiring a prostitute,' the woman laughs, and she turns to another woman close by. And just like that, my anger shoots up my spine like cold steel. I hear, but don't see, Alice sigh deeply.

'Go back to being a whore and leave the day jobs to women with husbands and children!' she yells, getting a few chuckles from the other stall owners.

'I'm not a prostitute—'

'Oh, you're not a prostitute, you say?' The woman has others around her now, all supporting her taunts. 'So you just like spending your days with them?' She nods in the direction of Sophie, who has reappeared with her friends from nowhere. Sophie looks on with sad, concerned eyes.

I feel a hand on my shoulder. It's Alice. 'Come away.'

The redhead laughs, pointing at Alice's face. 'Someone knows how to use your face well, don't they?'

No.

My mouth twitches and my muscles tighten, one by one. My gaze fixes on the woman as I slowly stalk towards her, and away from Alice, my rage mounting.

'Be careful what you say around me, especially of those who are *with* me.' My tone stops the basket-woman giggling. To my surprise, she stands up straight when I tower over her. My mouth twitches at her bravado.

'Elizabeth! That's enough!' Mrs Piddington joins Alice beside me. I cast my employer a fierce look, and then dart my eyes to Alice, who, with trembling hands, is covering her face, trying to hide the bruises.

'There's no point trying to hide that mug of yours, love, I'm sure there'll be more tomorrow!' the woman chides at Alice again, causing her to sob and the pulse in my neck to tick.

'Curse you for being so cruel!' Mrs Piddington spits at the stall owner. This seems to silence her once and for all, but my vision is clouded by a dark veil I just can't ignore. It's been too close to the surface all day. And I can't shake it. No matter how hard I try.

'What's your name?' I ask.

The woman smirks. She peers over her shoulder at her friend, who wears the same smug expression.

'My name? It's Hannah Hyfield,' she says, mocking a curtsy. This gains a few laughs from onlookers.

'Do you want to know my name?' I ask her, tilting my head to one side.

Hannah takes a step towards me. 'I know your name.' She takes another step. 'You're Elizabeth Wilkinson.' And another step. 'Widow of murderer Robert Wilkinson.'

A few gasps are heard rippling through the crowd that has gathered around to witness our exchange. I jut out my chin.

'Well then, *Hannah*, you know what's coming next.'

'And what's that?' She grins again.

It's my turn to smile. This feels good. Natural. I can feel the excitement build behind my eyes as my blood pumps through my veins.

'A challenge.'

CHAPTER 12

'WHERE AM I?' I groan, looking around the unfamiliar room. My head is pounding and my mouth tastes like it does after I've drunk too much gin, like rotted meat. Ugh.

'Where I stay – the Tippling House,' a female voice replies, not quite whispering but in a noticeably lower tone than that of the other women, who are still laughing and joking in the hallway. Our entrance obviously woke a few people. Sophie waves them away.

'You really should drink less, Elizabeth,' Sophie scolds me, like a parent would a child.

I frown and rub my forehead as if to wipe steam from a window for a clearer view.

'Tippling House?' I ask, squeezing my eyes closed, willing the throbbing to cease.

'Yes,' Sophie says harshly, cutting our conversation off. She hands me a mug of small beer that is sitting on a dresser table on the opposite side of the room. I sip at the bland drink while Sophie walks to the bedroom door, where she stands for a few seconds, peering out into the hall.

'Is this your room?'

'Yes.' Crisp and succinct.

'What time is it?' I ask.

'Late.' Sophie sounds impatient. I haven't seen this side of her before. She slowly pushes the door shut and rests her back against it. I raise my eyebrows, waiting for an explanation as to why I am in her room at the Tippling House.

Vincent Love's Tippling House.

I groan again and shake myself to life, trying to focus my gaze on my surroundings. I hear doors opening and closing outside, and footsteps passing the room we occupy.

Sophie's room. Ugh.

Realisation dawns. The footfall is of men leaving their bed companion. My skirt is gathered around my hips, exposing my petticoat and untied shoes. Confused, I sit bolt upright and cover myself.

'Do you remember challenging Hannah Hyfield to a fight? A "trial of skill"?' Sophie shakes her head, scolding some more. 'I thought you'd changed, Elizabeth. I thought you were going to make an *honest* living?' I vaguely remember challenging someone. Yes. The woman – *Hannah* – had called me a whore, thanks to Sophie. I snort. The fact that I'm now sitting in the brothel where Sophie and her friends work warrants a laugh. But the insult towards Alice, *poor Alice*, is something I won't forgive. *That* is what caused me to break. To challenge her.

I can't remember much of the night. I certainly don't remember Sophie and her friends bringing me back here, but I do remember drinking at The Black Hog after work, and apparently Sophie was too – or at least her friends were – and now, here I am, in Sophie's room at the Tippling House. A place I had hoped to avoid at all costs.

And then there's Mrs Piddington. I wonder what she makes of all of this. She'd been curiously quiet on our way back to the shop from Newgate market. The thought bounces around my head as if trying to tell me something, but my mind is too tired, or drunk, to pinpoint what exactly.

'I need to stop drinking,' I say finally, running my fingers down my face.

'Yes, you do.' Sophie dabs a wet cloth against my face. I snatch it and rub my eyes with it. 'So, you'll forget about this. . . this Hannah Hyfield? You'll just walk away from the challenge—'

'No,' I state. I won't walk away from a challenge. Not then, not now, not ever. I raise my eyes to meet Sophie's. She knows not to push me, and merely stands up to dispose of the bowl of water and cloth, after snatching it from my hands. I roll to the edge of the bed, where I let my head fall into both hands.

Thud. Thud. Thud. My head is pounding.

Thud. Thud. Thud. There it is again.

Thud. Thud. Thud. No, it isn't my head, it's the wall, and it's shaking. I look behind me at the wall and then turn back to Sophie. She bites her bottom lip, trying to hide her smile. And I can't help it, I laugh. Shaking my head, I stand up just as I hear reverberating footsteps approach Sophie's room. The door flies open, revealing a hefty-set woman in a black dress, fastened up to her neck. The woman's hair has a nest of grey piled atop a stern, elderly face. A cross dangles around her neck.

'What do we have here? A new client, Sophie?' she enquires, fixing her sights first on me and then around the room. 'Well?' the woman asks again without looking at Sophie.

'Mother Lavinia, this is my friend, Mrs Elizabeth Wilkinson, and I was merely. . .' Sophie starts to explain, her voice trailing off when Mother Lavinia steps towards me, holding up her hand, silencing Sophie. I look up at the woman, the Madam of the House, I'm guessing, and twist my neck to face her.

'Mrs Wilkinson, we do not rent rooms per night, but by the hour. I think it's time you were on your way. Sophie needs to rest,' Mother Lavinia says in a gentle tone, drawing her arm towards the door for me to follow. Sophie remains with her back against the wall, head down, picking at her nails nervously.

I couldn't agree more; it is time for me to return to Clerkenwell. Tomorrow I have work; I need to get some sleep, and away from Sophie and this bawd.

I nod my agreement, pushing past Mother Lavinia, whose haggard eyes are now focused on Sophie. I stagger a few steps, holding on to the door while I regain my balance in as steady a fashion as I can physically manage. I look back once at Sophie and her eyes meet mine. She gives a slight shake of her head that tells me not to argue. So I continue on my way, climbing down the stairs one at a time to the front hallway. When I'm at the bottom of the stairwell, I notice Mother Lavinia, Sophie and some other women have followed suit.

I look back up to Sophie, who is looking at me over Mother Lavinia's shoulder.

'Thank you, Sophie,' I force myself to say. I wanted to say sorry for hurting her earlier, but the words came out as a thank you instead. Sophie, wide-eyed, is silent. She nods, but still says nothing. I hold up my hands, retreating towards the door. 'Mother Lavinia, I apologise for my intrusion. It won't happen again. I assure you.'

This, at least, gets a smirk from Sophie.

I reach behind for the door handle and my hand finds nothing but air. I twirl and in front of me, where a door should be, stands a tower of a man, whose maleficent and abhorrent face is obscured by masses of stringy black hair. His presence is enough to hush the women in the stairwell, including Mother Lavinia, who shuffles nervously at his arrival.

Vincent. Twice in one day. How very unfortunate.

He cocks his head to one side and shifts his eyes between myself and the women, and back to me. His brow furrows but other than that he holds his body upright, resting both hands on his cane – which, up close, I see has a moulded gold top – in front of him. His attire is top quality but his person is unkempt. Money to spend, but no amount can hide his filth. A slow grin spreads, but doesn't reach his eyes.

I make a dramatic move to one side to let him past, determined to show him my indifference to his presence. The silence is eerie and I find myself wanting to break it. Sophie climbs past Mother Lavinia and stares at me. It's a concerned stare and causes my bluster to falter. I'm sobering up. But Sophie's alarm tells me I'm not quick enough. Something isn't right. The women are all looking downwards, except for Sophie, who continues to look at me and then darts her eyes to the door. It takes me a second but I understand her message. I need to leave.

I move towards the door, but Vincent blocks me with his cane. Without thinking, I push it out of my way, cocking my head to look at him. He pulls back his shoulders and raises his chin, looking down his nose at me. He doesn't look as old as he did at The Black

Hog. In fact, he doesn't seem as frail either. My eyes study the formidable man who has fooled me into thinking he is ordinary.

'Elizabeth, what a pleasant surprise,' he says, his tone full of venom.

'She was just leaving,' Sophie offers, edging closer to where we stand. Vincent takes two swift strides and grabs Sophie's hair, pulling her head back. 'Was I speaking to you, Sophie?' he snarls in her ear. I stand at the door, watching as his spit hits her flawless cheek. Sophie cries out, trying her best to free herself from his grip – the same feeble way she tried to fight me at the market, pulling at his wrist with both hands – but he's too strong.

For her.

'Leave her, Vincent. Sophie already has marks on her neck from a customer, no point in blemishing her further,' Mother Lavinia says calmly. I look at Sophie's neck. The red marks I gave her are starting to bruise. I swallow the lump forming in my throat. She lied about how she got them. Who gave them to her.

Vincent tugs Sophie's hair higher so he can inspect her neck, forcing her to stand on her tiptoes. Sophie wails again.

'Stop,' I order. I can see pain etched all over Sophie's pretty face. The familiar burn begins to build in my limbs as I watch Vincent torture the woman who was already hurt from my hand, and for no other reason than petty jealousy. I lick my lips and shake my head at the thought. That's *two* women hurt by me. My actions. My choices. *Zounds.*

'I'll go,' I try again.

Vincent finally releases Sophie, shoving her towards Mother Lavinia, and Sophie crumples at her feet. The other ladies swoop around to help her up and out of Vincent's reach. With Sophie away, I can focus on Vincent once again. He's not much taller than me, but he managed to lift Sophie off the ground by her hair, so he's strong. Stronger than I thought. My muscles are flexing, my limbs warm, ready for whatever is coming. The corner of my mouth is twitching, my heart rate accelerating. I'm going to explode; I need to leave before he makes me do something that can't be undone.

I move towards the door again but, as I do, Vincent's arm lashes out and he grabs me, slamming the door shut with the other. I inhale sharply as he spins me around to face the wall, pressing my face up against the solid wood.

'Leaving so soon, Elizabeth?' He leans in, his face close to mine. His breath stinks of brandy.

I instinctively push back and jerk my arm out of his clutch. 'Move.'

He laughs. 'You are feisty, aren't you? Have you finally come to your senses, left that wretched job to come work for me? I don't even have to do any introductions—'

'I'm not a whore,' I spit out.

He slowly shakes his head. 'No, my dear Elizabeth.' He shifts his weight to his back foot, repositioning himself. 'You're not a whore, *yet*.'

'Not now. Not ever. Now step aside before I make you,' I snap back. Vincent doesn't budge. I square off with him again, spreading my weight evenly between my feet, ready to move either way he comes at me. 'I'm feisty and *impatient*.'

His face lights up and he takes a step back, looking me up and down. He laughs, rubbing his chin with one hand, resting the other on his cane. He shrugs his shoulders and turns his back on me.

Well, that was easy.

I steal a glance back at Sophie, who shakes her head quickly. Before I realise my mistake, Vincent spins around and punches me in the face. Unprepared, I fly backwards.

'Now, Elizabeth, I finally get you through my doors and you think I'll just let you walk out? I think you should stay a while. I've been patient enough and we really should get to know each other better,' he says, stepping towards me, wiping his hand on his coat and shaking it out.

I spit blood on the floor and wipe my mouth.

'Yes,' I say, pushing myself up off the floor, 'let's get to know each other better.'

I hear gasping from our audience as I launch myself at him. I feel my arms and hands absorbing strength from everywhere in my body. Gone are the excuses I feed myself all day as to why I can't fight any more. I unleash my hatred. The man is not expecting my attack, so hitting him is too easy. He stumbles backwards and I pursue him. I grab his collar, swing him around away from the door and punch him again. He raises his arms to cover his face, but my blows keep coming, knocking him off balance as he stumbles backwards down a passage. The anger, hatred and rage flows from my pores as I let go of any restraint built up over the past few weeks. My heart races, not from fear but from excitement.

I like this.

I've *missed* this.

I stalk him down the corridor and when he stops I grab his head and knee him in the face, breaking his nose. Blood gushes all over his clothes.

I take a deep breath as he crumples to the floor, his face a mask of flowing blood. Typically, this would be where the fight would end and I would walk away. But this isn't the fighting pit of St Giles. There is an audience, but no organiser. No one telling me that the fight is over. No Robert.

I'm in control now. I decide when it ends. And this isn't over. The power I feel is liberating. I can feel my chest open up as I take air into my lungs – breathing in life, exhaling fear. I tower over the long, wiry, black-haired man who dared touch me, threaten me, something I will never allow again, and I kick him. I kick him in the stomach and then across his ugly, bloodied face.

'That's enough, Elizabeth!'

It's Sophie. She's standing in front of the other women, wide-eyed. I pause finally, and look around the hallway. Not one person is cheering. Mother Lavinia, concerned, is edging her way along the wall towards the fallen man. They look ... horrified. Scared. *Of me?* I return my sights to my opponent, broken and bleeding on the floor. Blood is splattered across the wood and if it isn't washed away soon, it will leave a stain like the blemish I've just dealt to his reputation. I shake my head, pursing my lips.

'If you ever touch me again ...' I wipe my mouth with the back of my hand. Vincent grins, showing bloodied teeth.

'You'll be back,' he seethes.

I kneel down beside him and grab his hair, pulling his head up off the floor. 'You don't *want* me back.'

I throw his head back and it bounces off the planks. I kick him between his legs and he howls in pain, curling his body up while cursing me.

Mother Lavinia and Sophie both rush towards him now, like he's a fallen soldier, returned from battle. I look around at the other women, all keeping their distance.

I straighten my clothing and make my way towards the door for the fourth time, shaking my head.

'It's not over, my Amazonian virago,' Vincent utters, his voice low and raspy, pushing himself up to lean on one hand. Sophie brushes his hair away from his bloodied face and pulls a handkerchief from her jacket pocket, pressing it over his nose to stem the flow of blood. He flinches at her touch. 'Trust me.'

I glance at Sophie again, but she refuses to meet my gaze. The man just assaulted her and she's nursing him? I shake my head. 'I know.'

I pivot, and swear I hear him laughing as I walk the dark cobblestones down Drury Lane.

I know it isn't over.

Vincent is just like Robert.

He bears grudges.

CHAPTER 13

AMAZONIAN.

It isn't the first time I've been called that. Christ, Halfinch also called me that the day we first met. Vincent's words keep replaying in my mind. As do the facial expressions the women wore after I broke his face. My mind fills with images of Sophie and concern gnaws at me.

Zounds.

I didn't think ... I didn't give a second thought to what my actions might mean for Sophie ... or the consequences she might face as a result. Vincent is vindictive – cut from the same cloth as Robert – and God knows what he'll do to her now. I scrunch up my face at the thought.

It's been months since my last fight at the St Giles rookery. My body had recovered until my run-in last night. I rub my jaw where Vincent landed his one and only strike. It's tender, but my teeth are still there. None dislodged from the hit I took. I stretch my fingers and see the swelling starting to occur from their use.

I think of the altercation last night. Of Vincent's fist against my face. Of the frantic feeling that fuelled my limbs after. Of the way my hands knew what to do. Of the blood pumping through my body. Of the feel of my fist hitting Vincent's nose. Of the cracking sound it made. Of his body crumpled in a heap. Of the familiar scent of copper as blood streamed from his nose. Of the warm comfort it brought me knowing I'd beaten him, surrounding my shoulders like a warm blanket. Of the gleam in his eye when he threatened it wasn't over.

As long as Sophie works there, I know Vincent will be a reoccurring threat. One I need to disarm.

I snort at the thought. Who am I kidding? Vincent and I go together like carefully made plans and London weather: opposing and improbable.

And ... I can't help but feel a little bit excited at the prospect of running into him again.

But I need to make sure Sophie is safe. She needs that pretty face to earn her living. And as much as I hate what she does, she doesn't deserve that prick controlling her. I have to make sure of it. She can't continue to work there. I blow out a slow breath when I think of the two women in my life I am now trying to save from the men in their lives. I sigh and rub my eyes; my knuckles ache from the brawl.

A loud bang thumps on the door of the room I slept in. I shuffle out of the bed, away from the two strangers I slept next to at the twopence house. The occupants of the lodge change daily, but it's always full. The stench from the number of bodies in their unchanged duds is so intolerable that only a truly desperate person would sleep here. The first thing I'll do with my winnings from my fight with Hannah Hyfield is find another place to stay, a better-smelling one that I don't have to share. No, wait, that will be the second. First thing I'll do is celebrate, because that's inevitable. Then new lodging, and then I'll give Alice her money back to get her away from her husband. I'll deal with Sophie later. She can put up with Vincent a bit longer. She seems accustomed to him and her surroundings so she'll be fine, I convince myself. After the way she took care of Vincent last night, I wasn't going to rush to help her if she didn't plan on giving up her whoring for that filthy bastard.

My stomach twinges with hunger pains, reminding me that I need to get up. I haven't eaten since dinnertime yesterday. No time between work, issuing challenges to a woman, getting drunk and fighting Vincent. And I'm gut-foundered.

I really need to stop drinking. I really wish I could. I wish it was that simple. Just say it and it happened. But every night, after work, I can't help myself. My feet take me back to The Black Hog to drown in gin and try to forget every single day of my life that brought me here.

I just wish I didn't wake up every time with a new person I needed to help.

Maybe I should just pocket the winnings from my fight and let Alice and Sophie deal with their own lives. I'm not helping them to live by actually helping them to survive. That they need to learn on their own. Whatever it looks like for them.

The bang on the door comes again, louder this time. Time to go.

I swing my legs over the side of the bed and pull on my jacket and boots, ready to start another day.

'You're gonna fight again!' Halfinch's voice near deafens me as I step out of the twopence lodging I've been staying at in Clerkenwell since Robert's death.

With my boots tied and jacket fastened, I give the boy a sidelong glance before walking my usual route to work, ignoring him. It wasn't a question.

London is waking up. The smell of freshly baked bread fills my nose one moment, while the stench of chamber pots being tossed out of windows consumes it the next. This city – never could there be another such contradictory place. Shop owners are removing boards from windows and mothers are dragging their children to wherever they are headed, protesting all the way. Which reminds me ...

'Do you go to school?' I ask, slowing my pace so he can hobble faster to catch up.

'School? Er ... no,' Halfinch says, quirking his mouth in disgust.

'Can you read?' I probe some more, stopping to let people past and allow Halfinch to walk in front of me. It's crowded with workers this time of morning, forcing us to walk one in front of the other, and I can't hear him if he's behind me. I frown. Not that I care what he has to say. A row of stone posts mark the edge of the street and we are forced to be on a constant lookout for potato peelings and chimney soot being tossed from windows above.

He scoffs as he slams a paper into my gut. 'Read this! Billy gave it—'

'Who's Billy—'

'My mate. Now read it!'

I frown at the boy. He didn't answer my question about him being able to read ... Nevertheless, to stop his rambling I pick up the paper, knowing full well what it says.

'"*CHALLENGE – I, Elizabeth Wilkinson, of Clerkenwell, having had some words with Hannah Hyfield, and requiring satisfaction,*

*do invite her to meet me on the stage, and box me for three guineas;
each woman holding half-a-crown in each hand, and the first woman
that drops her money to lose the battle.*'" I read out loud while the
boy limps along the road beside me. He beams over his shoulder.
'You're really going to fight again?'

I grab him by the collar and lift him back to walk in front of
me. 'So it would seem ...' My voice trails off as we continue to
manoeuvre around the masses of people hustling to work. I also
need to get to work. We pause to let a barber shake out a wig
before continuing on our way, and I hand the boy his paper back.

I need to face Mrs Piddington. The wench isn't going to be
happy, especially when she sees my hands and even more so when
she hears they're only going to get worse.

Back at work, Alice's work has piled up in her absence, keeping her
busy and giving me a chance to do some other repair work, which
makes a nice change from sewing whalebone casings for the ever
diligent and silent apprentice to use. I glance over at his working
board, sitting empty. Benjamin isn't in today. We were told he was
helping Mr Piddington with some deliveries, not like we care.

It's going to be a long day. My head is heavy from little sleep
and my limbs even heavier. My fingers aren't doing as they're told,
swollen and sore from the previous night. I've stuck myself a few
times with the needle, cursing every time and causing Alice to
frown. Mrs Piddington hasn't been in the workroom yet. She's in
the shop, dealing with customers and receiving orders. I chance a
look through the curtain and when I see Mrs Piddington turn her

back, holding up a finished gown to someone, I reach down under my skirt and pull my purse loose.

I count out six pennies and slide them across the table towards Alice. It takes everything I have not to snatch them back up and keep them. I promised her the day we went to the market that I'd give her back her money. I know it's too late, but I owe her, and every day I have to sit and watch her limp or wince makes me feel like my place in hell is getting more secure.

And I'm not ready to see Robert again.

She hesitates before taking them. And I nod.

'I know I still owe you more, and I'll get it all back to you, but you keep it for yourself.' I give her a stern look like Mrs Deirdre used to use on me when I did something I wasn't supposed to at the orphanage. 'Hide it. Anywhere you can that he won't find it. Don't make my mistake, Alice. Don't spend it on something that will only give you a temporary escape. It's a dark path if you do. One that's difficult to unfollow.'

I notice Alice shifting in her seat. She fidgets with her hands and the way her eyebrows are bunched together tells me she's thinking hard about something she wants to say but isn't sure she should say it.

'You can say it, Alice, I'm not him,' I remind her, coaxing her with my voice as best I can. Mrs Piddington is still occupied. She hasn't bothered me much since the market. She seemed happy enough to have the company that day, since Mr Piddington wasn't around to escort her. Alice made a joke, saying I'm Mrs Piddington's twang. I laughed and said that would make her a brothel owner and when I asked what that would make Alice, she fell silent, suddenly realising her role in her own joke.

'If he ever finds it—'

'Make sure he doesn't,' I push. I would offer to keep it for her, but I don't trust myself not to spend it once I get to The Black Hog after work. And Alice can't ask Mrs Piddington to keep it for her because then she will have to tell her why she's hiding money from her husband and where she's getting it from. Alice is an innocent. She can't lie. Her beatings from her loving husband say as much. And Mrs Piddington doesn't trust me; she won't believe I am helping Alice because I want to. She'll convince herself, and possibly Alice, that I have other, more selfish, motivations. Which isn't true, but she can think what she likes as long as she doesn't interfere with my plan to get Alice away from her husband, possibly to family. We need to work out the details, but we will.

No, Alice needs to do this. She can and she will. She has to. She has to escape her husband before he kills her. We are working on a plan to get her out of London, but we will need Mrs Piddington to help with that and Alice isn't ready to speak to her yet. The fewer people who know, the better. So for now, my part is paying back her money as quickly as I can. Alice has already suffered another bruised cheek since returning from the hospital. It can't go on. I can't let it. I couldn't help myself when Robert was alive, but now that he's gone, and I'm still here, I can help Alice escape her own Robert.

'I'll give you more once wages are paid at the end of the week. And after my fight. Until then, you find some place safe to hide it. All right?' I squeeze her hand and she finally smiles, nodding her agreement. I know it is going to take a long time for her to have enough to make her escape but I vowed to myself, and to Alice, that I'd help her.

Alice and I have talked a great deal since she came back from the hospital and I've learned a lot about her. She's from the country, a place north of London, past Enfield. I hadn't heard of it, but she grew up there with her five siblings, three boys and two girls – she is the middle girl, and fourth in years. She stayed until she met her husband, a butcher who was travelling to visit a farmer about livestock. His name is Henry Griffin. A name that is now etched into my memory, along with the others I am still trying to forget: Mrs Deirdre, Sir Frederick Stockton and Robert Wilkinson. They have no children, one of the many reasons Henry beats her. Her mother was a seamstress and taught Alice her craft. Alice hasn't been back to Enfield – or wherever it is she said she is from – since she left with Henry. She hasn't seen her five siblings in ten years and doesn't even know if they are still living in Enfield. Close to home.

Home. That's what she called it.

London isn't her home.

Henry isn't her home.

'You should write to them,' I blurt out.

Alice inhales a breath and just stares at me, her body rigid.

I take in her new injuries, which are on display because her arms and neck are difficult to hide; she's taken another round of blows from her husband. A lump forms in my throat and I feel heat behind my eyes, but I tense my jaw, refusing to let any tears fall.

Her tone grows thick. 'I should.'

While Benjamin and Alice eat dinner, Mrs Piddington chooses to sit down next to me – I haven't been allowed my dinner break due to my slow progress with work. I try ignoring her, even when she begins talking. 'You think you're so brave, Elizabeth, challenging that woman ... You might even think you're untouchable because of your past, and now your present relationship with Constable Boyle?'

Relationship? I look up at her, confused. I have no relationship with the constable, nor do I want one. I don't want another relationship with any man, for that matter. Nothing good comes from it.

Constable Boyle helped you find this job, didn't he? my stupid mind chooses to remind me. I roll my eyes but Mrs Piddington drones on, oblivious to my internal musings. 'But I assure you, you are not,' she continues. 'There are people with much more power. And you and I? Merely pawns.'

At that, I lay down my implements and stare at her. She has my attention after that remark. I'm nobody's pawn.

'I don't know what you're talking about.'

'Of course you don't,' Mrs Piddington snaps.

'She went after Alice—'

'Indeed, that was rather unfortunate, but also ... necessary, it seems. I was surprised it was Alice that made you snap. But then again, she's been a weakness of mine too.'

I look at my employer, confusion and pain etched all over her face. She finally meets my gaze. 'Would you have challenged Mrs Hyfield – a woman, I assure you, who also has a talent for bare-knuckle fighting – if she hadn't insulted Alice?'

'What do you mean?' I asked.

Mrs Piddington smiled. 'Just that, Elizabeth. Mrs Hyfield knew exactly what to say to get you riled. I wonder why that was?' She rose and walked towards the kitchen. My head was drowning with words and thoughts, all jumbled together, none of which were making any sense in my fragile state. Feeling desperation claw at me, I jump to my feet, angry that I don't understand what Mrs Piddington is trying to tell me.

'I challenged her to a bout. You should come watch – come see how I rip off her arms, and beat her to death with them,' I snarl, looking down at my employer, my tone causing Alice and Benjamin to appear at the kitchen door, aware of the tension between Mrs Piddington and me. When I see Alice's questioning look, I shake my head and sit down to begin stitching again.

Mrs Piddington stands motionless for a moment before returning to my side, facing Alice, who remains in place. She leans over and tucks a stray strand of hair behind my ear, leaning towards me. I freeze.

'Merely pawns,' she whispers, placing her hand on my shoulder, 'and I hope you do beat her, Elizabeth. For both our sakes.'

CHAPTER 14

B Y THE TIME I leave work, I'm ready to go to the twopence house and sleep for days. I am that tired, both mentally and physically. I am that tired my feet don't even want to take me to The Black Hog, which is saying something. My conversation with Mrs Piddington bounced around the inside of my head all afternoon and I still couldn't make sense of it. Her words felt like a warning, but no matter how I tried, I couldn't make out what I was or wasn't supposed to do. Should I not have challenged Hannah Hyfield?

As I pinch my the bridge of my nose, a high-pitched voice rings out.

'Elizabeth! Elizabeth!'

I sigh heavily. Not him again. Please God, I don't have the strength to deal with his excitable ways.

'Elizabeth!' Halfinch shouts again, hobbling along behind me at pace. 'She responded! Here, take a look!' He shoves the daily journal into my face, hitting me when he does. I jerk my head back, take a deep breath and will myself to remain calm before reading. Halfinch waits all of a few seconds before shouting, 'Read it out loud!'

I scowl at the boy, but decide to humour him.

'*ANSWER – I, Hannah Hyfield, of Newgate Market, hearing the resoluteness of Elizabeth Wilkinson, will not fail, God willing, to give her more blows than words, desiring home blows, and from her no favour: she may expect a good thumping!'*

A snort is my dignified response to the wench's threat of a thumping. I peer down over the paper to see Halfinch's eyes are large with wonder. Mine are closing from fatigue.

'I can't wait to see you pummel her!' Halfinch exclaims while he pretends to box the air, fighting no one but a figment of his imagination.

Not in the mood, I ignore him. When I turn around, I find Sophie standing there.

'Zounds!' I shout. 'Both of you? I don't have patience for this.' Sophie glances at me and to Halfinch and back. She's dressed immaculately as usual, but her demeanour isn't as refined, not as collected. I sigh, waiting for her to say what she needs to say so I can be on my way – away from people who know me and the day that is drawing to a close. I long for silence and day's end. A moment's peace. There have been times in the past when I thought I'd go crazy from loneliness, but now, with Mrs Piddington, Halfinch and Sophie constantly at my heels, hounding me, I'd welcome the solitude. I vow, again, to find a room for myself after my bout against Hannah Hyfield.

'Good evening, Elizabeth,' Sophie says solemnly. Her back straight and head upright, she wants to appear calm, but her eyes tell a different story. She can't meet my gaze, her eyes keep looking around furtively – telling me she isn't sure she should be here. I wait for more. She hasn't asked me anything yet and I'm in no mood for idle chat. I merely stare at her. Our meeting last night had not ended well and I made yet another enemy because of Sophie.

'I just wanted to warn you,' she said. 'Vincent ... he's – he's dangerous.'

My eyebrows arch up. This is nothing new to me. I knew I had put myself in a precarious position by fighting back. But it seems that no matter how hard I try, backing down and keeping quiet when forced into a corner isn't something I'm willing to do – and my unwillingness to yield has left me in dangerous settings my whole life. I eye Sophie up and down and notice no marks other than the slight bruising around her neck from me. Guilt over squeezing her neck hits me in the gut.

'And yet you seemed to escape his temper last night after I left,' I say through clenched teeth.

Sophie's lips part. 'He knows where to hit.'

This realisation causes me to step back. I take another look up and down at Sophie, wondering about the extent of the damage beneath her beautiful midnight-blue gown. My eyes flick from side to side, unable to fathom what I'd find if she removed her clothes.

'Sophie, I—' I try to speak, but the words catch in my throat. Zounds, I need a drink. The thirst begins to grip me, the need gnawing at my insides as I close my eyes and clench my fists.

'Elizabeth isn't afraid of anything!' Halfinch interrupts. He comes to stand in front of me like the obedient guard dog he is ... one I did not ask for, and even if I had, I'd have trained him better. I stare at the top of his head. I can't see his face but I imagine it's filled with defiant bravado.

Sophie is smiling at my new ward. 'And who is this brave young man?'

Halfinch softens immediately, blushing when Sophie strokes his cheek with her fingertips. 'My name is Halfinch, and may I have the honour of knowing the name of the most beautiful woman in London?' He removes his cap and bows, taking Sophie's hand and kissing the back of it. I roll my eyes. *Fool*.

'She's not bloody royalty, you pillock,' I hiss, pushing past them both.

I don't get far before I bump into Constable Boyle. 'Oh, please God have mercy!'

If Constable Boyle is taken aback by my outburst, he hides it well. 'Mrs Wilkinson, it's lovely to see you again,' he says. He gives me an abrupt nod and then clasps his hands behind his back.

'Constable,' I reply. I don't mean to sound impatient, but it comes out that way. My hands rest on my hips and I try not to scowl at the man blocking my way. I hear Halfinch and Sophie talking behind me; they are catching up with me.

This is the most popular I've been in my entire life. And I don't like it.

Constable Boyle regards me, then the boy and the woman who now stand beside me expectantly. I shoot him a quizzical look.

'Good evening. I'm Constable Matthew Boyle.' He bows and kisses Sophie's hand. She smiles and bats her long lashes.

'My name is Miss Sophie Dawson, sir. I'm a friend of Elizabeth's.' Sophie tilts her head towards me and I raise my eyebrows. Friends? I know her, yes, but she's a prostitute, someone from my past, not my friend. I don't have friends. Well, except for Alice. I have one friend. One is enough.

Constable Boyle returns Sophie's smile and then looks at Halfinch, bowing again, this time at the boy. Halfinch eyes him like a rotten piece of cheese; he isn't quite sure whether to reciprocate. Eventually, he gives a short bow back.

Constable Boyle seems bemused. 'And what's your name, young man?'

'What do you need my name for?' Halfinch asks. Subtlety is not a word Halfinch seems to be familiar with. I smirk at the boy; we have another thing in common.

'If you do not wish to give me your name, then I shall make one up for you. How about David?' Halfinch turns up his nose at this and shakes his head. 'No? Not David, all right ... how about Paul?' Halfinch rolls his eyes and stands behind me, crossing his arms.

'Never mind him,' I say, edging my elbow back to push Halfinch away from me. Halfinch stumbles but returns to my side in seconds.

'Right, well ...' Constable Boyle turns his attention back to me. 'I just wanted to make sure work was still going well?'

'I'm still there,' I retort.

'Still exhilarating?' the constable probes, waiting for me to elaborate, but I stand firm, staring back at him, refusing to engage.

'Did you help Elizabeth find work there, constable?' Sophie chimes in, breaking the awkward silence.

He smiles. 'Yes, I know the owner through my father, who owns a watch-making business over on Leather Lane.'

They continue their discussion as Halfinch and I wait on the sidelines, watching the beauty and the lawman engage with each other. Finally weary of Sophie's giggles, I interrupt, 'Do you need something, constable?'

'Yes, actually, I just wanted to confirm a rumour I heard,' Constable Boyle says, smiling a small smile again. 'Make sure you aren't indeed causing any *trouble*.'

My eyes widen and I bite my lip. *Zounds. Has he heard about Vincent? Has he come to take me to prison?* My heart races as panic sets in. My concern at his words must be obvious as Constable Boyle's smile fades and he takes a step forward. 'You haven't caused any trouble, have you, Mrs Wilkinson? You look pale, are you ill—'

'No, I wouldn't necessarily say she's caused any trouble ...' Sophie chips in, 'but she has challenged a woman to another fight.' I turn to glower at Sophie, who shrugs and gives me a *well, you have* look.

'I see, so it's true,' is all Constable Boyle says. 'Do you think that wise, Mrs Wilkinson? You have your job and ... forgive me, but I thought you'd given up that *pursuit.*'

Sophie nods in agreement and thanks him profusely. 'How refreshing it is to meet a man who doesn't condone physical violence,' she adds, placing her hand on his arm.

'I wouldn't say that, Miss Dawson. There are times when physical violence is necessary, unfortunately.' Constable Boyle turns to look at me, but all I see is Sophie's hand resting on his. He steps away, letting Sophie's arm fall, breaking my trance.

'Yes, well, the wench insulted me. Called me a *whore*. And *I'm* not a whore,' I respond, looking pointedly at Sophie, who stares at the ground.

'They're just words, Elizabeth,' Constable Boyle says. The use of my first name surprises me. I didn't think he was capable of it – seems the sort of thing he'd find impolite. Halfinch is shaking his head. I'm not sure what I've done to win over this little thief's heart, but I was starting to like him for it.

'It wasn't just me.'

'What do you mean?'

'It wasn't just me that she insulted.'

Matthew instinctively looks at Sophie.

I shake my head. 'Not her, another friend.' I wince as soon as the words leave my mouth. 'Have a good evening, *Matthew*,' I say, and walk away.

He doesn't follow, but Sophie does. I hear her shoes clacking against the cobbles. 'Elizabeth, please slow down, I have to talk to you!' But her voice only causes my pace to quicken. Halfinch hobbles along, trying to keep up. I see him look behind to where Sophie is trailing and he eventually stops to wait for her.

I do not wait for either.

After a few gins at my favourite tavern, I head back to the twopence house and secure my bed for the night. At some point, I need to bathe. I can smell myself, which is never a good sign. I was in a rotten mood after seeing Sophie and then the constable, and while I was determined to get a decent night's sleep, I decided that the only thing that would help my temper would be to hit someone or have a drink. I chose the latter. Seemed like the lesser of two evils.

I hear the door creaking and half open my eyes to watch as a small form slowly limps towards my bed. Halfinch stops in front of me and shakes my arm until I'm fully awake. He's eating a steaming hot potato. I snatch it from his hands and begin eating ravenously.

'That's mine!' he barks, sitting next to me on the bed. I take a break from eating and then, after one last bite, hand the remains of the potato back to Halfinch.

'How did you get in here?' I prop myself up, shuffling my bum along the bed to lean against the wall.

'SHHHHHH!' hisses one of the lodgers from the other bed.

Halfinch takes a bite from his meal before whispering, 'Wasn't hard,' with a cocky grin. As if he had a key and strolled in. I roll my eyes at him.

'What do you want, Halfinch?'

'Miss Sophie, she said to warn you,' Halfinch says between bites. I can see bits of potato dribble down his chin.

'She already did. Close your mouth when you chew. And finish your food before you speak,' I order, leaning my head back against the wall to stare at the ceiling. The cracks between the wooden boards seep nothing but darkness and cold air into a room that already has too much of both.

'What?' Halfinch says, another piece flying out of his mouth. I don't notice where it lands. I shake my head. Halfinch finishes the last bite and crumples the paper in his hands. The couple opposite hush us again.

'Oi, oi! Don't you bloody shush me! Do you know who this is – it's Elizabeth Wilkinson and she'll knock you to hell if you don't shut your mouths!'

The couple look at me, but I merely rub my forehead. Halfinch bounces off the bed.

'Miss Sophie overheard Vincent Love speaking with some other men ... he is out to get you. So you need to watch yourself. No more walking around in the dark by yourself,' Halfinch says, patting me on the head. I flick his hand away and he chuckles.

'Is that so?' I ask.

'Yeah.'

I watch him hobble to the door.

'Halfinch,' I call. He pauses, turning to look at me in the dimly lit room. 'How am I supposed to get to and from work then?'

The boy grins again, says, 'An escort, of course.'

I guffaw. 'Who is supposed to escort me?'

'Me,' he says, then winks, before pulling the door shut.

Splendid. Another stray to take care of.

I take a deep breath and let the darkness lull me to sleep.

CHAPTER 15

I<small>F</small> I <small>CLOSED</small> my eyes I'd think I was back in the rookery, the feeling is that familiar.

Hockley-in-the-Hole was the only place I thought of when I challenged Hannah Hyfield to a contest. It had been on my mind since Halfinch put it there. And in truth, it's as good a place as any. A narrow, rickety-looking building, surrounded by dire houses, where shady spectacles happen by even shadier characters. Hockley is a common watering hole where my fellow Londoners come to see sparring, and eat frumenty and hasty pudding. I know it well.

I take a deep breath and my nose decides I'm hungry, the waft of porridge infiltrating my senses. My mouth salivates at the thought of the frumenty being cooked. I wonder if they serve it with sweet or savoury dishes at this time of day? I sigh. I can't eat now, not this soon before my bout with Hannah. It's never a good idea to eat immediately before fighting. No one wants to see the remnants of your meal on the stage floor after taking a punch to the gut.

How did I get here? All these years, I've been forced to fight like one of the tortured bulls or bears you see chained and prodded. Robert never really posed it as a 'take it or leave it' option when it came to me fighting, nor did Sir Frederick. Maybe Sophie is right – like every other woman in London, my body is not my own; it's property, a chattel, to be handled and governed by someone other than me. But Robert is gone. And I haven't seen Sir Frederick since arriving in London. So why am I here?

Your temper, that's why. I hear Sophie's voice in my mind like she's standing beside me. My hands still haven't recovered, still tender from defending myself against Vincent. I open and close my fingers at the memory of him and his threat. The week has flown by without it transpiring, but that didn't stop me from looking over my shoulder everywhere I went. Being on guard all day every day is ... exhausting. When I placed the challenge in the newspaper, I chose to introduce some rules to the fight with Hannah to avoid getting another nasty bite mark, scratch or gouge. They take too long to heal. The instruction to fight with half-a-crown in each of our fists will hopefully fix that. It also ensures a time limit on our fight. I can't say I wasn't displeased that Hannah accepted my challenge. I have been giddy since my battle with Vincent and my body has been on edge ever since. Knowing I had this to look forward to has helped, a little. Facing Mrs Piddington and Alice every day has and hasn't, at the same time – good for fuelling my fury, but not so good for my willpower.

I made it through the week without causing any trouble – well, any more trouble than I usually do – and arrived at Hockley for my pre-fight ritual drink of gin with Halfinch in tow. He has kept true to his word and elected himself my chaperone most evenings. Every time I told him to go to hell, he'd reply that he'd take the route I was walking. For the most part, he stayed out of sight, but I always knew he was there, like a second shadow.

The gin I gulp runs through my body, along with the desire to inflict pain on Hannah, today's opponent. I let the anticipation of my first blow filter to my limbs. I close my eyes and visualise the fight, each punch I land to her chin, cheek and nose.

'Should you be drinking that?' Halfinch asks, looking up at me as I stand in front of the bar.

'You asked me if there was something you could do to help me get ready,' I reply, placing the tankard on the wooden bar top. 'I thought of something,' I say, looking down at him. 'Go home.'

Halfinch rolls his eyes and pushes my empty tankard away from me. 'I'm not leaving. Someone needs to make sure you make it up on to the stage.'

I frown, gripping the bar with both hands. My body sways slightly and I turn to face the dingy room. To my surprise, the venue is full of seedy spectators already. Robert always told me he placed a lot of advertisements to reel in people to watch him fight. I didn't have spare money to place many, but it seems the fight didn't need any draw. The venue was popular enough.

'There are so many people here,' Halfinch states, excited. 'It's packed! My friends are coming too! Cadge and Jack-Jack, they're both coming to watch you fight!'

Cadge? I grunt and roll my head around to loosen up my neck. I want another drink but one eyebrow-raised look from Halfinch tells me I shouldn't. I frown again at the boy and walk towards the steps to the stage. My head is clear and my limbs feel lighter than before. I sweep up the mounds of my long brown hair and tie all of it back on top of my head, piled up and away from my face. I rub my neck and shoulders and finally place my hands together. Halfinch hovers close by, watching me with a misplaced look of reverence. I'm not scared. I've never been scared to fight. Eager? Yes. Impatient? Definitely. I've done this time and time again. I'll win. Hannah may have some experience fighting, but she hasn't had to fight to survive before. The depths I'll go to pull every ounce of strength and stamina from within know no limits. You can throw one more punch? I'll throw two. You can stand another minute? I'll stand another two. Whatever my opponent brings, whoever they are – I'll bring more, I'll be more. Just more. More of everything. I know nothing but brutal dominance and I plan on showing Hannah and everybody watching just how much I want this. Winning isn't an option, it's a way of life. My way of life.

'Wilkinson, you're up,' the owner of the Hockley says, full of cockney swing. I nod in his direction. I think of Alice, Sophie, Mrs Piddington and finally Robert. A dull ache sinks in my belly, so I shake my arms vigorously to reawaken my spirit. Now is not the time to dwell on the past. It's time to fight. This is my time.

For the fight, I chose to wear my blouse, short petticoat, coming just below the knee, drawers and my boots. I refuse to strip down for this fight. It's not St Giles. I'm fighting on my own terms now.

Halfinch, wide-eyed, stares at me.

I wink at him and throw my jacket at his face.

He pulls it down, smiling.

The reaction of this crowd is different to the pit in St Giles rookery. They seem preoccupied with their drink, waiting for something. A spectacle – a spectacular spectacle. This audience isn't used to seeing women fight. Prize-fighting is a sport for men. I shake my head, opening and closing my fists repeatedly. It makes no difference to me what they expect as long as I walk away with the winnings.

I climb onto the stage without acknowledging the crowd. I make my way to the centre and wait for Hannah, pacing back and forth, a lion in a cage, waiting to be unleashed on its prey. A few minutes pass before Hannah arrives, accompanied by a man, presumably her husband. I eye him up and decide he isn't a threat. He's short and stocky – most likely a butcher, given Hannah works at Newgate market. He has more hair on his face than the top of his head, and his face is red, flushed from drinking. I'd know. Hannah is still wearing her coat but her husband, seeing me ready and waiting, motions for her to take it off. I see it immediately. Hannah's hesitation. My lips curl as my eyes narrow in on my opponent. *You're mine.*

Hannah finally removes her coat, revealing her belly. I hadn't noticed it at the market. Hannah didn't want for food, that's for sure. She crosses her arms and stands still, her chin raised. Hannah's bravado isn't fooling anyone, least of all me. I know Hannah is scared. I can see it in her eyes.

'This woman invited me here to box! She thinks she can stand and exchange blows with me!' Hannah shouts her abuse, her screechy voice piercing my ears, giving me yet another reason to punch her in the face. It also grabs the attention of the patrons. People start looking up at us from their tankards to see what the ruckus is about. Hannah is still running her mouth off. 'Well, here I am, Elizabeth! I've answered your invitation! Let's see if you hit as well as you say!' There are some jeers and laughter from the crowd. I ignore them. My sights are set on one person only: Hannah Hyfield.

The owner announces our names, outlining my challenge and the prize of three guineas. He wastes no time in setting out the rules before handing Hannah and myself two half-crowns each to hold in our fists. Hannah smirks as she bounces up and down, her tits flapping around. Occasionally she screams random noises that don't bear any resemblance to any English I know. I stand still. My fists will speak for me soon enough.

There's a bell instead of a mallet slammed against wood, which throws me, causing me to turn towards the sound instinctively. But Hannah knows what the bell means; she swings a fist, connecting with my chin. The smacking sound spurs shock through the spectators. 'Oooooo!' groan some of the men closest to the stage. Others choose to stand to get a better view after the opening seconds.

I recover quickly, side-stepping around Hannah to regain my balance and wits. After the first blow, it is all me. I dance around Hannah, taunting her with jabs to the face and body, always keeping her guessing where I'll strike next. I'm able to avoid another hit with ease.

The audience cheers each time I weave in and out, wounding Hannah with each advance and jab. To Hannah's credit, she stands longer than I expect and even manages to connect a few punches. We dance around each other for over twenty minutes. However, it makes no difference. Hannah's hands aren't held up high enough to block anything. I wait for my opportunity and when I'm within reach I unleash a string of punches to Hannah's face – two left-hand jabs bust her mouth and blood begins to flow down her chest and fat belly. I follow up with a right-hand hook to Hannah's left temple and she flies backwards to the floor, throwing her hands to her face and letting go of the half-crowns.

The roar from the crowd shakes the walls. They're all on their feet, screaming for more. The owner jumps in to check the battered woman, but she's alive. I can see her chest rise and fall in time with her breaths.

Halfinch is beside me, jumping up and down. He grabs a chair and stands on it, raising my left arm as high as he can. I shrug him off as Hannah's husband jumps onto the stage to help her; she's still knocked out cold on the wooden floor.

I grab my winnings from the owner, walk to the front of the stage and stare out at the crowd.

It's a peculiar sensation. Hearing what individual people are saying rather than the usual garbled message from the masses. I can hear people chanting my name, calling me 'city championess'. I hadn't thought of myself as that. I can't remember a time when I'd lost, except to Robert. I'd fought numerous women in St Giles. I'd never heard of Hannah but apparently she'd fought before – where, I have no idea. Another name comes to mind, an Irish woman called Mary Welch. I don't know her, just by reputation. And of course, she's *Irish*.

I scan the sea of faces, mostly strangers, until I reach the third line of tables and spot Sophie with her friends. Sophie is standing, applauding my victory in a very dignified way. Her friends, on the other hand, are swaying and jumping on each other, yelling. A mother hen with her unruly crew.

To my surprise, the best part about winning isn't the money, nor is it the pats on the back, and it isn't the gin, which seems to flow freely at no cost afterwards (a few celebratory drinks wouldn't hurt, would it?). It's the feeling of victory and the looks of acknowledgement from strangers. It's the knowledge that no one other than myself won up on that stage. And I can't wait to tell Alice.

But first, another celebratory drink.

CHAPTER 16

‘‘**B**oxing in public at a bear garden is what has lately obtained very much attention amongst the men, but until last week we never heard of women being engaged in that manner, when two of the feminine gender appeared for the first time on the theatre of war at Hockley-in-the-Hole, and maintained the battle with great valour for a long time, to the no small satisfaction of the spectators." Impressive, Elizabeth,' Mrs Piddington adds, after reading from the *Journal* with a smug look on her face.

Ah yes, this miserable wench. I knew my good mood wouldn't last. I glare at her silently, my hands sewing tirelessly. Mrs Piddington circles the table and tosses the paper down, front page facing up. She then turns and leaves.

My motivation to work at Piddington's is fast dwindling. The early mornings, long days sat huddled over a table and low pay were starting to wear me down. Especially after my victory against Hannah Hyfield. I smile at my winnings, carefully tucked away in my purse. I haven't yet found new lodgings and I long for a decent night's sleep – one where I don't sleep with one eye open on the strangers sharing my room, or covering my ears to stop the monotonous snoring. I stand to stretch, easing the tension and creaks out of my muscles and bones.

My mind drifts and I find myself wondering if I could earn money from fighting alone. I have no way of knowing how much of the money Robert earned was from fighting and how much was from stealing and other crime. I also don't know how many beatings my body could take before I'd need to find another source of income anyway. Probably best to stay put until I can figure out how to make money from fighting. Yes, I need to stay at Piddington's for longer. If not for any other reason but to ensure Alice gets away safely.

My eyes flick to my meagre co-worker sitting at the table working diligently. Alice is sporting another black eye and busted lip. I try not to stare, but the large mass of black and blue is hard to ignore.

Back and forth, back and forth; Alice focuses on her needle as if it were the only thing she could depend on in life, pausing occasionally to check her work. I slowly lower myself back into my seat next to her. Benjamin is finishing another beautiful piece, one of many I've now seen him make, all custom-made for people I never meet. After the boned layers are completed, the silver cloth is laid on top and attached to the underlayers at the other edges of the stay, making it one garment. The stay is lined with a fine silk. The front is embroidered with couched gold and lilac silk thread. It's a piece of art. Ben is an attentive apprentice, one Mr Piddington didn't want to lose.

I think about the type of woman who will wear the stay, a woman of high pedigree but who will ultimately belong to a man. He'll wear her on his arm like an accessory. She'll bear him an heir and so the cycle will continue.

I check to see if Mrs Piddington is near. She isn't. She's preoccu-pied with a customer. Since the magistrate's visit, we haven't been graced with any more introductions to customers. The magistrate is the only one who has been brought back here to the workroom to meet us: the workers, the hired help. I glance back up at Alice, who shoots me a soft look before continuing her trade. I pull my purse from my skirt and count out a guinea, before sliding the coins across to her. Alice's hands still, but she doesn't move to take the money. I nudge the coins towards her some more, trying to entice her to take them.

'Did you find a place to hide it?' I ask.

Alice looks at me. 'I did.'

I smile. 'Good. Take that and stash it away with the rest.'

Alice sighs, lowering her shoulders. She bites her lip before snatching the coins away. 'You're too kind, Elizabeth.'

'No, I'm not,' I say, rapping the table with my knuckles twice, giving her a wink so she knows I'm teasing. I shove the copy of the *Journal* away from me to create space, grabbing another garment in need of repair to begin working on it.

Alice stops sewing the shirt she is mending. She picks up the paper. The bold headline is visible for us all to read, including me, even from the opposite side of the table:

'*SECOND MAN FOUND DECAPITATED.*'

I rub my chin and eye up Alice, who is reading the main story. I lean over and peel the paper from Alice's fingers, breaking her concentration. I read the couple of lines aloud, "'Another man has been found decapitated on London Bridge. His head, pierced with a spike, was found in the early hours on Sunday. No arrest warrants have been issued ...'" My voice trails off. 'Well, that's one way to get rid of your abusive husband,' I say jokingly. Alice remains silent, deep in thought.

My eyes dart to Benjamin, who is no longer working on the stay, but listening, his brow furrowed.

It has been a long day, one I am happy to see the back of. I need to find another room to rent but my thirst is getting the better of me. I start making my way towards The Black Hog when I hear my name.

'Mrs Wilkinson! Elizabeth!'

I stop. It's Constable Boyle. Jogging towards me, hat in hand, pushing past people in the street, narrowly avoiding a carriage as he darts across the street to reach me. He pants heavily.

'Constable Boyle,' I say, looking past him to see if anyone is following him. No one is. 'Is something wrong?'

'It's Stephen – he's been arrested,' Constable Boyle says to me, as he takes deep breaths.

Who is Stephen?

'For pickpocketing,' he adds, regaining his composure.

Ah. I close my eyes and take a deep breath myself. I shudder, thinking of Halfinch sitting in the gaol.

'When is he to see the magistrate?' I ask, cracking each of my finger knuckles. A gust of wind blows my skirt against my legs, the wet hem sticking to my breeches, making me even colder than I already was.

'Tomorrow,' he replies. 'He's being held at the watch house in Covent Garden until then.'

CHAPTER 17

'WHAT ARE YOU looking at?' a hefty man with freckled skin and red hair asks gruffly, standing over me as I sit on the ground with my back against the wall. I shrug and pick up a piece of straw and begin cleaning my teeth. I had watched Halfinch being dragged out of prison and escorted by that other constable and beadle through a few streets towards Long Acre, where he disappeared into a residential house. Constable Boyle informed me that Halfinch had been accused of pickpocketing an older man near Covent Garden and that he would be taken to see the magistrate today. Against my better judgment, I followed. I wanted to shout at the boy for being so stupid. For getting caught. And maybe there's a part of me that wants to look into his eyes and make sure he's all right.

The large man grunts before turning to look down the street. A smaller, ordinary-looking gentleman is jogging towards us. They speak for a few moments before the smaller man hops up the steps and into the house. It is only after he has gone inside that the larger man leans back against the wall with his shoulder and sighs a deep sigh, shoving his hands in his pockets. His red cheeks match his hair colour and he is as wide as an ox.

'You Elizabeth?' he finally asks, gazing down at me once more.

I nod, rubbing my hands up and down my thighs before crossing my arms and tucking my hands under them for heat.

'The boy doesn't stop talking about you.'

I grin, but remain silent.

'You going to fight again?'

I lick my lips and tilt my chin up towards him. 'Maybe.'

He nods and turns his head to look over his shoulder, taking in the people emerging from their adjoining houses, scurrying to wherever their feet need to take them for the day. No realisation that a young boy might be transported to Newgate Prison to await execution for his crime after today. The sudden ache in my chest hits me harder than a kick to my stomach. The thought of Halfinch being hanged at Tyburn does not sit well with me.

After a while, I break the silence. 'The boy's foot ...'

The big red man looks back down at me, frowning. 'What about it?'

'Did you do that?'

His frown deepens. 'He tell you that?'

I shake my head.

'Good, because I didn't.'

My head shake turns into a head nod. I'm somewhat glad to hear this big red man isn't responsible for Halfinch's gammy foot. It's clear he has some connection with the boy, otherwise he wouldn't be here. We stay together in more silence, watching people pass us by, me on the ground and him standing leaning against the wall next to me, both waiting for the same boy.

After what feels like a long time, the front door is flung open and the elderly accuser stomps out, down the steps and up the street, mumbling as he passes, clearly disgruntled. I push myself up over the ground and dust off the dirt and straw that cling to my backside. Halfinch appears a second later with another man, the gent who earlier spoke to the big red man currently standing next to me. When Halfinch spots me, he gives me a wink and a smile so big it looks like it's been drawn on.

Cocky shite. He hobbles down the steps towards the street, and the short man continues past us, not making eye contact with the big red man. In fact, he acts as if he's never seen him before. I frown.

'Championess! You came! For me?' Halfinch asks, then turns his attention to the man next to me. 'Thank you, Big Red. Have you met Elizabeth? Elizabe—'

'We've met,' Big Red says abruptly. He nods at me, and I mimic the head gesture back.

Big Red. Should have guessed.

Halfinch's eyes dart between us. 'Let's go, Halfinch,' Big Red orders, clasping his hand around the boy's neck, guiding him away from me, back in the direction of Covent Garden. I watch as Big Red escorts the boy away and while I am relieved he is free, I find the aching in my chest grow as he disappears around the corner. I didn't get a chance to find out what happened. Annoyed, I bite the inside of my cheek, causing me to wince, and then focus.

'Are you making new friends, Mrs Wilkinson?' a deep voice asks, pulling my attention away from the distance. A constable stands on the last step leading up to the private dwelling. The same constable I met that day when Constable Boyle told me about Piddington's.

'No,' I reply abruptly, resulting in an uncomfortable silence.

'I worry for that boy,' the constable sighs, shaking his head before looking at me. 'Apologies, you might not remember me – my name is Nicholas Clayton. I'm parish constable over in Covent Garden. You're an acquaintance of Constable Boyle, correct?' Constable

Clayton enquires, breaking the awkwardness that was beginning to settle.

'I remember you,' I say, glancing down the street.

'I read in the *Journal* that you won your prize fight against Hannah Hyfield at Hockley. Not many venture to that place. You're a brave woman.'

I don't know this man and owe him no explanation. It might be rude, but there's no question in his rambling so I don't feel bad about not engaging in conversation. I can feel him studying me. I shift on my feet to make my way to work; I'm already late after coming to find Halfinch, but I'll deal with Mrs Piddington when I get there. Being here felt more important, more urgent.

'You know, Matthew – I mean, Constable Boyle – wouldn't have made it home to his family that night in St Giles if you hadn't intervened the way you did.'

I look at Constable Clayton, who slowly smiles at me. I nod at him. The only way I know how to acknowledge his sentiment, one he has repeated twice now.

'Was it you who arrested the boy?' I ask sternly. Constable Clayton's face falls, and when his eyes meet mine, I note the fleeting guilt passing over his features.

'The old man, Mr Thomas, brought Stephen – the boy – to me, says he caught him red-handed stealing a handkerchief from his pocket. I had no choice but to lock him up until the magistrate could see him this morning,' he explains, frowning before continuing. 'But that other man, the smaller one – you may have seen him leave here just moments ago – said he saw the whole thing and that it was another boy who took the handkerchief. As Stephen didn't have any stolen items on his person, Magistrate Trelawny—'

The name struck me immediately. 'Who?' He had my full attention now.

'Magistrate Trelawny, Charles Trelawny, he's a magistrate and resides here.' He points at the house behind me. I look up at the building, towards the window on the first floor, where someone stands, watching. A child. A young girl.

'Where have you been?' shouts the Mistress of Misery. 'You're late. Very late!'

'Too late,' a man's voice states.

I whip around to see Mr Piddington leaning on the railing outside his office. 'We need reliable people to work here, Elizabeth. I think it's best if you seek employment elsewhere.' He nods at his wife and then spins back into his office before slamming the door.

I look at Mrs Piddington, waiting for her to say something.

But for the first time since I started work at the shop, it seems the Mistress of Misery is lost for words. She shifts and finally snaps her eyes to mine. 'We are merely pawns, Elizabeth.' I purse my lips and glare at her. Alice appears from behind the curtain, breaking the tension. Her soft features force me to exhale deeply. She takes a step towards me, but I shake my head once, urging her to stay. Mrs Piddington returns to Alice's side, wrapping her arm around my co-worker. A gentle embrace that also calms my nerves. I take my coat and my leave from Piddington's Stay-making and Haberdashery shop.

People tend to get out of my way, which is normal given my size, but I think the scowl on my face is sending a different message tonight, causing people to scurry out of my path. I hug my coat around my waist, fighting to keep the bitter cold at bay, but it whirls around my head, burning my cheeks and ears. My feet, without any conscious instruction, began the walk down the street, then right on to Holborn. In and out, in and out, my feet march beneath my skirt. They don't stop until I see the swinging sign of The Black Hog.

As it is a weekday, the public house will be half-empty. Good. *More gin for me.*

The next day, I wake up, put on my boots and tattered coat and walk straight back to The Black Hog, where I drink gin until I can't walk straight. The innkeeper – a man I've learned is called John Adams – isn't happy with me.

'Any more problems and you'll be banned, Elizabeth!' John points a hairy finger at me. 'No more abusing the customers or you're out!'

I cock my head to the side and shoot him a sideways glance, as I raise my tankard to him. 'No problems from me today, John.' Then I neck the rest of my drink. I have enough from my winnings against Hannah to last me another week without having to worry about work, but it just means I am still in the twopence house each night, which is not what I wanted. Losing my job at Piddington's was not part of the plan. If I had a plan, that is. I'll drink today and then go and speak to Constable Boyle to see if he can help me. He's the only person in London who might be able, and willing, to.

I just need another day to wallow. I just need to drink today. Tomorrow will be different, I tell myself.

'Thought I'd find you here,' a familiar voice says from behind.

'Go away, Halfinch, I'm not in the mood.'

Halfinch hobbles up and hops onto the stool next to me. 'Why aren't you at work? I waited for you, but you didn't come out, so I figured you'd be here.' Halfinch rests both arms on the bar and interlocks his fingers, as if he's a grown man rather than a young boy who hasn't felt the warmth of a woman's thigh.

I sigh heavily and let my head fall onto my hands. 'I don't work there any more,' I reply.

'Good! You can fight now without worrying about your hands getting broken!' Halfinch exclaims, with no attempt to try and hide his delight.

'What? No, I'm not fighting ...'

'What? Why not?' he barks, holding his palms up. When I don't respond, but motion for John's attention, Halfinch lets his head drop into both hands. 'I'm going to piss,' he announces through his fingers, and he jumps off the stool, hobbling towards the back of the tavern. I lick my lips and finish my drink. *Tap. Tap. Tap.* I knock the bar top with my knuckles as a second attempt at getting John to serve me another drink. He gives me a long look before shaking his head at me.

Bastard.

I hear the heavy-set tavern door swing open and from the corner of my eye notice a few men enter. I don't turn to look at them, even when they approach where I am sitting.

'Amazonian,' the voice rasps behind me. I take a swig from my gin. 'We have unfinished business.'

I shift on my seat to see two men standing on either side of Vincent. He pulls out a stool and raises his hand to get John's attention.

'All these threats and warnings from you, Vincent, and then nothing,' I say, holding up both hands. 'It's rude to tease a lady. I was beginning to think you'd forgotten about me.'

'Oh no, not forgotten,' he smirks, as John approaches. 'Can I buy you another drink?' He points to my empty tankard.

WHACK! I slam my hand down on the bar, beaming from ear to ear. 'Yes, Vincent! You can buy me another drink, how very kind of you for a fanny-fucking-business-owner!'

'Elizabeth, I warned you—' John states, pointing at me again with hooded eyes. John is a big bloke, but harmless. Another one with many words full of empty threats. Still, not wanting to piss off my favourite tavern's proprietor, I simply nod at him and scrunch my eyes close.

Vincent slips a coin into John's hand. 'An ale, and a gin for the *lady*,' he orders, dismissing my earlier outburst. John arches an eyebrow. He knows me well enough to know I might be a woman, but I'm not a lady. None of the females who frequent The Black Hog are.

'Oi! You're in my seat!' Halfinch chimes from my side.

Vincent's men chuckle at the boy, while Vincent merely smiles. 'Cute boy. Does he belong to you, Amazonian?'

I peer back over my shoulder at the young cripple with crossed arms and a serious look on his face. I grunt, 'Sort of.'

'I thought so, for wherever you are, he is never far behind,' Vincent sneers. His yellow eyes stare into mine. Beneath them, his dry mouth curls into a vile grin. The hair on the back of my neck stands and a chill ripples down my spine. The warning permeates my body, causing me to jump to my feet, knocking over my stool, to stand in front of Halfinch, who leans to one side to peek around me.

Vincent laughs. 'Well, we best be on our way,' he remarks, downing his ale. He places a hat on his head and extends an arm. One of his men hands him his cane. I stand still, grimacing at the man, holding Halfinch behind me, while Vincent considers us both. 'No more Piddington's,' he states, shaking his head. 'Guess it's the workhouse or whorehouse for you after all, isn't it, Amazonian?'

CHAPTER 18

NEITHER. I CHOOSE NEITHER.

After leaving The Black Hog last night, Halfinch and I argued about my next employment. Together with the crippled pickpocket, I staggered back to the twopence lodge, where he dumped me onto a bed the landlord indicated I could have for the night. I woke to find my boots removed, but otherwise I was fully dressed. Halfinch reappeared with a smug look on his face and said he was taking my 'drunk arse' to see James Figg, who he was convinced would help me.

Me? I wasn't so sure.

Everyone knows James Figg, not everyone knows me, and not everyone wants to see women fighting on the stage. Not in public, at least. In the squalor of St Giles rookery and retrograde Hockley-in-the-Hole, women get away with a display of pugilism, but not in more reputable establishments. Establishments like James Figg's Great House.

I shift my weight beneath my feet, unsure of my next move. Figg's academy isn't what I expect. Off Tottenham Court Road, at the corner of Castle Street and Marylebone Fields, the detached roadside public house is isolated from other buildings and stands at the sign of the City of Oxford. A far cry from the windows of dukes and duchesses, lords and ladies or well-dressed wits, my mind turns to Alice and whether she's been able to protect the money I gave her. I narrow my gaze on the school for *the manly art of self-defence.*

'*Manly,*' I snort.

'Well, what are you waiting for? Go in and speak to him,' Halfinch says, motioning towards the building with his hand. 'It's either this or you accept Vincent's offer ...'

I frown at the boy as my feet take me towards the gym at the mention of Vincent's name. Pushing through the unlocked doors, I look around the building. It's eerily quiet.

My eyes settle on the elevated stage enclosed by wooden rails. Curious, I edge towards the enclosure.

'What do you want?' a man says. I spin on my heels to face him. His gravelly voice isn't familiar, but when my eyes adjust to the lighting, I recognise the face immediately.

James Figg. The proprietor of the academy and recognised boxing champion.

I squint at him, taking him in. He's tall, bald and has strong shoulders and grey eyes. He exhales deeply, flicking crumbs or dirt from his trousers. I can't tell which from here.

'My name is Elizabeth—'

'Wilkinson. I know who you are,' he states, his tone uninterested and his piercing grey eyes interrupting me. My mind blanks and words fail me. Why am I here again? I blink and take a moment to regain my thoughts. Yes, Halfinch convinced me to come. To speak to James Figg ... to try and convince him to let me fight ... James Figg or Vincent Love. Those are my options. I swallow and find my voice.

'I want to fight,' I say finally, tilting my chin towards the stage.

He snorts, and slowly shakes his head. His intense gaze causes me to shift on my feet, his stare going right through me. I massage the back of my neck in the hope it will help my brain to start working, to think of something else to say, string words together, but it isn't working.

James raises his eyebrows, as if waiting for me to speak. When my voice fails me, he rubs a hand over his bald head. I track the hand, unable to tell if he's naturally bald or if he just chooses to shave his head. Then he drops both hands to his hips, pursing his lips, considering me. All the while, his eyes never leave mine.

'I don't train women,' he announces at last.

'I'm not asking you to train me,' I state through gritted teeth, instantly regretting it the moment the words leave my mouth. I can't help it. I feel uncomfortable and when I'm uncomfortable my temper rises. Anger is always the emotion I resort to when challenged.

James's eyes flare and a vein in his neck pulses. 'Go back to your gin, Mrs Wilkinson.'

'I want to fight,' I snap. 'I can fight—'

'No, you survive—' he scolds.

'Fighting is surviving!' I shout, unable to contain my rage and the hammering in my chest. My jaw clenches as my teeth grind down.

A low chuckle comes from his chest as he raises his hand to run his thumb along his bottom lip and smirks, 'No, it isn't.' He pushes past me and ascends the stage. His stage. He's a giant of a man, taller than I'd initially observed. His knuckles are scarred and he has a mark below his left eye – a memento from a fight, I am sure – and a crooked nose, another souvenir from battle. He's been on the receiving end of a few nasty jabs, as have I.

Does my nose look like that?

My mind drifts to the first time I fought for Robert. My opponent was slighter than me and she was petrified. I won that fight handily. I've won every fight I've fought, tearing through each opponent, like a storm releasing hell on a busy street, destroying anything in its path. And still Robert brought more people for me to destroy, just like Sir Frederick had. I couldn't lose. Losing meant dying. Dying either at my opponent's hands, or Robert's. Violence came naturally to him, like the ability to walk and spit at the same time. Even now, losing this line of reasoning with James meant death, because I'd rather die than work at a whorehouse or workhouse – more hopeless than poverty.

My hand unconsciously traces one of my countless scars. My mind traces memories of Robert taking his sword to me before a fight, cutting me just enough to make me angry, but not enough to harm me seriously. Like a wounded animal, I'd been taunted, forced into battle, surrounded by screaming men and women all looking for some sadistic fix. By the time I was unleashed, my opponents never stood a chance.

I glance up at James Figg, appreciating the space he fills with his presence on the stage.

Halfinch is right. The man is formidable, but he isn't Robert. He's controlled. Relaxed. Secure. He's no criminal.

He's a prize fighter. The champion.

I hear voices entering the premises – several men, all tall and broad, come in through the wooden doors, ignoring me as they approach James, who hasn't given me a second glance since alighting the stage. My jaw unclenches as my body releases the tension I had no idea I was holding until now. I blink several times, willing my feet to move. Maybe I should listen to James and seek refuge at the bottom of a gin, pushing the worries of my future until another day.

But then I think of facing Halfinch outside, of Alice's broken face, and Sophie's lightless eyes at the Tippling House. Vincent is right, I'd be forced to go to the workhouse. To work among dead women walking. I don't want that. I've *survived* too much to succumb to that fate and I am not going to whore my body.

I have to fight.

I want to fight.

I *need* to fight.

I lift my head and roll my shoulders back, having made my decision. I follow the men up on to the stage, a couple of them tossing questioning looks over their shoulders at me. I stare at James. His eyes narrow, sharp, focused on me. He picks up a short dagger, tossing it in front of me before choosing one for himself, and stalks towards me.

He juts his chin at the weapon on the ground.

'You'll change your mind,' I state, bending over to pick up the dagger. I feel the weight of it in my hand, studying it.

'We'll see,' he replies.

'Yes, we will,' I smile, beginning to circle the enclosure. The men step back, creating space for us, sensing the upcoming battle. A few heckles carry over the air and my head. My concentration is firmly on the imposing man mirroring my movements.

I stop and brace myself for his attack, but again, he copies me, holding position across from me.

Quit your games, Figg, I think to myself, steadying my breath. A minute passes, possibly two. The heckles and laughter from our audience grow louder. I can feel my heart beating faster, my breaths shallowing; a trickle of sweat falls down my neck under the gaze of James. I blink and as I do, James launches at me.

I feel the sting at my right hip.

'Zounds!' I yell, spinning around to shield my wounded side.

'That's one,' he smirks. I instinctively reach for my hip and see blood on my hand. I look up at James and see the short dagger in his hand, the hint of crimson over the blade. He lifts it and wipes the blood away with his middle left finger, his calculating stare remaining on me.

James points the dagger at my chest. 'Your turn.' He drags his eyes down my blouse and heaving chest. His gaze lands where his dagger nipped my flesh and he cocks his head to one side.

I seize the moment and throw my forearm across to knock his outstretched arm away. I follow the momentum with my body, spinning behind him, and swipe at his back, drawing blood of my own.

James's scowl causes me to grin. I thrust my dagger at him again but he blocks my advance and jumps back, creating more distance between us.

'You've used a blade before, I see,' he says, breathing quickly. 'I shouldn't be surprised given Robert's skill with a blade.' I don't respond, allowing *my* skills to speak for me.

He lunges at me and this time he manages to scratch my shoulder and I wince.

'That's two; one more and I win,' he says, withdrawing. These are his rules. Never had I partaken in such a test until now.

James takes advantage of my hesitation as he steps in and knocks the dagger from my hand. He reaches for my hair, which I haven't pinned, and spins me around into his embrace. His chest is pressed against my back as he holds the dagger at my throat, his cheek pressed against mine.

'If it's just money you want, there are other ways for a woman to earn a coin or two,' he whispers into my ear. My rage boils at his breath in my ear. I instinctively throw my head back and hit his nose, followed quickly with an elbow to his left temple. He stumbles back but doesn't drop his weapon, so I swiftly pursue and kick him in the groin. He drops to his knees and the clatter of his dagger to the ground says he's done. I'm not. I punch him with all my might across the face, sending him to the floor.

I pick up his blade and point it at his chin. He holds his head up, his eyes watching my every move. I lean down and whisper, 'Yes, I can use a blade. Yes, Robert taught me a little. And yes, there may be other ways for less fortunate women to earn money, but I'm not a whore and I'm getting *really* tired of people thinking I am.' I stand back up and fling the short dagger across the floor towards him, the clanging from the metal bouncing off the wooden planks echoing around the chamber. I push my way through the crowd of men and descend from the stage towards the doors.

I hear James chuckle behind me.

'Elizabeth,' he calls, recovering quickly. 'Come back tomorrow.'

'I wasn't sure you'd come back,' James says, without looking at me as I enter the doors to Figg's Academy.

'Neither was I,' I lie.

He snickers and continues to roll up rope around his arm. 'Come, I'll show you around.' I follow quietly, taking it all in. It's a large room with cudgels and swords lined against one wall, a bench rested against the opposite side, and in between a wide open room where a number of men are standing, sparring in pairs. And that is that. My induction to James Figg's fighting academy is over. James calls over one of the other men and asks him to spar with me. He's a stocky bloke by the name of James Stokes. He has dishevelled black hair and several scars on display – another regular in the prize-fighting arena. With his dark eyes and lightly bronzed skin, he could pass as European, rather than a Londoner. But a Londoner he is. His accent can't be mistaken for anything else.

'Another James?' I ask, looking between the two men.

'Welcome,' James Stokes greets me, smiling, holding out his hand. I glance back at the other James, who is watching us, before shaking his hand. 'Call me Jimmy – everyone else does. Avoids confusion.' He flicks his head towards the other men.

'I'm Elizabeth.'

He nods. 'We all know who you are. First woman James has taken in and has knocked him down. Sorry I missed it yesterday.'

I don't respond to that. I can sense James's eyes on the back of my head. So I wait for Jimmy to speak again. For direction, from anyone.

'Shall we spar?' Jimmy asks, raising his fist. I nod once and copy his stance.

We dance around for a bit before the jabs start – quick but light, so as not to cause any serious harm. I'm not used to the boxing practice and several times I accidentally connect with Jimmy's face or stomach. I apologise each time, but he doesn't seem to mind.

He just grins and shakes his head, beckoning me to continue. The sooner the men know I can fight, the better. I don't want to have to look over my shoulder when I'm here. Jimmy takes a few punches in good faith, but by the fourth connection his patience evaporates and he lashes out with a punch of his own, straight at my chest. He immediately apologises, holding up his hands, but it's too late. I'm raging. Blood pumping, muscles twitching, I pounce with an angered mind and wild limbs. I swing left and then right, connecting both times, forcing Jimmy backwards. Before I can collect myself, I feel strong arms envelop me, restraining me. By smell alone, I know it's James. Another two fighters gather around Jimmy. He waves them off, laughing.

'You weren't lying – she does have a temper!' Jimmy says, rubbing his jaw. This breaks the tension and they all laugh, dispersing back to their training. Jimmy walks away with the two men, joking, though not without glancing back at me and winking. James is still holding my arms, only releasing me when there is ample space between us and the other fighters. I shake him off and crack my neck. I feel the tension drain from my body.

James turns me to face him. 'You need to control your temper.' I roll my eyes at him and watch as the others spar. 'If you want to train here then there are a few rules you need to abide.'

'When can I fight?' I ask, choosing to ignore his comment.

'The first is no drinking. I don't want you showing up here drunk and unable to train. The second—'

'When can I fight?' I press him.

'When I say you're ready. The second is that you will stay at lodging I choose for you because I don't trust you not to drink and show up on time unless I can keep an eye on you. Gin is potent and damaging, Elizabeth, and will only lead to your ruin,' he says, his warning a cold, brutal truth I have been reluctant to face. 'Finally, if you cause any bad will among my students or damage my or my academy's name, then you will no longer train with or fight for me. Understood?' His tone holds no emotion. His voice didn't soften as he reeled off his rules. He simply stated them. He's a grumpy bastard, I decide.

I let his words take root. I'm not the kind of person who follows orders easily, but judging by the way he stands, unflinching, I know I have no choice. I can swallow my pride and adhere to his conditions or I can let Alice and Halfinch down. They need me. So does Sophie.

James grabs my chin with more force than necessary and holds it so that I can't look away from him. 'I need to hear you say you agree to my terms.'

'I agree to your terms,' I seethe, hating the part of me that wants to punch him in the face and head to The Black Hog in defiance.

His eyes twinkle with amusement, sensing my struggle at verbalising my consent. 'You're going to cause trouble, aren't you?'

I stare at him incredulously. *Why does everyone think I am going to cause trouble?*

'No, I'm not,' I sigh.

James chuckles then, as if I am some amusing child. 'Yes, you are.'

CHAPTER 19

J AMES HAS UNDERPLAYED the lodging I am to stay in. I thought I'd be forced to share, but it seems as the first woman fighter he's agreed to train, I get my own room. To avoid temptation. As if I want to share my bed with another person, let alone man, again. The idea of intimacy holds no interest for me whatsoever. All I have to do is recall Robert's touch or the sight of Alice's bruised face or Sophie's dim eyes and any thought or desire for a man touching me disappears like that of the heat from a dowsed fire.

My new residence is situated on Henrietta Street, just north of Figg's own house off the Oxford Road. It's sparsely furnished – a single room, bright and airy, free from the congested smell that sickened me at the twopence house in Clerkenwell. It has a double bed with a straw and feather mattress – which I'm not to share – an armchair near the window, just to the right of a small fire, and a chamber pot in the corner. But it's clean. It's mine. And I love it.

Despite the late warming up of the weather, it's June. The start of a new season in more ways than one.

After stating the rules of my employment at the Boarded House, James tells me I'll be on a trial period. If I can follow his rules for a month, then he'll let me stay. The rules are simple: train, respect the other fighters, and win. And no drinking. My posture slumps every time I think about the no-drinking part. But James repeats himself when he shows me to my room, to make sure his message is clear: 'I mean it, you're no good to me drunk.'

He hands me a parcel before sticking his hands into his pockets as he watches me open it. 'Tea?' I ask, my face scrunched up. He nods and points to the bucket by the door. 'Water pump's just outside, boil it first,' he grunts, pointing at the pot suspended over the unlit coals. 'Table beer or tea. That's what you drink from now on.' He points at me with one of his large, hairy fingers. 'No gin.'

I look down at the box of tea in my hands, then at the bucket, and settle my sight on the small fireplace. I sigh and nod, pivoting to take in my new abode. I pull my hair together in my hands, twist it and pin it all up on top of my head.

'Your hair is beautiful.'

I freeze at the unexpected remark. My hands tighten around my tresses, pulling tighter than necessary. Robert used to remark on how long and luscious my hair was. It was the only compliment he ever voiced. That was reason enough for me to keep it piled up; I hate my hair being noticed. James's words cause me to shiver.

'Are you cold?' he asks, tilting his head as he studies me. 'I can start a fire for you.' I turn to face him, shaking my head once. My hand rests on my belly as it rumbles, longing for food. James frowns and digs his hands into his pockets before handing me some money. 'Here, take it. Buy yourself some food.' He holds the coins out for me to take. It feels as if his grey eyes pierce through me every time he looks at me. I tentatively reach out to take his offer but when I try to pull on the coins, he doesn't let go. 'For food, not drink, understood?'

I stare at him, wide-eyed. I can feel my mouth salivating at the thought of a drink, of the warmth washing over my body and numbness over my thoughts, slowing the world to a near stand-still. I lick my lips and nod. I don't want to break his rules, but the thought of not tasting gin again is starting to gnaw at me from the inside out.

'Do you need anything else?' James asks me, taking a step back, as though he knows I need space. I shake my head again.

'Very well. I'll leave you to get settled.'

Settled? No, I doubt I'll be able to get settled here. I want a drink. My mind is already thinking of ways I can get a tipple without James knowing. I wonder if Halfinch would help get me something to drink? No, I won't ask the boy. He'll tell me I'm being lazy or ask too many questions about why I'm not getting it myself. I won't let my weakness control me. I can beat my thirst.

I can.

The best thing about having my own room – apart from the lack of snoring – is not having to worry about whether it will be there for me the following week or even the next day. When the door closes at night, it stays that way until I open it the next day, despite James's incessant banging on the wood to wake me up most mornings. Many of the other fighters have their own rooms, but they share, and some choose to live elsewhere with their wives and families. It strikes me as odd that some of the men have families, watching them spar and bleed in one moment and then picturing them sitting around the table eating supper with their bairns. My inability to conceive a child with Robert saved me in some way. While other young women were giving birth, I was fighting to keep myself alive and out of the life I'd been born into – one destined for few prospects.

James remains true to his word – as long as I show up for training, he leaves me alone. If I want to stay, if I want to win and help Alice, then I have to wake up and put in the time. Follow James's direction and rules.

I find avoiding temptation is key to not drinking, so I haven't been back to The Black Hog since starting at the Great House. In fact, I avoid Covent Garden altogether. How I will visit Alice will be challenging as I have to walk past my old haunt to get to the shop, but I will leave that problem for another day. The withdrawal is torturous. Most days I suffer from the shakes and at night I get cold sweats. Every morning I vow I'll have a drink. Just the one. To take the edge off the fire searing through my body and mind. But by the time training finishes, my body can barely carry me back to Henrietta Street, and certainly no further. Desperate for bed and sleep. I think that is James's plan – to work me to the point of exhaustion each day so I can't physically get myself to a gin shop.

James splits our training among three disciplines: pugilism, short sword and cudgel-play. I don't know why we need to practise with weapons, but it adds variety and passes the time more quickly. Of course, I've sparred with men before, but this is a far cry from Robert's taunting jabs to rile me up the day before a fight. The men who I train with are all respectful, despite being of the working class.

James makes sure they aren't lenient on me because I'm a woman; the time he gives me to rest between training sessions is the same as for the men. He makes sure I eat regularly and, while he dictated I stop drinking, he has never told me I cannot leave the house. I want to visit Alice. I need to reassure her I haven't forgotten about her.

On the Sunday, a week into my time at the Great House, Halfinch is waiting for me outside my new home on Henrietta Street, looking giddy. As annoying as he is, I've grown used to his presence. I won't say I enjoy his company, but I can tolerate the boy now. I'm also secretly relieved he no longer has to act as my escort since starting my new routine with James.

'How's the training going?' he asks, not getting up from the ground where he sits, legs outstretched like it's a comfortable chaise lounge.

'Bloody tiring,' I reply, hovering over him.

'When you fighting again?'

'Don't know,' I say truthfully, because James hasn't given me any indication when I'll be ready according to him. Halfinch looks up at me seriously now. 'You'll let me know when you do though, won't you?'

I nod, watching the boy, and when my gaze falls on his gammy left foot, my chest tightens. Curiosity gets the better of me. 'Tell me something,' I say, nudging the foot with my toe before taking a seat beside him, 'what happened to your foot?'

Halfinch cocks his head to the side, looking at his maimed foot. 'I was run over by a carriage,' he explains. 'After a job. . .' He takes off his hat and scratches his head. I frown, unable to think of anything to say to that. Because what can you say? I'd normally tease him, but this time humour seems like an inappropriate response to a child getting crushed. I look down at him as he rubs the tops of his thighs.

And just like that, my heart catches.

In a matter of seconds, he's gone from being the lippy squirt with an answer to everything to a disabled young boy in need of protection, or comfort. Love, even. But I don't know how to love, having never experienced the feeling myself. Just pain and despair.

I close my eyes and rest my head back against the wall, sitting next to my little pickpocketing cohort. I allow the silence to grow, comfortable in the feeling of his shoulder resting against my arm. I can tell Halfinch wants to talk about something, but I won't press him. It's not often the boy is quiet. I'll enjoy it while it lasts.

CHAPTER 20

I GUESS JAMES THINKS I'm ready because I'm standing to the side of the stage at the Boarded House, a bear garden in Marylebone Fields off Oxford Street. It's my first fight under James Figg and my nerves are getting the better of me.

Flyers have been plastered all over the streets and advertisements promoting the fight were published in the local papers.

'Are you ready?' James asks me. I say nothing, fearing I might be sick all over his shoes. He steps towards me and grabs my chin between his thumb and forefinger, forcing my face up to meet his gaze. 'What's wrong? Are you ill?'

I swallow and shake my head. He considers me a moment longer before someone calls his name, drawing his attention from me. He hesitates before leaving me, probably fearful that I am going to drink. The temptation is everywhere and if I'm being honest with myself, I'd say I feel naked without my pre-fight gin. It's unusual to be this sober before a fight. Nevertheless, the sounds of the audience stamping the floor shake the ground, but not my courage.

I can do this, I tell myself. *It's just another fight.* I haven't lost a fight and this Martha Jones, a fisherwoman no less, will not be the woman to end that record. And with that, my jittery insides settle.

James told me Martha is known for her vile tongue, and she's crossed many women with her rhetoric in the streets, backed with a quick beating on different stages. He also told me this to prepare me for any insults she throws my way in an attempt to rile me. 'Don't lose your temper,' he said. 'Focus on her movements, not her tongue.' James's words replay in my head. The fact that I remembered them is surprising.

Ours is the first fight scheduled for this day. There are two men's bouts arranged afterwards. James told me that as my reputation grows I could maybe headline a prize fight myself, but not yet. Spectators need to see what I'm capable of. What women are capable of.

I smile.

Devastation. That is what I intend to bring to the people of London. They love a good beating, the bloodier the better.

There's a hushing of the crowds before James announces the first fight. Martha's name is followed by a loud booming from the crowd as she makes her entrance on to the stage. I watch the woman as she stalks around the enclosure.

I hear James call my name but I don't hear the rest. I make my way to where the stage is set, my presence completing the picture. I bound up the three wooden steps to climb over the planks on to the square stage. My hair is tied on top of my head in its usual way and my blouse is fastened around my body, holding my breasts firmly in place for this bout. I take my position opposite Martha, who is still pacing back and forth.

A voice yells, 'Christ almighty, that's a bloody big woman!'

Martha laughs at the jibe. She starts mimicking my stance, which pleases the audience as they roar laughter. I tilt my head to one side and narrow my glare on Martha. The Boarded House looks different when the pews are filled with people. Voices fill the air, as does the excitement.

James calls us both to the centre – another ritual I'm not used to, but James had mentioned it to me beforehand, so I approach at his beckoning, as does Martha. James explains the rules – fight until the other drops – and then sends us back to our respective corners. James steals a glance at me, giving me a subtle nod as he leaves the stage. Moments later, a mallet drops against a slab of wood. *Smack!*

Martha wastes no time, advancing and swinging at my face, forcing me backwards. I circle around to find the centre of the stage, pursued all the while by Martha, throwing her arms at me. It reminds me of a game I used to play as a child. I snort. It's easy to dance around the stage and I find my place. Soon, the crowd joins in with my laughter as I taunt Martha. I look up to where James stands, the only audience member not delighting in the moment. His steely grey gaze reminds me to concentrate on the task at hand.

A beating.

Martha grows impatient and begins yelling abuse at me, calling me names, daring me to retaliate. Just like James said she would. She holds her fists up, ready for battle. Still seeking my opportunity to advance, it's only when she utters the word 'whore' that my composure drops. The darkness descends as rage spreads from my head down my arms and into my stomach.

I raise my fists and stalk towards Martha. I throw a lazy punch, which Martha easily avoids, and she lands the first hit to my stomach, causing me to double over. I stagger backwards with Martha following me, landing two more jabs to my face. The crowd roar and Martha stops her assault prematurely, allowing me time to regain my breathing. By the time Martha begins her next attack, I'm ready. I feint a few punches to get Martha's guard down and then throw a jab that connects with Martha's chin. I throw another and crunch her nose. Each time, Martha's head snaps back, exposing her neck. The next time I try a combination that James drilled into me earlier in the week, jab-jab-right-hook out from the side and into Martha's left temple, rattling her skull. Martha stumbles back, recomposes herself and launches her body towards me again. She manages to clip my cheek with a punch, but I avoid the full brunt of it by jumping to the side away from her fist.

I start swinging. I hit Martha's face, ribs and gut as many times as I can. Martha endures it as long as she can, but soon drops to her knees. I'm still angry about the 'whore' comment and so I punch Martha in the face again, toppling her over to the wooden floor. It takes James a minute to get on to the stage to announce the winner. He takes a strong stance between me and the now inert Martha Jones. We stare at each other for a few long seconds and then he moves towards me with purpose. I raise my arms as if to fight again but he doesn't attack. Instead, he grabs my left wrist and pushes me towards the middle of the stage, announcing me as the winner.

Confused, I stand still next to James. The crowd begins applauding and I raise my arms, only spurring the audience more. They don't stop even when James escorts me off the stage and back up the steps, away from the masses.

'Well done,' he says, as I sit down on a stool next to Jimmy, who fights next. James grips my chin, turning my head from side to side, inspecting my face. I swat his hand away with mine.

'I'm fine,' I state. 'Where's my money?'

Jimmy chuckles as James arches his eyebrow at me.

'You'll get it.'

I nod, taking a deep breath as I lean my head back against the wall. My job is done.

'You'll be wanting a drink,' James says, motioning at Jimmy to get ready.

My brow furrows. 'I thought drinking is against your rules.'

James grunts and the corner of his mouth curls. 'You've earned a celebratory drink tonight.'

A slow smile spreads across my face. 'Or two?'

James shakes his head and walks with Jimmy back towards the stage.

CHAPTER 21

'Do you want another, Championess?'

I look at John, considering his words. The noise in The Black Hog, which has risen to a considerable level, is giving me a headache. So far, I've had three pints of ale. After stopping my gin drinking, I felt it best to abstain from the taste, to save finding myself having to give it up again – it was near impossible to stop the first time. The cold sweats. The shaking. And the thirst! It was hell's torment, to be sure. No, best I stick to ale. To my surprise, the first drink in what feels like a year, but in actuality has only been a few weeks, tastes heavenly. I've trained, fought and won, all while keeping to James's asinine rules. The man said I could have a celebratory drink. Surely he didn't think that meant just one? But after three pints, I feel perfectly giddy and ready to go home.

I inhale deeply and purse my lips. 'No,' I say, setting my empty pint down on the bar.

'No?' Halfinch asks me, confusion etched across his features.

'No,' I repeat, pushing my stool back and standing. 'Good night, John.'

'Good night, Championess,' he nods, clearing my tankard and serving another patron.

I push open the door and step out into the fresh air, wrapping my arms tightly around me, as if they would miraculously create more warmth. They don't. There is a thin mist hovering above the cobblestones. I hear Halfinch's steps behind me.

'Zounds, it's a fine night!' he says with a laugh.

'Watch your language,' I tease, bumping his shoulder with my hip. True to his word, Halfinch watched my fight and was waiting for me after I left the Boarded House. I didn't bother staying to watch Jimmy fight. I hope he won. After our first day at the gym, we've found a respect for one another and more often than not he is the man that spars with me.

My legs feel heavy and my arms heavier. My jaw and brow ache from the blows I suffered from Martha; the ale hasn't taken the sting out of them the way gin would have. I know it will take a few days to feel like myself again. James hasn't mentioned whether I need to train in the morning, but I hope not. I want to sleep all day in my quiet room. Take the time to recover.

I also want to see Alice. I need to give her some more money and check in on her. It's been too long and I haven't seen or spoken to her. Guilt grips me, adding to my weariness. I've been a bad friend. I should have asked Halfinch to look in on her; he wouldn't like it, but for some reason I know he'd do it if I asked him. The boy seems almost willing to do anything I ask. I frown and cast my sights down on the boy hobbling along next to me. He's rambling about the fight again. He can't get enough. He asked if I wanted to stay for the other contests but I wasn't in the mood. James said I could have a drink and that was the only thing on my mind once the words left his mouth. Nothing, or no one, was going to stop me from getting to The Black Hog and enjoying some booze. God, how I missed it. The warmth. The haze. The freedom.

My mind flits to Sophie. I haven't seen her either; she wasn't at my fight, as far as I could tell, nor was she at The Black Hog tonight. Maybe it was for the best. I sigh and continue our trudge back towards Oxford Road.

As we make our way across the cobblestones, I hear them.

Footsteps.

I slow my pace, trying to home in on the sound, but Halfinch's incessant chat prevents me from hearing.

'Quiet,' I hiss, as I stop walking. The sound of footsteps behind us halts also. I cast my eyes left and then right and see men flanking us on either side. 'Run, Halfinch.'

He looks up at me, wide-eyed. 'What?'

'I said run, go to Big Red,' I command, pushing him away from me and the men. His eyes dart to the men approaching and he disappears into the shadows.

Thank Christ.

I turn around, trying to calm my heartbeat. Vincent Love's men. I recognise them from The Black Hog that night. I swallow as more footsteps approach, getting closer. I slowly spin around to face the greasy-haired man.

'Vincent, lovely to see you again.'

Vincent surveys the street. His neutral expression gives nothing away, other than a general distaste for what he sees. He turns his attention to me.

'Where's your crippled orphan?' he sneers.

'Gone.'

'Probably for the best, would hate for the boy to get hurt... You and I have unfinished business,' he reminds me, as if I needed the reminder. Halfinch is a walking, talking reminder.

I raise one shoulder in a shrug. 'If you say so.'

Vincent nods slowly, as if preparing himself. 'Is now a good time?' he asks, revealing a dagger in his right hand.

I sigh. It isn't a question, not really. I squeeze my eyes closed, and fist my hands at my side. When I open my eyes, two things happen. Vincent motions me to move towards the alley and his men appear at either side of me.

I pivot slowly, mentally preparing for what's to come, when Vincent, noticing a couple of figures approaching through the mist, stops me. With a flick of his wrist, his two men leave.

'Mrs Wilkinson?' It is Constable Clayton, emerging from the veil of grey. He looks at Vincent and watches him slink away, out of sight. 'Is everything all right?'

I nod my head, releasing my breath, not aware I had been holding it. I look at Constable Clayton and the member of the night watch accompanying him.

For once, I'm relieved to see the officers.

CHAPTER 22

'WHAT HAPPENED?' HALFINCH barks, as I exit my building on to Henrietta Street.

'Christ, Halfinch!' I grumble, rubbing my eyes with my hands. I take a deep breath and gain my composure before looking at the boy. 'Nothing happened, constable and nightwatch appeared.'

'Phew,' Halfinch sighs, swiping his brow. 'By the time I went back, you were gone.'

'You came back? Big Red let you back out?' I demand, my voice rising, incredulous.

'He came with me! Why are you so angry?'

We stand off, staring each other down. After a long moment, I shake my head, shove my hands in my coat pockets and turn to leave. I hear Halfinch's feet dragging behind me. 'Go away, Halfinch, I have to see someone.'

'Who?'

'None of your business! Don't you have somewhere to be? Someone to mill?' I toss the callous words over my shoulder, aware I am walking too fast for the boy to keep up. His tiny steps quicken, the sound of his dragging left foot shortening as he attempts to stay with me.

The walk to Holborn takes longer than I anticipated. I lose Halfinch just before I pass through St Giles. My stomach twists when I think of the way I spoke to him. But I was angry at his carelessness, putting himself at risk like that. I'd need to have words with Big Red about letting the boy out so late, following me around all the time. It couldn't continue, especially with Vincent showing up like he did last night. I saw the snarl on his lips when he spotted the night watch. Constable Clayton said he had been summoned to investigate a broken window and just happened to walk by. I'm not going to lie and say I wasn't pleased to see him. I wasn't in the best condition to be taking on three men, even if I hadn't just fought and drunk three pints at The Black Hog.

I stand opposite Piddington's, waiting for Alice to finish work. James gave me a day's reprieve from training. I think most of the men took the day. It seems to be a ritual after a fight night. Not all the men train as much as I do either, having other commitments or because it is not to earn a living. They come to James for tutelage because he is the champion, and high society wants to learn from the best. James also gives private tuition to some of the more wealthier families – fathers wanting their sons to learn the art of pugilism.

Leaning against the alley wall, I look around at the Londoners scuffling along the street. I haven't been back since finishing at Piddington's, but now that I stand on King Street, I feel nothing. I don't miss it. I don't miss sitting all day. The monotonous tasks and daily routine. Of course I miss the feel of the extravagant fabrics against my fingers and Alice's smile and gentle presence – it was calming to my soul. But I don't miss seeing her hurt. Waiting to see what bruises and marks she'd show up wearing on her skin.

As if I summoned her, Alice appears at the front door of the shop. I stiffen at the sight of her – she's wrapped up in a green jacket and carries a bag over her arm. As she shuffles along the path I jog across to greet her, not wanting to startle her.

'Alice!' I call, as I approach. She turns and smiles upon seeing me.

'Elizabeth! How nice to see you again,' she replies, standing still. I notice the injured cheek immediately, and the gap hiding behind cracked lips where a tooth is missing. Her hand darts to her mouth, sensing my annoyance at her wounds. My eyes flit to hers, but she doesn't meet them, choosing to gaze at my jacket buttons; her expression is frozen, like me being here reminds her of how horrid her life is. I take a breath and yank my purse from my hip, counting out ten shillings, which I hand to her. She reaches and takes the money without saying anything.

'Are you still saving it some place safe?' I ask, my voice low.

She nods, but doesn't say anything.

'I think it's time to speak to Mrs Piddington about contacting your family. Begin arrangements to get you moved.'

She glances back in the direction of the shop. 'I already have. After you left... Well, she knows. She's already written to my sister. We're waiting a response.'

'That's good, Alice,' I say, licking my lips and nodding. I try to smile, but I fear it looks forced. Because it is. She's broken and I'm not certain she can survive for much longer. I should have visited sooner. Reassured her.

'I heard you are training with James Figg ...'

I nod, this time my smile genuine. 'I am. I won my fight last night—'

'I don't doubt it,' she states, her smile matching my own. 'You don't know how to lose, do you?'

I laugh. I can't help it. 'I don't like losing, that's for sure.'

A clock chimes and Alice looks at me, signalling she has to go. I don't want to keep her, to make her late. I lift my chin in the direction of her home. 'Go.'

Alice nods, reaches out and rubs my arm with her hand, giving me a gentle squeeze before turning. 'Alice!' I call after her, causing her to spin and look at me again. 'I don't know when my next fight will be, but I'll let you know. Be ready.'

She stares at me, nods once and walks away.

I pray she can hold on until then.

Arriving back home, I notice women's voices coming from upstairs – an unusual sound among what are normally male-dominated noises. I strain to hear what is being said, but their voices are muffled.

I climb the steps slowly, my legs heavy from the fight and walking all day. Sophie is on the landing, leaning against Betty, propped up by her large waist. Some of my fellow fighters peer at them curiously as they pass. I move to let them by, nodding at them to let them know the women are welcome to stay.

Betty gasps with relief when she sees me. 'Ah! We came to find you and when you weren't home I insisted we wait.'

Sophie's eye is swollen shut and her lip is bust. There is bruising around both sides of her face. I can't tell where else she's hurt under the glamorous red dress she is wearing. I've never worn anything like it. I watch the women a moment, cautiously, unsure of what they want from me.

I slowly approach them and open my door, allowing both women entry. I continue to watch Betty as she escorts Sophie to the only chair in my room. Betty instructs me to fetch some water, and I oblige.

'She needs a doctor,' I state.

'I'll go,' Betty replies. She pulls me to the side. 'It was Vincent,' she tells me. 'He was so angry when he got back last night. Barged into Sophie's room and dragged a client off her. I've never seen him so enraged!'

I grunt. 'What did he say?'

'He didn't say anything ...' Her voice trails off as she glances at Sophie, slumped in the chair. 'He just went mad!'

'He didn't say anything at all?' I ask, confusion etched on my face.

'After ... as he was leaving, he just said it isn't over. Not sure what he meant by that – Sophie hasn't done anything to him,' Betty states, resting her hand on her protruding gut.

I sigh. *I know*, I think to myself, turning my attention back to Sophie. 'Why did you bring her here?'

Betty throws up her hands. 'Where else could I take her?'

'The hospital?' I bark back.

Betty shakes her head. 'I brought her here. You can protect her. Mother Lavinia will look in the hospital—'

'She can't stay here!' I shout, wincing when I notice Sophie shrink back further into the chair at my tone.

'Fine, you take her to the hospital and leave her there where one of Vincent's men can come claim her back!' she spits in a hushed voice, before turning to leave.

I roll my eyes at her back.

As Betty reaches my door, she pauses, leaning on it. 'We're people too, Elizabeth. Born into a life we didn't choose for ourselves ...

We all survive the best way we know how. Your judgment changes nothing and helps no one. All it does is blind you to what could be, to *who* people could be.'

I swallow as her words hit me. She nods at Sophie. 'Once you are indebted to Vincent, you are never free of him.' Then Betty shuts the door, leaving me alone with Sophie. I stalk over to the table, fill a mug with beer from the earthenware jug and offer it to her. She sniffles away tears and thanks me.

I grunt, before spinning and removing my jacket and boots, then sitting on the edge of my bed. I study Sophie as she shivers.

She's cold. I can fix that. I drape a blanket around her shoulders, pulling it tight before lighting a fire. I busy myself gathering some cloths and a bowl to clean Sophie's wounds. As I begin wiping her down, Sophie grabs my hand.

'I-I ...' she stutters. She touches her lips with her other trembling hand.

'It's all right, Sophie, you're safe here. You can stay.' I pull my hand free gently and continue cleaning her face, before moving down her body. I strip Sophie of her clothes and carefully tend to her wounds as best I can. I don't have any pumice to rub over her broken skin, and pray Betty returns with a physician soon.

Having done all I can, I empty the water out of the window on to the street. As I grab the pail to fetch more water, Sophie squeaks, 'Don't leave me. Please.'

My lips curl into a smile. 'I'm not leaving you, just getting water. Don't open the door for anyone but me.'

She stares at me, her eyes wide, before blinking and nodding. I close the door and lean back against it, closing my eyes at the thought of Alice's battered face, then Sophie's broken body and Halfinch's sad eyes as I shouted at him earlier.

I haven't cried in years. After all the torment and strain of living with Robert, I gave up crying. The number of times I wanted to, but no tears came ... and while I feel my eyes burning, the thought of these people who have found their way into my life causes an ache in my chest I don't know what to do with. I press my palm against my rib cage in an attempt to dull the pain.

But still no tears come.

CHAPTER 23

ANG! BANG! BANG!

B The banging on the door causes me to sit up, startled by the sound. My gaze drops to Sophie, who is lying next to me, close to the wall.

BANG! BANG! BANG!

It's a different sound to the loud knocking James usually makes, signalling my wake-up call to get up and over to the Great House for training. I push out of bed and take two large strides to open the door, only to come face to face with Big Red, Betty and Halfinch, who peeks up at me from behind Big Red.

'What the hell are you all doing here?' I growl as Big Red pushes past me. He swings his eyes around the room until he finds Sophie, who is sitting up on the bed, clinging to the blanket, covering herself. He inhales sharply through his nose as he takes in her damaged, pretty face.

'God's blood,' Big Red says, crouching next to my bed. I look back at Halfinch, who shrugs, so I turn to Betty and raise my hands, gesturing for an explanation.

'He came to see Sophie last night, but when he couldn't find her he waited for me. After we were done with the physician here, I went back to the Tippling House to find him sulking on the front steps ...'

He wanted Sophie. I understand. But that doesn't answer the question as to why they are all here, in my room, now.

'Vincent do this to you?' Big Red asks Sophie, reaching for her. To my surprise, she lets him pull her to him. I observe him holding her on my bed, comforting her, his frown deepening as she presses her face into his bushy beard and begins to sob, nodding her head.

'You should report him,' I state, crossing my arms. Halfinch looks on, wide-eyed, as the scene unfolds, leaning against my door. Betty stands next to me, in front of the now dying fire, the embers barely burning.

'You aren't going back there,' Big Red states, leaning back to look at Sophie and completely ignoring me.

'Where will I go?' she asks, her eyes pleading him. Big Red exhales, dropping his hands from her.

Zounds. Fine. 'You can ...' I start, rolling my eyes, knowing I am going to regret this but all of these people in my room are putting me on edge. 'Stay here. For a while,' I add at the end, to clarify this is not a long-term solution.

All eyes turn to me, looking at me as if they aren't sure they heard me correctly. Christ, I'm not even sure *I* heard me correctly. The words were out of my mouth before I realised what I was saying. Why did I offer this? Sophie is a burden I neither want nor need.

'Are you sure?' she asks softly, her eyes wide. Big Red eyes me, rolling his hands into tight fists.

The fact that the tension in my chest, deeply rooted since I laid eyes on her last night, starts to ease isn't a good sign. Even if I didn't want her here, I'm not willing to let her go back to the Tippling House and I am not sure what relationship she has with Big Red...

the last thing I want is for her to flee one man to land in the arms of another. Not until I know he won't hurt her. Although, with the way his eyes glisten, I dare say Big Red has a soft spot for Sophie. Regardless, he hasn't offered for her to stay with him and Sophie doesn't have family out in the country, like Alice does. She doesn't have anyone except those in this room. I don't like prostitutes, but that is my irrational prejudice, as Betty pointed out last night. My eyes dart to Betty, who has a smug look on her face. Maybe Big Red will offer now and save me from my stupidity.

'Thank you,' Sophie whispers. Big Red nods at me.

Zounds. My hands fist at my sides as another knock on my door sounds. I close my eyes, stomp to the door and throw it open to find James standing, hands on hips, his expression neutral. His eyes take in the room and the people crammed into the small living space.

My living space.

James sighs and points his finger at me. 'Tomorrow. I expect you back at training tomorrow.'

I nod and slam the door in his face.

He might be my landlord and trainer and promoter, but he isn't coming in.

No one else is coming in. Into my room, or my heart.

There's no more space.

A week passes with Sophie residing with me and me returning to training at Figg's Academy, indulging Halfinch's tall tales and looking over my shoulder everywhere I go. When I ask Sophie about her relationship with Big Red, she blushes. She actually blushes. I don't probe more as it is clear from her face that Big Red isn't just a customer of hers, which begs the question of why she is staying with me if the big red, bushy bearded man harbours romantic feelings for her.

'Who is she?' James asks, grabbing my arm and yanking me towards him. He lifts my hands and begins wrapping them with cloth, to protect them during training, apparently. He hasn't asked me about my visitors until now. I wondered if he just didn't care or didn't want to know the answer. I suspect a bit of both. He's made it clear he isn't interested in getting his name sullied. I try to think what Sophie is to me – an acquaintance? A past co-worker? No, definitely not, not in the way he'd understand. In the end, I settle on the only label I can give Sophie. 'An old friend.'

James's eyes meet mine. 'Is she safe?'

Is she safe? That's an open question. Safe from Vincent? Yes. Safe from me? That's to be seen … Safe for him? No. Absolutely not. Too much sullying of him and his reputation, but I'm not going to share that with him. After a moment, James quirks an eyebrow and I realise he is waiting for my response. I nod, holding his gaze while he continues to wrap my hands. When he's done, he flicks his head in the direction of the men behind us. Jimmy and the other fighters are already getting warm. Jimmy smiles at me and motions me to join them. Happy to be away from James and Sophie and Halfinch, I jog over to him, ready to get lost in a day's hard work, because yes, this is my work now.

The session goes well; better than well, despite my lack of sleep due to overthinking about all the people I now find in my life. I didn't realise how much my body needs the physical exertion. The release it brings. An escape from all the tension I'm carrying these days, weeks even. James must sense it too, as he calls me over after training.

'You want to fight again?'

Yes. My answer is and will always be yes to that question.

I tell Halfinch to deliver the message to Alice that I have my next fight and to be prepared to leave London. I don't want her spending any more time with her husband. I just hope that Mrs Piddington does in fact care about Alice and wants to help her as much as I do.

It wasn't hard for James to find me an opponent. My reputation for prize-fighting is spreading further than the English borders. The Irish woman, Mary Welch, has written to James and the papers challenging me. He seems excited about the prospect of me receiving this challenge, but says the fight has to wait. I'm not sure why, but assume he doesn't think I am ready to fight this Mary Welch. Halfinch has heard of her, which is testament to her abilities as the boy knows his prize fighters, from James Figg to Richard Stinson, William Broadmead and Ned Sutton. Halfinch could tell you their favourite punches and how many bouts they've fought, won and lost. His passion for the sport inspires me. The fact that he has chosen me as his personal favourite makes me feel warm and fuzzy, and that has nothing to do with booze. Indeed, I haven't touched the stuff since my last fight.

With Sophie residing with me and my daily training, I don't find a lot of time to venture out and about. I am too tired and anxious about Vincent to stray far from Henrietta Street or the academy. Sophie is too afraid to go out as well. Unless Big Red comes by, or

I am with her, she stays in my room, cooking and cleaning for me. I didn't ask her to, she just does it. Big Red has visited a couple of times this week, as far as I can tell. I really hope she isn't having sex with him on my bed. I haven't asked for those details and I do not want to. She cannot hide the embarrassed colour in her cheeks when confronted with Big Red's name the way I can hide my big feet in men's boots. It's painfully apparent they are intimate. And I don't take umbrage with that fact, I just do not want them being intimate where I sleep.

Several times I've returned home to find Sophie's friend Betty lying on my bed, engaging in idle chat. I'm thankful for her efforts towards Sophie. More often than not, I feel like I am staying with Sophie, rather than the other way around.

I frown at this thought. I told her I'd be home later this evening, as I'd need a drink after my match. For the fight, James accepted a challenge from another Londoner, Joanna Hatton, on the condition that Joanna fought me at the Boarded House in Marylebone.

As I wait to be called to the stage, I take a few moments to study the surroundings. The venue is becoming eerily familiar. I focus on Alice and getting her as far away from London and her sadistic husband as possible. Having a goal to focus my thoughts on helps me prepare, similar to the way a pre-fight drink did before.

The time comes and I fight Joanna Hatton and win easily. Like so many of the others, my opponent jumped around, pumping up the crowd, wasting her energy on words when fists are the only true measure of success on the stage. The dance lasted twenty-two minutes. If you've ever tried punching someone for twenty-two minutes you'll know how hard it is. My arms feel like they're weighed down by sacks of grain, they are that heavy. My muscles ache and I am in dire need of a wash – my skin is covered in blood and dirt, and I am fairly certain the smell in the air is emanating from me rather than the bucket in the corner. James asked me to put on a 'show' for the audience. If I'm popular, more people will pay, which means more winnings for him, and me, in future bouts.

Unfortunately, I did lose my temper when a man groped me on the way to the stage, demanding I take my blouse off ... so I spat at him and kicked him in the groin. I then took the rest of my anger out on Joanna Hatton, insulting her when she missed strikes and teasing her when she couldn't raise her arms to defend herself against my attack. Not quite the image I'm supposed to develop. At least, that was James's opinion on my performance.

'How many times do I have to tell you?' he shouts, rubbing a sticky paste over my busted eyebrow, shoving my head back. 'Don't lose your temper! You need to exercise control on the stage!'

'I won, didn't I?' I snap, scowling. He's my trainer and promoter, but he's also a condescending bastard at times.

His eyes narrow. 'Yes, you won the fight, Elizabeth, but as far as the likeability contest goes, you're losing. Badly,' he snaps back, the vein in his neck pulsing as he struggles to keep his control. I can tell my reliability to disappoint is wearing thin on his patience.

I stand and push past him, seeking to join Jimmy and some other prize fighters at The Black Hog. We get a few days off from training following our fights so I see no harm in entering the tavern, especially if my fellow fighters are there. They'd allowed me to pick the venue for celebratory drinks, a sign I'm winning them over at least. While Jimmy lost his bout, we had broken down the barrier between people who train together, who live next to each other – to now people who drink with one another.

The smell of the tavern is exactly as I remember – stale and dense. My lips curl into a smile as I sit with the men and order my first pint.

'Ale? Not gin?' Jimmy asks, rubbing his busted nose. He's going to have a pair of black eyes in the morning. He took a few hard shots to his nose, courtesy of James, who walked away rather unscathed, unsurprisingly. James is the superior fighter when it comes to the two Jameses.

There is much chatter and clinking, shattered only by the arrival of Jack-Jack, a blonde haired, brown-eyed lad I know to be Halfinch's friend. Jack-Jack is tall, all lanky and leggy. While Halfinch is shorter, he still manages to overshadow Jack-Jack with his over-optimistic personality. I look around for my boy, and when I can't find him my heart sinks. I turn to Jack-Jack and lift off my stool. He's out of breath and I feel a sense of foreboding.

'Slow down, boy!' says a man, attempting to kick Jack-Jack as he pushes through the throngs of people. 'Watch it!' another patron yells as Jack-Jack bumps into him. Jimmy stops the boy before he runs into me. 'What's the hurry, son?' His calm tone seems to reach the boy, who is shaking his head vigorously, taking a moment to catch his breath.

'Halfinch,' says Jack-Jack, then he hesitates, reluctant to tell me the news. 'He's been hurt.'

Jimmy looks at me. 'Halfinch? Is that the cripple who is always following you around?'

I nod, without taking my eyes off Jack-Jack. 'Where is he?'

CHAPTER 24

I N King's Coffee House in Covent Garden, all talk is of business, but talk of business is, however, of no interest to me. I'm here for the boy.

My boy, I have decided in my haste over here. I'm claiming him.

Following Jack-Jack, I find Halfinch being tended to in the kitchen. Cadge is sitting beside him with his brown haired head resting in both hands, while one of the serving maids, a pretty girl with ebony curls and skin the colour of roasted coffee beans, cares for him. Big Red hovers, arms crossed, with a grimace over his face.

'What happened?' I ask curtly.

Heads fly up to look at me. The serving maid stills her hand and faces Big Red.

'Keep going, Beatrix,' he orders.

'Championess!' Halfinch says, clearly happy to see me, hiding any sign of hurt from the bruises and scrapes all over his face and arms. I stomp over, lift his chin first, and then each arm, carefully inspecting the wounds. Halfinch winces when I raise his right arm above his head, pulling it back down to his side. Beatrix dabs his face with a wet cloth, creating a clean patch on his skin.

'Who did this to you?'

'I'm all right. Honest. Just a few bruises, is all.'

'That's not what I asked you,' I say through clenched teeth. Guilt, worry, fear and rage swirl inside of me. All the things I want to say and ask disappear behind a haze of emotion.

Halfinch looks at Big Red, then down at his fingers, picking dried blood from between the creases of his knuckles. A heavy-set man – the cook – hands him a cloth to wipe away the blood stains. Cadge shifts uneasily in his seat when I focus my attention on him. The chubby boy's eyes flit past me to the door. I look over my shoulder curiously, and immediately see what had caught Cadge's eye. Or rather, *who*.

Vincent Love is putting on his coat when he spots me. He backs away from the door, retreating quickly to the corridor off the kitchen. I leap up to run after him.

'Elizabeth, leave it!' Big Red barks, but I only feel fury. Vincent makes his way down the corridor towards the back of the building, with me chasing after him. I catch up with him as he opens a door at the end of the hall leading to the back alley, and I kick him in his lower back, sending him flying down the few steps. I stalk him down, taking my time with each step. I sense people gathering, watching, waiting.

Vincent is lying on the floor, groaning and holding his leg. I kick him across the face. He howls and spits blood. I squat down next to his battered body, assessing his likely wounds: possible bruised ribs, leg and lost teeth.

'You'll have a real need for that cane now,' I spit.

Something catches my eye – a short dagger wedged in his belt. I pull it out from under his coat and hold it in front of his face. Vincent lets go of his leg to shield his face from the blade. I grab a handful of his greasy hair and tilt his head back, exposing his neck.

He tries to fight me off, but when I hold the blade to his neck he stops struggling.

'Tell me, why on earth would you flee a crowded public house to out here?' I ask, pushing the blade, piercing his skin. Blood trickles down his throat.

'Elizabeth, stop!' Big Red booms, grabbing me and hauling me away from Vincent.

'He did this! He hurt Sophie and now he's hurt the boy!' I rage, kicking my way free from Big Red's grip. Vincent takes the opportunity to flee down the side alley. 'Why did you do that?' I shout, pushing at Big Red. 'Why did you let him go? Look at what he did to the boy! One of *your* boys!'

Big Red grabs my arm and pulls me to him. 'Stop, Elizabeth! Look around you,' he whispers into my ear. 'There are greater forces at play here.' As my fury subsides, my eyes take in all the people watching. 'Listen to me and walk away. Halfinch needs you. Sophie needs you. You're no good to them dead!' he spits, and I stumble backwards as he releases me. Big Red stills, watching me closely. My chest heaves as the haze lifts from my senses, my vision clearing. I shake my head and my thoughts flood with images of Halfinch, Sophie and Alice. Halfinch's face – black, blue and red. Just a boy. Orphaned. Crippled. But still full of light and life. Even now. As I stand here, arguing with Big Red.

'You should have protected him.' I point my finger at his chest and hop up the steps into King's Coffee House, barging my way through the crowd who gathered to watch the drama unfold.

'At least he's not dead, and besides... he doesn't listen to me,' Big Red barks, following me into the building. 'It was a message.'

'Make him, he's a child, you're an adult,' I tell him, marching down the passage.

'You make him—'

I spin on my heels. 'Fine! But he's coming home with me. Now. Tonight. I can't protect him if I don't know where he is.'

Big Red stops, and I turn to see him looking at me.

'That wise?'

Christ. I don't know. But seems I'm saying and doing a lot of things lately I'm not necessarily thinking through. I stand there a moment, letting it sink in, then say, 'Yes.'

'He's staying here with us?' Sophie's angelic voice hums from the chair in front of the fire, as she stirs the pot suspended over the flames.

'Yes,' I reply, busying myself with a bowl of the beef stew Sophie prepared. I close my eyes as I savour the salty flavour. *Tastes good.* I look at Sophie and Halfinch as realisation sets in. I have two more mouths to feed. I press my eyes shut and take a deep breath before uttering the next question. 'Do you need me to buy any food tomorrow?' I ask Sophie, not raising my eyes to meet hers, although I can feel her eyebrows raise at me.

I know. I'm just as surprised as you are, trust me.

She nods. 'I'd like some bread, potatoes and maybe some salt and nutmeg, if that's all right?' My eyes flick to hers as I blow on another bite of the hotch potch, the tender beef falling apart in my mouth as I chew. Halfinch squeezes in beside me with his own feeder, ready to serve himself. I nudge him back and Sophie glares at me, reaching for the boy to come around to her side for access to the late supper.

'Nutmeg?' I ask, ignoring her disapproving stare.

She smiles as Halfinch takes a big bite of her creation and moans appreciatively. 'Yes, for pottage. You need wheat and milk—'

Her voice drops as she sees my face – it's my turn to raise my eyebrows at her. She has to be suffering from some lunacy if she thinks I will buy all of that.

'Well, I can use water for frumenty—'

'You can make frumenty?' I ask, excited at the thought. I've had dreams of it since smelling it at Hockley. Sophie helped in the kitchen at Stockton Estate. She can probably cook a great number of things I've long forgotten.

Hmph. Maybe this lodger business isn't so bad.

'Yes, but it tastes better with milk and butter. Nutmeg also adds a nice taste to it.'

I nod. Thinking. I have a few stops to make after training tomorrow. Halfinch and Sophie's giggling interrupt my thoughts. 'What's so funny?'

They look at each other but say nothing. I continue my stare, waiting for one of them to give in and tell me what's got them laughing like a pair of children sharing a secret. Halfinch finally grins at me. 'Where am I sleeping?'

That's a good bloody question.

I initially told Halfinch to sleep between Sophie and me with his head down by our feet, but after the third time he kicked me in the face with his good foot, I threw the blanket off, picked him up and tossed him to the other side of Sophie, wincing when I recalled his injuries. I silently chastised myself for being so rough with the boy, but made no apology at the time, nor do I intend to this morning. Sophie didn't mind him cuddling up to her and we all slept after that, which made me less irritable – I'm still irritable, because they hog the blankets and the two of them stayed up giggling when I was trying to sleep. We all ate leftover bread before I dragged Halfinch away from Sophie, much to his annoyance. The two have already formed a bond, much to my annoyance. She needed to stay hidden, but he needed to stay near me so I could keep an eye on him. I'm tired, cranky and not in the mood to train.

'Why am I here?' Halfinch asks, hobbling through the doors to Figg's academy. 'Why can't I stay with Sophie?'

'Sit down and shut it,' I reply. My fellow fighters laugh at the boy's outburst. Some nod in agreement. I see James studying the cripple suspiciously, surveying the boy – his clothes, his movements. He glances towards me, then seems to lose interest, moving on to one of the other fighters.

Satisfied James is no longer paying heed to Halfinch, I prepare and then get set to spar. Wary of the distraction, my training partner waits for me to strike first before reciprocating.

After training finishes, Jimmy tosses a paper from his coat pocket in front of Halfinch. 'Congratulations are in order, Halfinch,' he nods as the boy glances down at the paper. 'Your Elizabeth here has been hailed the "London City Championess".'

I frown at the boy as he looks at the newspaper. It's upside down. I raise my eyes to meet Jimmy's and he quirks an eyebrow. I shake my head, not wanting to have that conversation here, but remind myself to ask Halfinch about his reading ability later at home.

Wait. Home? Not home. He's not staying forever.

'Let's get going, we have a few shops to go to before heading ho—'

ZOUNDS! I almost did it again. I take a deep breath and try again. 'We have a few shops to go to. Move it.'

Jimmy's chuckles follow us out of the doors.

After visiting several shops to buy the ingredients Sophie requested for frumenty – everything but nutmeg, we could only find cinnamon – we make our way back to Henrietta Street, Halfinch blabbing the entire way. I recall Big Red's words – *is this wise.* Hell, I don't know. But Vincent has lashed out at both Sophie and Halfinch in the space of a few weeks, all because of his anger and hatred towards me. I don't understand his actions. They seem reckless, fueled by some other motive, but I cannot for the life of me figure out what that motive is. My mind flits to Alice and I squeeze my eyes shut, responsibility for these people bearing down on my mind and shoulders. The weight is becoming too heavy. I need assurance. Security. The knowledge that Vincent won't come after me or my friends any more. I pinch the bridge of my nose and grind my teeth.

I didn't ask James's permission for Halfinch to stay, nor will I. It's my room and I am living by his rules. He never mentioned anything about me not sharing my room with others. It's a tight squeeze with both Sophie and Halfinch staying, but we'll make it work. We have to.

We climb the stairs and enter my room to find Sophie boiling water over the fire. Halfinch takes over the wheat, seasoning and bread to her, along with the mortar and pestle the grocer insisted I take. I spent a lot of money on everything. The irony of buying food and cooking utensils for Sophie to make me a meal, rather than buying gin to forget about Sophie and everyone else, is not lost on me. The cheerfulness on her face as she takes the items from Halfinch and hugs him is, however, worth it. She stands and carries the items to the table in front of the window, spreading out her goods, and starts soaking the wheat. I'm intrigued by her process – having never really watched her, or anyone for that matter, cook. I always ate what was given to me or, once Robert was dead, bought – bread, potatoes, cheap beef and gin. On rare occasions I'd eat salted pork and carrots, but I often forewent those and settled for stale bread to have more to buy drink with. It all comes down to priorities. Right now, watching Sophie busy herself over preparing the wheat for her frumenty had me salivating the way gin used to make me.

Halfinch falls on to the bed and kicks off his boots. I frown, stand and place them next to the door before spinning to face him. 'You need to wash, you smell like horse.'

'Elizabeth ...' Sophie purrs from the window, scooping the wheat into a sack with a wash beetle. I'm momentarily distracted from my mission by Sophie's movements.

'What? He does,' I state, refocusing on the boy, who is now holding up the newspaper Jimmy gave him in both hands. His eyes flicker over the words, and again I wonder if he can in fact read. I motion for him to come to the edge of the bed and I sit next to him, finally taking the weight off.

He grins at me. 'London City Championess?'

I shrug. 'If that's what it says. Are you hungry?' He looks back down at the paper and shakes his head. After a few minutes, he tosses the paper to the side. I continue to watch him. 'Take off your clothes and get changed.'

The boy does as he's told, but pauses when he gets to his drawers. 'Those too,' I point.

'I'm not taking them off in front of you two!' he cries. I look over at Sophie, who looks back at me and presses her lips into a flat line. I can tell she's trying to stop herself from laughing.

I shake my head and place my hands on my hips. 'Why not? Go behind the chair if you're shy.'

Halfinch scowls, but limps behind the chair and turns his back to me while slipping off his drawers.

'Be careful not to burn your arse on the fire!' I shout as he balances against the chair. I grab his bag and unpack his clothes – two shirts, trousers, drawers and socks. His staple hat and coat are hung up on the back of the door, next to mine and ... Sophie's.

Huh. I cast my eyes around the room and notice a small case at the foot of my bed. I continue to turn until my eyes land on Sophie, who is now beating the wheat. I slowly walk over to her, careful not to get within striking reach of her right arm as she batters the sack.

'Did you have a visitor today?' I ask her, when she takes a pause to catch her breath. She wipes her brow and leans against the table. 'Yes, Betty brought me my things from the Tippling House.' She swallows and I can see her grip the table. Her whole body tense, like a frightened fawn, ready to flee a predator.

She's lying to me.

My eyes narrow. 'Betty?' I ask, studying her reaction. She nods and blushes.

Zounds! Big Red was here again. I stare at the bed before scowling at her as she giggles and then continues hitting the sack with more force than before. Not wanting to press further – I really want her frumenty – I decide to leave it. For now.

CHAPTER 25

'THE BOY, HOW long is *he* staying?' James asks as I stand among my fellow fighters, waiting my turn to practise the skills James has been teaching us with the cudgel. I haven't fought in a cudgelling duel in quite some time. I can't say I am overly keen on it – I much prefer to use my fists.

I slowly turn around, my eyes focusing on my trainer and promoter.

'As long as he needs,' I reply.

He looks at me curiously. 'Doesn't he have anywhere else he can stay?'

'No.'

'Where did he stay before?'

I ignore him, choosing to watch the two men swipe at each other with the single sticks, one finally drawing blood from the other's face. I smirk. *Good strike.*

'A head!' Jimmy yells, indicating the successful hit in his role as umpire of this practice match. It isn't easy. Cudgelling. You have to be strong and agile to break your opponent's head with the stick, which can take quite some time. To be clear, you don't actually break your opponent's head – well, it's really hard to with the cudgel – but rather, you lunge, stretch, duck and weave while swinging the stick to cut the skin on your challenger's head. A cut to the head, face or neck drawing blood counts.

'He can't stay, Elizabeth.'

I sigh, dropping my shoulders. 'If he goes, I go.'

I hear Halfinch and what I assume are his friends before I see them.

'Be merry my hearts, and call for your quarts,
and let no liquor be lacking,
We have gold in store, we purpose to roar,
Until we set care a packing.
Then hostess make haste, and let no time waste,
Let every man have his due,
To save shoes and trouble, bring in the pots double
For he that made one, made two!'

I slowly open the door to my room, not wanting to startle the boys. Sophie sits in her usual spot – the chair in front of the fire – laughing at the sight of all three boys jumping on the bed singing a tune I've heard many a time at The Black Hog tavern, and elsewhere for that matter. Amused, I listen as they make their way through the song verses, each one including instructions for more mugs to be fetched and drained. I too remember playing this game on more than one occasion, getting through thirteen helpings of beer by the end of the song.

'Then Hostess go fetch us some, for till you do come
we are of all joys bereaven,
You know what I mean, make haste come again,
For he that made ten, made eleven!'

At the last verse, I join in, wrestling them all to the thin mattress as I do.

'*Then Hostess lets know, the sum that we owe,*
twelve-pence there is for certain,
Then fill tother pot, and here's money fort
For he that made twelve, made thirteen!'

They all laugh and giggle while I hold them down, tickling their stomachs. I haven't laughed this way in years ... not since I was a girl. For a moment, I forget about Vincent, James and Alice, and in this moment it is just me, playing and singing with three young boys. One, in particular, makes my heart physically hurt. Halfinch is still trying to tackle me when I spot the paper sticking out of his trouser pocket. I snatch it and hold it up in front of him.

'What's this?' I ask, still chuckling while unfolding it.

Halfinch pants, trying to regain his breath. 'Oh, your old employer stopped by. Said to give it to you.'

His friends collapse on the bed, wiping the tears from their faces with their sleeve cuffs. I read the note, silently: *Alice is ready. If you still care. Sarah.*

Bloody wench! Of course I still care. Yes, I may have gotten a bit distracted with all my house guests, training and Vincent, but haven't I given Alice money every chance I got? I'm the one who put this plan in motion, not her! Who is she to presume to know what I do and do not care about! Like she knows me, or ever tried to know me – after she told me to leave her shop, too!

'Elizabeth?' Sophie says my name with a nudge to her tone. She clutches her hands in front of her and stands. 'Is everything all right?'

I grit my teeth and focus on my breathing.

It isn't Sophie's fault. It isn't Halfinch's fault, I repeat to myself over and over, willing myself not to lash out and yell at them both because of the anger I feel towards my old employer. It isn't fair to them. Focus, Elizabeth, control your anger.

My breathing slows and I open my eyes. I didn't realise I'd closed them. I look at Halfinch. 'Did you read this?' I ask.

He shakes his head. 'Can't.'

'Can't what?'

'Can't read,' he says, licking his lips.

I consider this. 'We'll have to fix that, won't we?' I nod at him, then wink at Sophie, easing her concern. Her lips purse as I order Halfinch's friends to say farewell.

'I have to go out,' I tell them both once Cadge and Jack-Jack leave, sulking.

'Where?' Halfinch asks, standing to reach for his coat.

'No,' I say, a bit too curtly. His eyes snap up to mine.

'No what?'

'No, you're not coming with me tonight,' I clarify, then give Sophie a serious look. She bites her lip and nods. She knows what I am saying, even if Halfinch doesn't. Neither of them can know about Alice.

'Why the hell not?' he shouts.

I slap the back of his head. 'Watch it!'

Halfinch rubs his hair, a cheeky grin spreading over his face. 'You won't know if I go out, you're not going to be here—'

'But I will,' Sophie interrupts him, startling us both.

After a second of staring at Sophie for her firm tone, I nod. 'Exactly, Sophie will know—'

'Pfft!' Halfinch exhales, throwing his arms in the air, shaking his head in defiance. I don't have time for this. I pick him up, toss him on the bed and point at him. 'You. Stay here. No arguments, Halfinch!'

Sulking like his friends, Halfinch lies back and crosses his arms over his chest, not looking at me as I leave. Only when the door closes do I mirror the boy's cheeky grin.

The sun is setting and I hesitate only momentarily before embarking on the long walk to Holborn. I want to speak to Mrs Piddington and find out the plan. I won't have time tomorrow before training and James's regimented rules. There's a smog settling over the streets so I keep my focus on the path in front of me, carefully placing one foot in front of the other, avoiding shite and holes in the road.

Londoners are still aplenty this time of day, where the sun says farewell and the moon bids its welcome. Twitter-light. I recognise the corner signpost with the broken window beneath it. I'm making good time and will pass The Black Hog tavern soon.

Do not get distracted. Get to Holborn, get home, I chant.

I don't notice the three men following me until it's too late, until they are right behind me and I feel the sweep of adrenaline rush through me. My heart pounds as two men grab my arms. I instinctively pull against my assailants, but they restrain me and throw me against a metal post. Then, darkness.

When I wake, I hear men laughing. I'm lying on my front, the cold cobblestones pressing against my cheek. My skirt is raised up over my back and one of the men is pulling at my breeches.

'What—' I croak, straining to see. My head hurts.

One of the men notices me stirring. 'She's awake! Oi, fellas, get over here and hold the cunt down,' the closest man barks.

I try to force myself up, but I don't move quickly enough. The other two are on top of me, holding my arms down at my sides while the original assailant continues to pull at my breeches. My brain snaps to attention and my body finally follows suit. I thrash my hips from side to side, trying to make it difficult for the man to undress me. My movements slow but do not stop the man from pursuing his goal. I feel a rip and the cool-night time air on my bare arse.

'No!' I shout, flailing to free myself from their hold. I hear the man unbutton his trousers and I scream again, as loudly as I can. The man straddling me grabs my hair and rams my face against the road. He leans down, holding his face close to mine, and I can feel his prick against my exposed skin. Rage explodes through my body. He releases my hair and tells the man on my left to get something to gag me with.

However, as soon as the man lets go of my arm, I throw my head back and make contact with the ringleader's nose. *Craaack!* He gasps and clutches his nose, and I follow up by throwing my left elbow back over my shoulder towards his temple. In the confusion the third man loosens his grip, giving me the opportunity I need to snatch my right arm back and push myself to my feet, just in time to meet the second man head on. My skirt falls back down, covering my nakedness, but I don't care. My heart is pumping too fast for me to care about my nudity. I throw a right hook across his cheek, sending him spinning. I turn to kick the third man in the gut, following through with an uppercut that leaves him sprawled on his back. With the two henchmen on the ground, I walk over to the ringleader, who is still holding his nose, lying on the ground, his dick out on display. I take the time to quickly pull up my breeches to avoid getting tangled in them, fuelled by adrenaline and anger.

I stand over him, blocking the light from the full moon. The man lets go of his nose and holds up his hands in surrender. It matters not. I stamp down on his naked crotch and then kicked his ribs repeatedly. But as I pull my foot back to deliver a final kick, I am struck by a heavy blow to my back. I pitch forward and roll to the side.

In my fury, I failed to see the fourth man in the shadows. I recognise him immediately. His long greasy hair is unmistakable. *Vincent.*

I push myself up but he kicks me in the face, busting my nose, and I fall to my knees again. My left eye feels like it is about to explode. He continues his attack with swift kicks to my stomach and ribs. I tuck into a ball to protect my torso and face but the man starts stomping on my legs.

'Get up! Get up, you whore!' he yells. Even if I want to comply, I can't, as the blows continue to rain down.

Vincent eventually stops his assault and crouches down next to me, grabbing my hair and forcing my head back so my face lifts towards his, blood dripping from my nose and mouth. In my delirious exhaustion, I begin to laugh.

Vincent punches me in the face, hard. My lip is bust. I know without feeling it with my hand. I lick my lips and spit out the blood on to the stones. The liquid shimmers in the moonlight, making it look black.

'What's so funny, Amazonian? Did you honestly think I'd let you insult me in my own establishment and live?' he spits, releasing my hair. I roll onto my back and hold the side of my face where he struck me.

'Quit your teasing,' I quip, spitting out more blood. I need to think of something. How can I get out of this? I look around to see if there is a weapon I can use, but there's nothing within reach. I silently vow to remember this feeling for my next fight. And there will be a next fight. I'm not giving up on Alice, Halfinch or Sophie. Not giving up on myself. Not yet. My eyes spot Vincent's cane a few feet away, but he picks it up as soon as my eyes land on it. His men have disappeared, fleeing the scene. Vincent takes a step back.

I turn onto my side, one hand covering my left eye, the other struggling to see where Vincent stands.

'I told you I'd get you, Amazonian.'

He is standing above me. But what happens next is a blur. Unexpected.

BOOM!

The loud bang spins Vincent around and he falls to the ground in a heap. Panting, I struggle to look around, my eyes clouded from the beating I endured. Vincent lies lifeless on the ground beside me. He doesn't move again.

'Championess! Elizabeth!'

I hear Halfinch's voice but I can't see him. 'He ... He ... He was going to kill you!' he whimpers. 'I had to protect you!'

'*Go. Go, Halfinch. Go back to Sophie,*' I whisper, my voice strained.

'I can't leave you!' he cries.

'You can't be here, Halfinch, go!' I yell. It's then I spot it. The pistol in his right hand, dangling by his side.

I hear his feet pitter-patter away from me. Lanterns flicker against the walls, threatening the night. For what is darkness, but the absence of light? I lay there, unable to move, heaviness sweeping across my body, then blackness descends over my eyes. There are sounds of horse hooves on cobblestones and drunkards singing some distance away. Then, a more definite sound of footsteps approaching, the shuffling of clothes. I feel someone tugging at me. Worried one of Vincent's men has returned, I begin groaning, trying to muster any strength I have left. The man pulls me upright, and then slowly lifts me from the ground, carrying me away.

'Easy, Elizabeth, I've got you. It's all right,' the familiar gravelly voice says, like a balm to my soul. Jimmy. I'm safe.

I think of Halfinch, Vincent and the loud cracking sound that stopped him.

Where did Halfinch find a pistol?

CHAPTER 26

T HERE IS NO banging on the door, no shouting in the halls, no one kicking me and demanding I get up.

I'm lying on my bed; the embers of the fire that had been lit are dwindling. My bones are stiff and my muscles scream when I move. My head feels like a drum and someone is beating it, loudly.

I have no idea what time it is, but it must be early still. The building is quiet. I collect myself as much as I am able and stumble out of bed. Sophie leaps up from the armchair, reaching for me. 'Elizabeth, no! You mustn't move!'

She grabs my arm and tries to haul me up, but her slight frame is no match for my much larger form. The thought of her trying to help me causes me to giggle. Sophie tries once more before giving up. She turns the chair instead, allowing me to pull myself up on to it, taking her seat close to the hearth. I hold my ribs and lean back, grimacing as pain shoots through every bone in my body. Sophie pours fresh water from the glazed earthenware ewer into a bowl next to it, sitting on a silver tray. She soaks a cloth and dabs it across my face. The liquid is still hot – she must have just boiled it. No matter, the wetness feels sublime on my skin and wounds. I moan and close my eyes, letting her tend to me.

She wipes my mouth and pats my cheeks dry with her skirt. I pick up the silver tray and hold it up, staring at my reflection.

Sophie gasps and it startles me – that, or the sight of my damaged face. I haven't seen myself in a long time. My features look foreign, like they don't belong to me, but someone else. One of my adversaries, perhaps. I trace my fingers over my bruised cheek and the rest of my marred features. The battered image serves as a reminder of all the gruesome injuries I've inflicted on others. The distorted nose, busted lips, swollen eyes and matted hair all aid in jogging my memory of the events of last night.

Halfinch!

'Where's the boy?' I croak, dropping the tray to look at Sophie. Her wide eyes tell me he isn't here. 'Did he not come back last night?' I ask as panic slowly begins to unfurl in my chest. Where is he? Who brought me home last night? I have to find Halfinch, but my battered body betrays me when I attempt to stand.

Knock. Knock.

Jimmy stands at the door, holding herbs and a small bowl. 'I told James to leave. That you aren't well. He seemed annoyed, but left all the same.' Jimmy enters my room; with a firm set of his mouth, he studies me for a moment, then waves a hand at Sophie, taking the damp cloth from her. 'Step away.'

He takes over my care, holding the cloth over my wounds. I flinch; it stings. He then crushes what looks like comfrey plant roots in the bowl and sprinkles a touch of water over them, creating a paste. Once he is satisfied my cuts are clean, he smears the poultice over them. I didn't like Sophie helping me, but I'd prefer her than Jimmy. He scowls at me and tells me to hold still as I lean away.

Jimmy finishes tending to my wounds, then sits back on the floor in front of me. My stomach grumbles and Sophie leaps to fetch me some bread and a mug of table beer. I make a face at the mug, but accept the bread. Big mistake. Chewing hurts my jaw, and when I swallow even my throat feels bruised. Sophie smirks and holds the beer back up to me. This time, I take it. I gulp the beer down and feel a tad more human. I'd feel a hell of a lot more human if it were gin I was drinking. A wash wouldn't hurt either. Or maybe it would. I need to do it sooner rather than later and I need someone to help me. My eyes flit between Sophie and Jimmy.

Definitely Sophie will be helping me with that task.

Jimmy looks at me. 'Tell me what happened.'

I sigh, wanting to roll my eyes and clasp my bloodstained clothes to my chest. I'm exhausted, but I need to find Halfinch. I look to the left and then the right, avoiding eye contact with Jimmy. I slowly roll my head from side to side and then stretch my arms, testing them. Test fails. The pain is too severe, causing me to wince. The attack is still too fresh, in memory and in body. Sophie winces too. A pity wince.

Jimmy frowns. 'Are you hurt anywhere else?'

I push myself up off the chair to get away from his questions. I'm not ready to talk about last night.

He mimicks my movements, shoving his hands into his pockets. His sleeves are rolled up, displaying his muscular forearms. 'Come fight with me.'

Confused, I stare at him. What a ridiculous statement to make at such a time.

'I'm leaving the Boarded House. I want to fight at another amphitheatre – rival James Figg—'

'No.' I cut him off, mid tirade.

'Just listen to me for a minute. Come join me. As my partner.'

I shake my ahead again.

'Elizabeth, last night—'

'What about last night?' I shout, tired of him badgering me.

'I went to The Black Hog, hoping I'd find you there. I was walking back when I heard the gunfire. You were lying on the ground down Dyott Street and I saw the boy, *your* boy, standing with his arms raised, holding a pistol. Another man lay on the ground. You said something to the boy and he fled ... I- I- I couldn't just leave you there. Not in St Giles. Not at that time. So I carried you home.'

I narrow my eyes on my sparring mate. 'And?'

Jimmy sighs. 'By the time I went back, the night watch were there – looking at the body.'

My breath catches. 'Where's Halfinch?'

'The boy?' Jimmy shakes his head. 'He wasn't there. I haven't seen him.'

I slump onto my bed, letting out a sigh of relief, my legs still shaky from the night before. Praying Halfinch has returned to Big Red, I turn to face Sophie. 'Can you go and see Big Red? Find Halfinch for me?' I plead.

She nods but doesn't move.

Jimmy studies me. 'He shot him, for you. Brave boy.'

I open my mouth and close it, unsure of how to respond to that statement.

'Come with me,' he implores. 'Start over. Get away from all of this mess!'

But I say nothing. The awkward silence is broken by the rapping on my door. Another visitor.

Jimmy opens the door to find Constable Boyle standing in the hallway. He looks tired, stressed, which only worsens when his eyes find me. 'Good Lord, Elizabeth, are you all right?' he asks, stepping closer to me. His eyes look to Sophie, then narrow at Jimmy.

'I'm all right,' I state, my head still spinning. 'Jimmy fights with me at Figg's Boarded House—'

'I know who he is – but why is he *here*? Why are *you* hurt?'

'I was worried about Elizabeth, she wasn't at training. I told James I'd check on her and helped Sophie to dress Elizabeth's wounds when I arrived.'

Constable Boyle blinks several times. 'You were worried about *Elizabeth*?'

Jimmy clears his throat and I roll my eyes. 'Yes, thank you, Jimmy. And now that you have helped, you can leave.' Neither man moves, so Sophie walks past them both and opens the door. I'm grateful for her in that moment. For her action. Jimmy takes the bowl and remaining herbs and walks out of the door, stopping to face me.

'Think about it, please?' he asks.

'I will,' I reply, placing my hand over my ribs, 'and Jimmy, thank you.'

He nods and closes the door behind him. I sink into the bed and Sophie comes to sit next to me. 'Can I get you anything?'

'No, thank you,' I say, my voice thick with strain. Constable Boyle stands next to the window, looking down at the table, picking up the bloodied cloths. 'I came to tell you that the night watch found Vincent Love's body last night. They think it was a drunken brawl that killed him. Constable Clayton and I have been told to ask around, find out if anyone saw anything ... Nicholas – I mean, Constable Clayton – mentioned seeing you and Vincent a while ago outside your favourite tavern.'

I sit there, holding my side as he shifts his gaze to me. 'He said it did not look like a friendly chat.'

Still I remain silent. I want him to leave so Sophie can go and find Big Red and, even better, Halfinch. But she can't do that until Constable Boyle leaves.

'So, Elizabeth, care to tell me how you ended up like one of your opponents?' He cocks a brow. 'Did *you* see anything?'

'No,' I say finally.

'Where is the boy – Stephen?'

I freeze at the sound of Halfinch's real name. After a moment, I reply, 'Not here, obviously.'

Constable Boyle nods, his blue eyes fixing on mine. 'And neither of you knows what happened to Vincent Love last night?' he probes, his voice soft, barely louder than a whisper. I tell myself he has to ask these questions, it's part of his duty. But part of me wishes it weren't him, someone I feel beholden to after he helped me get the job at Piddington's.

Zounds! Alice!

The thought of Mrs Piddington and Alice causes me to tense up. I don't want Constable Boyle to mistake my fears for Alice and Halfinch as a guilty conscience over Vincent. I mean, yes, I have a severe guilty conscience about a great many things, but Vincent's death is not one of them.

I gather my thoughts and shrug. 'I don't know what happened, but I am not surprised to hear of his death.' Constable Boyle's shoulders slump. If he suspects me of lying, he doesn't confront me. Instead, he makes to leave.

'Is he really dead?' Sophie asks.

Turning to her, I nod once.

She stares down at her hands, which are twisting her skirt. Vincent's face flashes in my mind. He'd followed through on his threat. Everyone told me he would. Part of me didn't believe it. But he did. And now the bastard's dead, but not by my hand. No. By a hand much smaller and younger than mine. One that should never have been faced with that choice. Sophie moves in front of the bed. 'I'll go speak to Big Red. Find out where Halfinch is.'

Unable to look at her, I roll down onto the mattress and close my eyes, fear curling in my chest as I hear her leave.

Alone at last, I let the pull of sleep take me.

CHAPTER 27

'WHAT DID YOU do with it?' I ask through clenched teeth.

'Wha-what?' Halfinch stammers, looking up at me with those big brown doe eyes of his that make me want to throttle him and embrace him at the same time, making sure no harm comes to him. Wee bastard saved my life and I have no idea what to do with that knowledge. He makes me so angry at times, and at others my heart is so full it feels like it'll burst out of my chest.

No. I can't be soft with him now. He shot a man. Killed a man. People are hanged for less. Way less. 'Where is it? Where did you get it?'

'From me,' Big Red states, sliding into my room behind Sophie. He leans one shoulder against the wall and stares at me, only softening when Sophie glances back at him. She smiles nervously, before shifting her eyes back to me.

'Sorry, Elizabeth, he insisted on coming ... to speak to you,' Sophie whispers, biting her lip. I don't budge or respond to her. Instead, I cut my eyes to Big Red. 'Where is it?'

'It's hidden,' Halfinch sputters to my side, looking down at his shoes, his entire stance rigid. Poor boy is terrified.

I look down at him. '*Where?*'

'At the coffee house,' Big Red replies, giving me a smile that doesn't reach his eyes. I shake my head. 'Why did you give him a pistol?'

Big Red sighs deeply and pushes off the wall to stand behind Sophie, who tilts her head towards him ever so slightly. The gesture is so small, and yet it speaks volumes about their relationship. They are definitely fucking. But the way her body relaxes when he's near, the way the tightness in her eyes disappears and she gets a flush of colour across her face – she has feelings for him. And by the way Big Red responds to her mere presence ... well, let's just say he doesn't seem to be the courting type so yes, I'd say he enjoys her company through the day as much as he does at night, when no one can see or hear them.

'Halfinch was beaten. By a man who wanted to harm *you*,' he explains, pointing a thick finger at me. 'And since I can't keep the boy away from *you*, I gave him a pistol to protect himself. Didn't think he'd *need* to use it to protect *you*.' His voice gets increasingly colder as he directs his tirade at me. He blames *me* for this?

I swat his hand away from me and narrow my eyes at him. 'Constables are going to blame *me* for Vincent's death.'

Big Red grins briefly, then shuts his expression down almost instantly. 'Perhaps, but they don't have any evidence, no witnesses.'

Jimmy. Zounds.

But no, Jimmy won't report Halfinch. He would have already. I think. I sigh and rub a hand through my hair, which is half down. I still haven't bathed and can't imagine what kind of foul smell I am oozing into the air. I need Sophie to help though. I can't fill a basin and replace the bandages without someone's help and she is the only woman I can ask.

I feel myself calming down, relieved Halfinch doesn't have the pistol on him any longer. I reach out and pull him into an embrace, kissing the top of his head. 'I haven't thanked you, have I?'

Halfinch shakes his head. I tilt his chin with my forefinger and stroke his cheek. His eyes widen as he looks up at me.

'Thank you.'

After Sophie helps me to wash in a basin, I put on my boots and shrug into my coat, wincing when I lift my left arm through the sleeve. My body needs time to heal. Time I don't have. If I'm not fighting, I'm not earning money. Not earning my keep to allow me to stay at Figg's, or in my room.

I haven't been this hurt since Robert. I'd hoped those days of healing were behind me. More fool me. I pull my coat around me and lick my lips before making the trek to Holborn. My thoughts are filled with Halfinch, Big Red, Sophie and, quite randomly, Jimmy. I need to speak to him and make sure he isn't planning on saying anything about what he saw. I also need to face James at some point. He isn't going to be happy about me missing training and he'll be wanting to schedule my next fight. That isn't going to happen soon. I'll be out for a couple of weeks recovering. No, James is not going to be pleased about that. I wonder if there is something else I can do to help while I am unable to train with the others. Perhaps, clean? No way am I cooking, unless he wants to be poisoned. I could offer to clean and do any repair work on the men's attire. It's something at least.

Big Red, Sophie and I agreed that Halfinch should return with Big Red. My injuries will need to be cleaned and now that Vincent is dead, the threat to Halfinch and Sophie is no more. The thought of living in my room without them is hard for me to swallow. I frown, not liking where my head is at when it comes to my current living arrangements and boarders.

By the time I reach Piddington's it's dinner time and my eyes have adjusted to the daylight. My breathing is laboured because of my injured ribs and I'm so fatigued I fear I'm going to pass out in the street. Mrs Piddington scurries out of the shop, pulling her collar up and hugging herself before turning to walk down the street.

'Mrs Piddington!' I call out to her, startling her. She looks at me wide-eyed, shock and confusion flit across her face.

'What are you doing here?' she hisses, scowling at me. 'What happened to your face?'

There's the Mistress of Misery I know so well. 'Lovely to see you too, *Sarah.*'

She rolls her eyes at me. 'Don't be clever, Elizabeth, it doesn't suit you. I prefer you direct and insufferable.'

I scoff. All right. Direct it is. 'How is Alice? When does she leave?'

Mrs Piddington looks over my shoulder and waves at someone behind me, smiling a fake smile at them – a teeth-baring one, it's quite frightening really. I flinch.

'Coach is taking her Thursday. Have you got more money for her? I've had to pay for her transport in advance to secure her seat—'

'You didn't pay it all, did you?'

'No, I didn't,' she spits, shaking her head at me. 'I'm not senseless, Elizabeth, I do run a business, you know.'

Yes, I know. It might be Mr Piddington's reputation and skills that got them up and running, but it is his wife's shrewd business mind that keeps it a success. Mrs Piddington smoothes her hair down and her eye twitches. It's then I notice the dark circles beneath her eyes, the pale, ashen tone to her skin and sunken cheeks. The woman looks like she hasn't slept in weeks.

'What's wrong with you?' I ask, looking down her body for more clues of what is troubling her. She straightens herself and glares at me.

'Nothing is wrong, just busy!' she hisses again, trying a bit too hard to convince me, if not herself.

I shake my head slowly. 'Something is wrong. You're—'

'I'm what? You have no idea what I am! You haven't been around in weeks, leaving me to deal with Alice, the business, the robbery—' she gasps, clutching a hand over her mouth.

My brows furrow. '*Robbery?*' I repeat, my tone revealing the question in that one word.

Mrs Piddington closes her eyes and drops her hand from her mouth. 'We had some goods stolen from the shop, shortly after you left.'

I blink, thinking about what she is telling me. 'Alice didn't mention it—'

'After you saw her,' she cuts me short, giving me a pointed look. 'The *one* time since you left.'

Ouch. Yes, I deserve that. I've been a bad friend to Alice, but it isn't for this woman to judge. I'll happily deal with Alice's anger and disappointment but not *this* woman's. I cock my head to the side and give her my hardest look, one that normally makes people quiver. I'm not surprised that it has absolutely no effect on Mrs Piddington. The woman is made of steel. She simply glares back at me, waiting for me to deny it. But I can't. I won't. So I point to my swollen face. 'We've *both* been busy.'

Yes, direct and insufferable. That's me.

When I get back to Henrietta Street, I spot James with Constable Clayton immediately. They are standing outside the door, deep in discussion. James throws up his arms and shakes his head. He isn't happy about whatever it is the constable is saying. I slow my pace, not wanting to draw their attention just yet. My stomach growls, reminding me that it is almost suppertime and Sophie promised me a stew tonight. My mouth salivates at the thought of a nice salty beef stew. I can almost taste it. Lost in thought, I fail to notice them both looking at me.

'Here she is,' Constable Clayton says. James says nothing, he just scans my body. Oh no, this is not how I wanted him finding out about my current physical state. I swallow and step towards them, hugging my coat tighter around me.

'Are you looking for me?' I ask, cautiously approaching the two men.

James's stare pierces me. 'What happened?' The vein in his temple pulses and his jaw tenses.

I decide to ignore his question and direct my attention to the constable. 'Why are you looking for me?'

Constable Clayton's eyes flick from me to James and back again, clearly unsure how to take my complete disregard for James. 'Yes, Elizabeth, I've been told to bring you to see the magistrate about Vincent Love's death. It seems there are some questions he'd like to ask you.'

I nod. 'Which magistrate?'

'Magistrate Charles Trelawny,' he replies.

Of course. Another name that I really didn't want to hear.

Goodbye, Vincent. Hello, Charles.

CHAPTER 28

'FATHER! FATHER!' A young, feminine voice cries, reaching out for Magistrate Trelawny, a servant quickly in tow, trying to catch her, passing Constable Clayton as he stands by the door to the front room that Magistrate Trelawny has made into his office – a large room with many books lining the back wall, tall windows bordering the street and two matching armchairs positioned in front of an ornate desk.

'I'm sorry, Mr Trelawny, I tried to stop her—'

'It's all right, Miss Lilly,' he says, reassuring her, before turning back to the child. 'Anna, my dear, remember what Father told you, this room is not for little children. Run along now.' And with that, the little beauty does as her father instructed.

'Beautiful girl,' I observe aloud.

'Just like her mother,' Magistrate Trelawny remarks, sitting back behind his desk. Back at the magistrate's residence in Covent Garden, I am hungry and angry. I'm hangry. I scoff, laughing at my own joke. Magistrate Trelawny's raises his eyebrows. 'Something amuse you, Mrs Wilkinson?'

I compose myself by focusing on the man's wig. The white horse hair is curled and coiffed to perfection, sitting atop his head like he doesn't remove the thing every night. I shake my head and he nods, resting his elbows on his desk and interlocking his fingers. Considering me.

'Well, Mrs Wilkinson, it seems our paths cross yet again,' he says finally, leaning back in his chair. He takes out a watch from his front pocket and studies it for a few seconds. 'I knew you wouldn't remain long at Piddington's shop. That place is much too mundane for someone like you...' he says, as he snaps his eyes back up to mine. 'So, tell me, how did you know Vincent Love?'

'Who says I do?'

He gives me a pointed look, popping the watch back into his pocket.

I shrug. 'I didn't. Not well, anyway.'

He clasps his hands together, resting them on his protruding waistline. He studies me as I try not to speak. My nerves are causing my heart to race and I'm convinced I am sweating. Does he have a fire burning?

'I understand you had an altercation with Mr Love at his establishment on Drury Lane, the Tippling House—'

'I—' I go to explain but he silences me with his raised palm.

'Let me finish,' he demands, his eyes not leaving mine. 'I also understand one of his... *employees* is residing with you at Henrietta Street – she has been for some time now. And that you came home the night of his death, looking like ...' His eyes trail down my body before rising to reach my face again. 'Well, like you do now.'

I stand still. His eyes rest on me, scalding me like a hot flame, following my every move. He certainly knows a great deal more than I had anticipated. My mind works to think of who could supply him with those facts – Big Red wouldn't, neither would Sophie. Possibly Betty or one of the other women from the Tippling House?

'Nothing to say?' he asks, sitting up while motioning to the constable, who hasn't moved. I'd forgotten he was there. Unable to think of something to say, I choose to say nothing. Anything I say now will not help my position. I can't lie and say I didn't fight Vincent – too many witnesses to contradict me. I can't think of a reason Sophie would be living with me if it hadn't been for her being assaulted by Vincent, and then the magistrate will think I killed him to protect Sophie or as revenge. And I can't lie about my injuries. I didn't have a fight that night. I could of course say I was attacked but didn't know my attackers ... no witnesses to support that. The only thing I can do is tell him the truth. But there is no way in hell I am doing that to the boy. As I try to think of a plausible explanation to help my defence, footsteps enter the room, followed by a strong waft of lavender. I crook my neck to see Mother Lavinia standing next to me.

I'm really, *really* going to struggle to explain myself now. I run my tongue along my teeth and drop my gaze to the floor. Nothing to do but wait to hear my fate. Mother Lavinia will see to it.

'As you can see, Mrs Wilkinson, I've asked Mrs Lavinia to be here tonight to help with the chain of events that have led us here. A man being shot to death in my ward.'

I'm about to confess when heavy, persistent knocking comes at the front door. Magistrate Trelawny stands as Constable Clayton sees to the noise. Loud voices come barrelling down the hall, louder the closer they get to the room. I smile as recognition sets in.

Big Red comes to stand at my other side, opposite Mother Lavinia, who glares at the man and all of his gingerness. Not quite certain what she has against Big Red, I find myself liking the man a bit more because of it.

'Albert ...' Magistrate Trelawny utters through pursed lips. 'What brings you here so late?'

I raise my eyebrows at the revelation of his first name, but don't look at him. Big Red, or *Albert*, points a finger at me. 'She does.'

Silence.

Magistrate Trelawny looks at Mother Lavinia, then the constable, before returning his sights to Big Red. 'All right, what do you want with Mrs Wilkinson?'

Big Red takes a breath and shoves his hands into his pockets. His signature stance, I realise. I smirk. 'Elizabeth didn't kill Vincent, she was too busy fighting with me that night.'

Shocked, my head flies up to look at Big Red, who has bruising on his face and neck. Marks that weren't there this morning. He doesn't meet my gaze, but continues his stare at the magistrate, who is just as surprised by Big Red's statement as I am, it seems. His eyebrows rise so high they are hidden by his wig. 'I see,' he states, matter-of-factly, his jaw clenched. 'And, *ahem*, why were you fighting?'

Big Red shrugs one shoulder, narrowing his eyes on the magistrate before turning to look at Mother Lavinia. 'She had something that belonged to me.'

'Ah! She stole from you—'

'No, she didn't steal anything. It's my own fault she had it. I was just angry about it.'

I am completely lost and confused by the discussion going on around me. I have no idea what Big Red is talking about. Is he just making this up as he goes along? He's a convincing liar if he is; a talented plumper. I glance at Big Red, who still avoids making eye contact.

A minute passes. Two.

Then, after what seems like forever, the magistrate reluctantly agrees to let me go. The annoyance is evident on both his face and Mother Lavinia's as I try to hide my grin upon leaving the room behind Big Red.

When we're back outside, away from curious ears and eyes, I finally use my voice. 'Thank you … *Albert*.' I can't help myself.

He snorts and shakes his head. 'Don't thank me. Didn't do it for you. And I'm not sure I should have...' Big Red glances back at magistrate's house.

I frown. 'Oh?' I don't ask him who he did it for or why he's having second thoughts. In truth, it doesn't really matter. He lied and I am free because of it. Not more than ten minutes ago I thought I was heading to Newgate Prison. My, how quickly things can change, and in my favour too for once.

'Who did that to your face? Because we both know it wasn't me,' I say.

He smirks. 'Someone I love.'

BANG. BANG. BANG. Like clockwork, James and his bloody personal wake-up rounds. I groan. I've slept in. Again. I sit up on the thin mattress, shove back my tangled hair, and massage my head as I stare across at Sophie's body lying next to me.

'Elizabeth? Open up,' James orders through the door. I roll out of bed as Sophie stirs. I fling the blanket back over to cover her. The cold floor jolts me awake as I hurry to let James inside and then back to the bed, not bothering to see if he follows. It's cold this morning and I'm still in my nightwear.

'You going to tell me what happened? You've been avoiding me,' he states, standing in front of me, crossing his arms. 'You haven't been at training and a constable appeared to take you to see a magistrate.'

'I'm sorry—'

'Not good enough. I want answers.'

'I know, and I'll give them to you ...' My voice trails off, not entirely sure I will give him what he wants to know. Sophie rolls over to face us, pulling the blanket up to cover herself. James glances at her before returning his focus to me. 'I'm waiting.'

I sigh, rubbing my hands together and blowing warm breath through my fingers. He frowns before spinning on his heel to start a fire. Once done, he turns to face me, hands on his hips, impatience in his eyes.

'A man died the other night,' I begin, my throat parched, my voice hoarse. 'Can I have some beer?'

He steps forward and scowls at me. 'I'm not your bloody servant,' he spits. I roll my eyes and jump out of bed, my unsupported chest bouncing as I land and make my way over to the ewer. Taking a long drink, I brace myself against the table and look out of the window. I can feel James watching me.

'Like I said, a man died the other night. The same night I got into a ... disagreement with someone.' I decide to continue the lie Big Red told the magistrate, the importance of keeping our stories aligned resonating strongly within me. 'Someone had told the magistrate that they believed I killed the man, but I didn't—'

A knock from the door stops me. I look over my shoulder as James stomps over to answer it. Jimmy stands holding more herbs and cloths. I smile at the sight of him. He's here to check my injuries. Not necessary, as I have Sophie for that, but kind of him all the same. The normal tension I feel when a man tries to exert himself into my life doesn't arise. I scowl, annoyed that he is here and that I am happy about it.

'What do you want?' James asks him, frustrated.

'Good morning to you too, James. I came to check on Elizabeth—'

'You do that frequently these days ...' James gives him a hard stare. 'I need to speak to Elizabeth—'

'And I want to check her injuries. She's healing, as you can see,' Jimmy retorts, walking further into the room and setting down the items he's carrying.

'You are not her husband. And I can see she's healing, I want her to tell me why she needs healing!' James shouts, hovering over Jimmy. 'How she could let someone do this to her!'

I frown as Sophie sits up in the bed, eyes wide. I step between the two men, not wanting another fight so soon. Aware of James's rugged temper, I place one hand on his chest and one on Jimmy's, gently nudging them back and away from each other. Only when I'm satisfied they aren't going to lunge at one another do I drop my hands to my sides.

'Thank you, Jimmy, Sophie can help me with my wounds,' I say to Jimmy. Then, turning to James, 'And I told you what happened, I got into a fight—'

'Yes, you did. Who was he?' he asks, his tone sharp and full of authority. I stand there and let him scold me like a child because I don't have it in me to argue.

'No one—'

'We have an agreement, Elizabeth. You train every day and fight and win, and you *do not* bring disrepute to my name or gym. Being accused of murder is not something I want one of my fighters known for!'

I turn to face him, feeling some of the fire I've worked so hard to tone down these months. 'I have trained, I have fought and won, haven't drunk except for when you've said it's allowed in celebration and I haven't brought *disrepute* to your bloody name or gym!'

'You can't train now, can you? Not in the state you're in!' he shouts back.

'I'll clean, help sew, anything—'

James steps into my space, his chest hitting mine, unfazed that the only thing shielding me is my thin sleep blouse. 'I don't want you to clean or sew, I want you to fight!'

'So do I!'

I feel Jimmy tug my arm, pulling me away from James. I exhale deeply and skulk to my bed, dropping down on to it. Sophie reaches out to rub my back, comforting me. I don't want her comfort, though; I am so tired and sore, and the gentle caress is enough to push me over the edge. I can deal with anger, disappointment, envy, even resentment, but not sympathy and not from Sophie. It's too much. I shy away from her touch, pressing my eyes shut.

'Was it because of her?' James asks. When I open my eyes he's pointing at Sophie. She inhales sharply behind me.

'What? No!' I spit, irritated that he is seeking to blame Sophie. She's a victim in this. In this mess. This mess of my life.

James just shakes his head. 'So, it was just you being you?'

I stare up at him.

'What's that supposed to mean?' Jimmy asks, inserting himself back into the conversation, reminding us he's still there.

'It means her bloody temper! She can't control it!' James shouts, his voice rising to an almost bellow. 'And now look at her!' I recoil at his words. I feel like I've been slapped. He says *my* temper is a problem? I'd laugh, but he is already in an odious mood. I've done everything this man has demanded of me – I even gave up drinking gin, my favourite thing in the world, the only thing that helped me escape everything, and he's giving me a hard time about being attacked and defending myself? He doesn't know all the details, and he certainly doesn't know enough to be making assertions like that.

'Leave her alone—'

'This doesn't concern you, Jimmy! She fights for me! She trains at my gym!' James bellows, his chest rising and falling. 'Why are you still here? She told you she doesn't need your help,' he says, gesturing in Sophie's direction.

Jimmy nods. 'You're right.' He looks at me as if trying to understand me, then back to James before heading out of the door.

James continues to assault me with his stony stare. 'The boy doesn't come back here.'

It's a threat. And we both know it. But then my stomach drops. *Why is he talking about the boy?*

CHAPTER 29

'WHAT ARE YOU doing here?' I ask, barring my doorway with my arm to prevent the Mistress of Misery from entering my room.

'Oh stop. Just let me in,' Mrs Piddington snaps, glancing over her shoulder, checking the corridor. I mimic her movement of scanning the hallway before letting her inside.

'Never thought I'd be in your home,' Mrs Piddington says, making her way from the door to the hearth, before stopping in front of the window. She's breathing quickly and all the colour has drained from her wearied face. The strain of life is taking its toll on the woman.

'What do you want?' I ask, following her with my eyes. She places her hands on her hips but immediately lifts her right hand to her mouth, stifling a cry. She is more than angry – she's *scared*.

'Is it Alice?' I ask her, gently cajoling her back to the room, away from the dark place her thoughts must be taking her. 'Where is she?'

Mrs Piddington shakes her head.

'When was the last time you saw her?'

'Yesterday, when she finished work.'

'Do you know where she lives?'

Mrs Piddington closes her eyes and takes a deep breath, composing herself. 'Yes, it's not far from the shop – Portpool Lane, opposite the Gray's Inn.'

Mrs Piddington insists I accompany her to Alice's house. As in, now. We're on our way, navigating the city streets through the busy roads, ominous alleys, and every path in between. Although we don't walk together. No, I follow the sour-faced wretch a couple of paces behind, like a dog would its owner. My breathing has become less laboured, even in the last couple of days, but my face still pains me, especially my lip – it keeps splitting.

When we approach Alice's dwelling, I immediately notice the front door is slightly ajar. Frowning, Mrs Piddington knocks while I scan the dark windows. Their street is quiet, despite opening on to a main road, and it isn't dark enough for us to hide from any passers-by, nor is it bright enough to warn us if anyone heads our way. We have to rely on sounds – footsteps, voices and the like – to let us know if someone nears. There is no answer at the door so I motion for Mrs Piddington to enter, but she refuses. I sigh and push past my old employer, who pushes me back. I can't help but chuckle at the woman's bluster towards me. She's afraid to go into a building but not to shove me back. Shaking my head, I stop and stare at her, the scowl she adopts completely unintimidating. She's so frail that if I blew on the woman, she'd topple. Ever the actress, she snaps her fingers and ushers me into the dark house.

It's darker inside. The only light emanates from a dwindling fire in the parlour to the left of the entrance, the embers a mix of black and bright orange, struggling to stay alight. We exchange glances before edging along the wall, slowly making our way through the house.

'Alice? It's me, Elizabeth ... and Mrs Piddington,' I call out, annoyed that I again find myself in a less than ideal situation. If someone reports strange happenings to the night watch, they'll find us snooping around a house that doesn't belong to us. Not ideal. And having had my fill of the magistrate recently, I'd rather avoid him if possible.

'You weren't at work today,' Mrs Piddington adds. 'We just came to see if you are all right?'

Nothing.

Then, as my eyes focus on the door frame where Mrs Piddington's bony finger points, a whimper. It's quiet, muffled.

There it is again.

We look at each other for a moment and then I stride into the room from where it came.

'Alice? Is that you?' Mrs Piddington inches her way towards the sounds, around what is clearly a kitchen, while I feel for a candle. I find one on the table and run to the fire to light it. I carry it carefully back to the kitchen, shielding the flickering flame from the draught. I have almost reached Mrs Piddington, who is crouched in the corner near someone, when I see a mass of black liquid covering the floor, etched through with footprints. I follow them to Mrs Piddington and see her dress hem is drenched in the black-looking liquid. I freeze, looking down at my own dress. I haven't stepped in the liquid, fortunately. So I turn and walk around to the other side of the table, where I find a man lying, face down, a knife in his back. I swallow.

Mrs Piddington is comforting Alice, who is pale and shaking. Blood covers her hands and most of her clothes, and is smeared across her cheek and forehead, where she must have brushed her hair away from her face.

'Mrs Piddington?' I call.

'Not now, Elizabeth!' She turns back to Alice, trying to get her to speak. Alice's eyes are fixed on the dead body, which Mrs Piddington has evidently not yet seen.

'Sarah!' I shout, and finally Mrs Piddington turns around.

'What is it?'

As the recognition of what lies before her sinks in, she slowly rises. She blinks, and I glimpse a flash of panic in her eyes, so quick I would have missed it if I hadn't been so focused on her. I see Alice look up anxiously at her employer, watching as she slowly makes her way towards the body on the floor.

'Christ! Is that your husband, Alice? Is that Henry?' I look at the man, at the knife in his back, and then at Alice. I can't help but think of Robert. All the times I imagined doing the exact same thing, killing him, over and over again. It never gets old. I know what drove Alice to this. Fear. Desperation. Hopelessness. Sheer hatred. If I hadn't fought all those years, this could have been me, sitting in a dark room, my husband lying dead on the floor. I would have snapped. Just like Alice.

'I'll get the night watch,' I whisper.

'No! Wait! Let's think about this,' Mrs Piddington pleads. Alice is hugging her knees and begins rocking, mumbling words that I can't make out.

'There's nothing to think about – her best chance is to say she killed him in self-defence. We've all seen the evidence! She's still got marks all over her face and body to prove it!' I hiss. 'If we wait, they fade. And with them any chance of explaining this!'

I need a gin. People are always telling me drinking gets me into trouble, but these days, not drinking gets me into just as much.

'What if they don't believe her? The knife is in his back for Christ's sakes!' Mrs Piddington asks. 'She'll be executed!'

I hold up my hands in frustration. 'So what are you going to do? Cut off his head and display it on London Bridge?'

'Alice needs to sit,' Mrs Piddington says. I push the chair closer to them. Mrs Piddington smoothes Alice's hair back, and finishes wiping the blood off her face. Then, looking into her eyes, she says, 'It's all right, Alice, take a drink.' Mrs Piddington gives me a pointed look as she hands Alice some beer. I shake my head, unable to hide the scowl on my face. I'm not happy with this decision.

Alice drinks the beer in two gulps. I swallow instinctively, parched, longing to quench my increasing thirst. Alice raises her hands to return the cup to Mrs. Piddington and I notice they are trembling. Shock. It's settling in, taking over, whether she wants it to or not. She needs sugar and sleep, before she breaks.

'She'll need to be ready in the morning, the coach leaves early.' Mrs Piddington leans across and steadies Alice's hands. Damn Henry. One more night and Alice would have been free of him. One more night! Henry had taken Alice's innocence. He'd left her with the same demons I fight daily. I'll be damned if he is going to take her soul from the grave too. I sigh. Mrs Piddington is right, Alice must leave on that coach in the morning. That's something we could give her. I'm stuck here, but she doesn't have to be.

'We'll get her a bed at one of the twopence houses in St Giles. But as soon as they find him, an arrest warrant will be issued—' I sigh again, exhaling deeply. 'They'll assume she did it, especially if they can't find her.'

'We just have to pray it takes them a few days before they find his body,' Mrs Piddington whispers, again stealing a glance back at Alice.

I nod. 'What do we do about those?' I point at the woman-sized boot footprints clearly embedded in the dense liquid.

Mrs Piddington looks to the pool of blood surrounding Henry's corpse. 'We'll throw some water down, wash them up.' She looks down and collects the hem of her dress, studying the stained edges. 'I'll burn this.'

CHAPTER 30

A FEW DAYS PASS and I pass them by sleeping.

Alice should be up north with her family. Mrs Piddington swore to me that she'd get her on that coach. She also insisted that I shouldn't see either of them again. I hugged Alice before bidding her farewell. It was hard saying goodbye, but I know it was for the best.

After Henry was reported missing for failing to show up for work and there'd been no answer at his home, beadles entered the house and found his body, not more than a day after his death. Sophie said the rumour was that Alice had left to visit family in the country – a rumour confirmed by her employer, Mrs Piddington, who had agreed to her temporary departure from the shop and knew nothing of Henry Griffin's murder. There was a semblance of truth behind that rumour. But the rumour that Henry had been killed by a disgruntled acquaintance – he liked to drink and was known for his temper – *that* was not so true.

Sophie's motherly concern for me is starting to annoy me. She doesn't need to stay cooped up inside any more. Vincent is dead. The threat to her gone. It's time she moves on, back to the Tippling House or wherever she wants. But not here. Not with me.

The waft of her frumenty cooking gives me pause. Her food might be enough to change my mind on whether she stays or not. I roll over and check my wounds. Happy they are healing, I no longer need any ointment but my ribs still hurt when I move a certain way. Nothing to do but breathe through the pulsing ache until it eases into discomfort. Sophie assures me the bruising on my face is starting to change from bluish purple to greenish-yellow. The exact colour one wants to hear one's face described as, I mused.

'Have you spoken to James recently?' Sophie asks, stirring the pot.

I shake my head. I haven't seen or spoken to him. His comment about Halfinch grated on me; I'm not entirely sure why he made it. I feel Sophie look at me and realise she's still waiting for a response, clearly not seeing my head shake. 'No.'

She nods, turning back to her grains, which have soaked on a soft fire overnight. We don't have a pan she can use so she has to do everything in the same pot. Scouring it after every meal just to start all over again. Seems horrendous to me, doing that over and over again, but not to Sophie. The routine seems to calm her. Gives her purpose. Other than what is between her legs. And we all need purpose. It is, after all, what separates us from beasts.

'And Jimmy?' Her gentle voice carries over the crackling fire embers.

No. Haven't spoken to or seen him either. The thought of Jimmy has me thinking about his offer. To join him as a partner. To leave the great James Figg – is that what I really want?

'I'm cooking your breakfast, Elizabeth. The least you can do is speak to me, I can't look at you for your unspoken responses and not burn the frumenty at the same time.'

'No, I haven't seen Jimmy either.' I yawn, rubbing my hands over my head then letting them fall to clasp my neck. 'How long until it's ready?'

The corner of Sophie's mouth twitches. 'Not long.'

'How long is not long?' I ask, irritated and hungry.

We both know how I get when I don't eat.

'It means, not long.'

I scowl at her then flop back down on to the bed. 'Wake me up when it's ready.' I hear Sophie shuffling around, moving things and humming to herself. When she stops I peel one eye open to find her looking my way. I press my eye shut again. 'What?'

'Edward Stockton...' she whispers, 'did he... I mean, did he—'

'No,' I answer, knowing the question. 'He didn't.' I roll to my side, propping my head up with one arm. 'But after you, I knew exactly what his intentions were when he cornered me.' I smile, remembering the pompous son screaming as I beat his face.

'They whipped you,' she states, reminding me of my punishment after they yanked me off him. I nod. 'They did.'

'Did it hurt?'

'Yes.'

'Was it worth it?'

'The whipping?'

She nods, wringing her hands in front of her stomach.

I flop back onto my back and close my eyes. 'Every lash.'

'Stephen has been arrested,' Constable Clayton states. Sophie holds the door open for him, her mouth hanging open at his words.

I set down my bowl before taking my first bite. 'What for?' I ask, panicked.

'Murder,' he replies, the hard line of his lips telling me he's as affected by the giving of this news as I am receiving it. I spring to my feet, knocking the bowl to the floor, spilling the contents everywhere. I can't ask what I want to ask for fear of giving anything away. I don't know what he knows, or what he doesn't. My chest rises and falls with my heavy breathing; I feel like I've just done a solid training session with James. I'm light-headed and it isn't from gin. Once it subsides, I look at him, gathering my wits. 'Who did he supposedly murder?'

'Vincent Love.'

I shake my head. 'No, not murder—'

The constable holds up a hand. 'Magistrate received information about the murder of Vincent Love. It led us to King's Coffee House, where we found the boy—' His voice drops as his gaze lifts to mine. 'And the pistol.'

I'm still shaking my head. 'How— Who—' My thoughts are a jumbled mess, incapable of forming the questions I want so badly to ask him.

'A witness saw your attack, he saw the boy ...' Constable Clayton takes a deep breath, holding it for a few seconds before slowly breathing out through his mouth. 'The magistrate couldn't ignore the report. I didn't think we'd actually find anything. Didn't think the boy could ...' He stops again, placing his hands on his hips, his brows bunched together in a deep frown.

Emotion overwhelms me. 'Nicholas, it wasn't the boy, it was me – I did it. I killed Vincent. He attacked me, I shot him—'

Constable Clayton takes two long strides towards me and grabs my shoulders, shaking me. 'No, you didn't. Vincent attacked you and the boy shot him. Big Red and you are already in the magistrate's disfavour for lying to him! You both made him look a fool in front of the Aldermen!' he says firmly, catching himself before shouting at me, ending up hissing the words instead. I lick my lips and swallow back bile; the acidic taste burns my throat. Oh God. I can't breathe. I can't get enough air. Before I know what is happening, Constable Clayton spins me around and forces me down on the chair, pushing my head down between my knees. He's hushing me as he rests a hand on my back. I feel Sophie crouching next to me. She's sniffling back tears. After a few minutes, my breathing slows again. I don't sit up.

'He-he was-he was protecting me,' I stammer, the tears stinging my eyes. At the thought of my boy being arrested, held, tried and possibly hanged ... all for me. The pain is too much and suddenly I can no longer contain it. My sobbing breaks through my chest, and my heart breaks too.

I sit in The Black Hog for hours, John giving me concerned looks from the other end of the bar. He approaches me a couple of times but I am unable to speak. Finally, without asking, he places a tankard down in front of me and fills it. With gin. I stare at the tankard, wanting to drink it all and then demand a second, followed by a third and possibly a fourth. I long for enough gin to make me fall asleep and never wake up. I've heard it happens.

The door swings open and slams shut, followed by heavy footfall towards me. The man pulls out the stool next to mine and takes a seat.

'Ale,' the familiar deep voice says. Big Red doesn't acknowledge me at first. 'Magistrate won't see me, and no straw men will help. They've been told not to intervene.'

I frown. *What does that mean?*

He doesn't say anything else, thankfully. I can't handle this conversation right now. It seems Big Red can't either because once he is served, he doesn't hesitate – he guzzles the entire pint and orders another. 'Keep them filled,' he orders John, who nods after looking at both Big Red and me.

I don't thank him.

I drink.

And when my tankard is empty and refilled. I drink some more.

'What are the rules, Elizabeth?' James asks without preamble. He's in my room, sitting in Sophie's chair. I peel open my eyes, my head screaming at me not to move. The warmth from the booze still permeates my body, fuelling my intolerance for visitors at this hour. I kick my leg out towards Sophie's side of the bed, but it's empty. I roll over to see she isn't there. I prop myself up, much to my head's dissatisfaction, and look around the room. Sophie isn't here.

'She's outside. I asked her to give us a few minutes alone,' James says, pushing himself up out of the chair. 'I gave you a chance, the chance of a lifetime, and you wasted it. I want you gone. Clear this room of your things. Today.'

I don't argue. I can't fight at the moment and the only thing I'll be doing anytime soon is drinking to forget about Halfinch's upcoming trial. I recall the words James drilled into me when I joined his gym: *train, respect the other fighters, win, and no drinking.* They were clear enough, but clear doesn't mean easy.

Sophie enters as James leaves, not saying anything further to me, nor giving me a second glance. She comes to sit on the bed next to me and picks up my hand, holding it.

'Did you get your fill?' she asks, bowing her head.

I look up at her and shake my head slowly. She purses her lips and pats my hand.

'Well, that's a shame, because Halfinch needs you. He'll be scared and want to see you. He needs to see you, Elizabeth—'

'No, he doesn't—'

'Yes, he does,' she interrupts me. 'He did this for you. He'd do anything for you. So you go see him. You *will* do that for him.' Her chest rises and falls with her breath.

I feel the wetness brimming my eyes. A single tear falls down my cheek. 'I can't.'

She gives me a smile that doesn't reach her eyes. 'Yes, you can.'

CHAPTER 31

THE OLD BAILEY is full of professional-looking people, most of whom I've never seen before. A few familiar faces are scattered around the room. Constables Nicholas Clayton and Matthew Boyle sit together, with others I don't know. Sophie and Big Red sit with me, Sophie wedged between us. To my surprise, Jimmy appears and takes a seat on my other side. I've decided that I am going to admit to killing Vincent. I can't let Halfinch die for me, for protecting me. He just needs to plead not guilty, as we agreed, and I'll get my chance to speak as witness, give my testimony to the Chief Magistrate. Make him listen to me. He needs to listen to me. I don't care what Constable Clayton said.

The set-up is as I remembered it from Robert's trial, even down to the flowers hanging around the open room. They're purely decorative, for I can't smell the typical scent flowers normally air.

The Chief Magistrate enters and everyone stands. Several speeches are made and then the clerk announces the first case. There are several cases before Halfinch's full name is read aloud: 'In the matter of Crown versus Stephen Hatfield.'

Halfinch is escorted in and searches the room, his eyes frantic until they land on me, his face lighting up when he sees me. I wave at him and return his smile, trying to remain stoic through this ordeal. I mouth to him, *Look at me*, but he doesn't understand, giving me a curious look.

The clerk reads out the murder charge against Halfinch and I shuffle in my seat as the moment for Halfinch to plead arises. 'How does the accused plead?'

Halfinch looks at the clerk, at the Chief Magistrate and then to the benches, where his eyes meet mine. The corners of his mouth twitch and he winks at me. I feel a sinking sensation in my stomach. I lean forward and nod at him, encouraging him to answer. Halfinch's smile fades and he turns again to face the court.

'I plead guilty.'

The gasps and shock ripple throughout the court. My eyes widen. A guilty plea means no witness testimony. I won't be able to have my say. Before I can think, I jump to my feet. 'No!' Murmurs echo through the court officials and spectators.

Sophie and Jimmy grab me, trying to sit me down, but I won't budge. 'No! It wasn't him! It was me!' My eyes dart from the Chief Magistrate to Halfinch and back again. The sound in the courtroom increases from rumblings to louder, outraged voices. 'It was me! He didn't do it! Don't listen to him!' I repeat, but my voice is drowned out by the crowd. Many of them are on their feet, straining to see who is causing the disruption. The Chief Magistrate orders my removal from the court, again. Jimmy starts pulling on my arm, dragging me back, before more patrols arrive to help, with a worried Sophie and grief-stricken Big Red following us out of the courtroom. My eyes lock with Halfinch's for a moment; the last thing I see is him turning to face the Chief Magistrate.

I make it out of the courtroom before a scream escapes my throat. Jimmy catches me as I collapse, sliding with me down to the floor. He holds me and doesn't let go, squeezing me tightly. 'Wa — was it you?' I ask between gasps for air.

'Was what me?' Jimmy asks, still holding me tight, my back to his chest.

'Did you tell Magistrate Trelawny it was Halfinch who shot Vincent?' I cry, trying to pull away from his grip.

'What? No! I wouldn't do that—' But I don't care, I turn my head into his chest, no longer wanting distance. My sobs echo in the open air. I cry without care of who is watching or listening. I weep until there are no more tears, and even then the sobs rack my body, my heart broken by love for a child.

I want to turn back time.

By the time I reach Newgate Prison, my eyes are dry and my voice has returned to its normal pitch. Constable Boyle and Jimmy escort me from the Old Bailey to the prison, where Halfinch is to be held until his execution. At the ripe age of eleven, he is to be hanged at Tyburn the following week. Another hanging day in London.

Halfinch is huddled in a ball in the corner of his cell. Constable Boyle speaks to the guard and he agrees to let me enter the cell with Halfinch; he will watch us. Jimmy waits outside, giving me my space. He told me he'd wait for me, whenever I'm ready, however long it takes. I want to be grateful for him, but I'm not convinced it wasn't him who reported Halfinch to the magistrate. Who else could it have been? I think of the possible reasons why he'd do it, but none seem likely. I am grateful for Constable Boyle, knowing I can't be around Constable Clayton – it isn't safe for him to be near me after he arrested Halfinch. I know he hated doing it, and it isn't fair of me to hold it against him, but I don't care. None of this is fair.

I enter the cell and Halfinch hobbles into my arms. He fits perfectly. I smooth his hair back from his face, exposing his dimples and long eyelashes. He is a cute child, and would be even to someone who didn't know him – he's fun and funny. Kind and mischievous. The light in an otherwise gloomy world, the beat to which my heart ticks. And despite my best efforts to deny it, I care for him. I kiss the top of his head.

'I … I'm sorry,' he says, sniffling back tears.

'Don't be. I'm the one who should be sorry.' I tilt his chin up and wipe the smudges from his face. He stands still while I fuss over him, like a child on his way to mass. But that's another story, belonging to someone else's life. We stay like this for a few minutes. Pretending to be normal. A woman and a child, sharing a moment.

'Why? Why did you do it?' I ask him, begging to understand his plea.

Halfinch blinks back the tears. 'Because you're the City Championess. And I'm a nobody.'

'Not to me … To me you are *everything*.'

Halfinch squeezes me tighter. 'I did it. I killed Vincent Love. Not you.'

'He was after me, you only killed him because of me,' I say, fighting back my own tears. As if sensing it, Halfinch looks up at me. 'It's all right. It'll be all right, Championess,' he says, trying to console me.

I laugh and wipe my eyes. 'I'm supposed to be telling you that!'

Halfinch grins.

'*A-hem.*'

Constable Boyle's cough means we don't have much time. I kneel before Halfinch and look at him, taking his hands in mine. 'Anytime you need me, you tell the guard and I will come. Do you hear me?' Halfinch nods.

'Now, don't be scared. Stand up straight,' I order, taking a more forceful tone. Halfinch straightens his stance.

'Good, that's good.' I kiss the top of his head again and stand up. 'I'll come back to see you as soon as I can.'

Halfinch watches me walk away. The constable holds the door open for me. Before he closes it, Halfinch calls out, 'Elizabeth?'

I pause. 'Yes, Halfinch?'

He starts to sway on his right foot, dropping his gaze to the floor where I stand.

'I ... I love you. I want you to know that.'

I run back to him, clasping him into my arms again, and hold him tightly against me. This boy, who hobbled into my life, who cheered me on in my fights, who survived the streets of London with a gammy foot, protected me at the cost of his own life.

'I love you too, Halfinch.'

When I finally release him, he wipes away the tears and snot on his sleeve.

'Tell me something,' he says.

'Like what?'

'Anything. How's Sophie? When you fighting again?'

I laugh.

'Sophie is fine,' I reply, ruffling his hair.

'You'll watch out for her?'

I sigh. Even now he's thinking of others.

'I'll try.'

'That's good. I like Sophie.'

'Most men do,' I snort.

Constable Boyle approaches. 'I'm sorry, Elizabeth, but we must be going.'

I nod and hug him one last time.

Halfinch blinks a few times. 'Make sure it's quick.'

I frown. 'What do you mean?'

'At Tyburn. Please, Elizabeth, make sure it's quick.'

I can feel the constable's eyes on me. I can't believe what Halfinch is asking of me. Dumbfounded, I rise. 'I'll see you tomorrow.'

'Elizabeth!' I hear him call after me again. Constable Boyle winces, shooting the guard an apologetic look. We turn around to see his little face peeking through the bars. 'When you fighting again?'

I shrug. 'I don't know.'

'But you will fight again, for London?'

'She will.' Jimmy speaks up, assuring Halfinch.

I smile, looking at Halfinch. '*Vis et armis.*'

'Vis and what?' he asks, leaning forward.

'*Vis et armis,*' I repeat. 'It means, by force and arms.'

Halfinch smiles the biggest smile.

'I'll fight again.' I walk back and rub my thumb across his cheek. 'I'll fight for you. With everything I have, giving everything I've got.'

Halfinch nods. '*Vis et armis.*'

CHAPTER 32

E VEN THE SKIES know this is to be a dark day. The clouds huddle together, refusing to let the sun shine through. Any sort of light would bring ill-judged hope and that isn't welcome.

Today is Hanging Day; another public holiday for the citizens of London to feed their inexplicable thirst for death and booze, and for me to say goodbye to a friend, a child, a thief of handkerchiefs and hearts, Halfinch.

Many in the crowd are already drunk by the time I arrive at Newgate Prison. I chose not to drink. Not today. I've drunk every day since Halfinch's trial. But now? Today? I want to feel every emotion the events of this day offer. I deserve as much.

I'm not allowed to see Halfinch this morning, but he knows I'm waiting for him outside the gates. I won't leave him to go through this alone. We talked about it. We both knew it was coming.

Finally, the guards open the gate and the convicts are marched out one by one. The crowd start throwing apples, offal and shite at the people to be executed. It's part of the circus. The convicts who buckle under the pressure and cry get it even more. I told Halfinch to hold his head up, not to cry. Not to shed one tear, not to give the people the satisfaction. But above all else, I told him to keep his eyes on me. I told him not to look at anyone or anything else. That's proving difficult now. As Halfinch emerges squinting into the daylight, I wrestle to get to the front of the mob, Jimmy and Big Red helping to clear the way for me.

'Halfinch!' I call out, pushing women and men alike out of my way. 'Halfinch! Here! I'm here!'

But he can't hear me. His eyes scan the thick crowd of people surrounding him. I punch a man in the jaw when he gets gobby with me for pushing. I step on someone else.

'Oi! Watch it!'

'Damn your blood!'

I push and pull, getting closer to the horse-drawn carriage that transports the murderers, rapists, traitors and Halfinch from Newgate to Tyburn.

*Criminal*s.

Halfinch may have killed a man, but he isn't a murderer. A criminal? Yes. Murderer? No. He saved me. He's been saving me since long before that dreaded night when Vincent Love followed through on his threat. I fight back tears at the thought of the boy being brought now to his death for helping me. And he is a boy. Just a boy trying to survive. Like Alice, Sophie and me.

I look around and see drunken men and women everywhere. One man hits a woman so he can take a bottle from her. There is no semblance of humane or tender feelings among these savages. I don't understand why they take such pleasure in watching another person fight against death. How can they go on with their day when people are about to be executed? Not just people, but a boy, my friend, my little champion.

I finally make it to the front of the crowd just as the carriage starts pulling away. I run alongside, calling out Halfinch's name.

His eyes dart from side to side, searching to see where I'm calling from.

'Behind you! Here!' I yell, waving my arms over my head. Halfinch turns and his eyes finally find mine. I see him breathe a sigh of relief, smiling slightly. He tries to wave but his hands are chained. He's on the verge of tears.

'Don't!' I warn. 'No tears! A champion knows he's won before he's stepped onto the stage.'

Halfinch nods and a single tear rolls down his cheek. I point to my chest, mouth and nose, motioning for him to slow his breathing.

I manoeuvre through the tangled masses, trying to watch where I'm walking and maintaining eye contact with Halfinch at the same time. I come close to tripping a couple of times. I don't turn to see where Jimmy and Big Red are; I know they'll be close.

'This is the time, before the fight, when I can hear the roar of the crowd!' A drunk grabs at me and I throw an elbow to knock the wind out of him. I pick up my pace to get closer to the cart.

'I start to focus on what I'm about to do, just me, no one else. No one else gets on the stage to fight for me,' I say. Halfinch is listening.

Before too soon, the cart stops; they are at the Tree.

Halfinch starts to panic, calling out for me, 'Elizabeth!'

'Halfinch! Halfinch! Look at me! *Look* at me!' I yell, pushing past a group of men who were waiting for the convicts to arrive. They curse at me, calling me a cunt, but I don't care. Halfinch's face is pale, his eyes are wide and his breathing is quick and shallow.

'I've entered the stage, I see the crowd, I see you! You're cheering me on! My opponent is there, but she doesn't matter!'

I can see the executioner checking the ropes, one by one, before placing them over the heads of each prisoner. The crowd surges, eager for the show to begin.

I raise my fists up. 'I'm not afraid! Never afraid!' I lie. Halfinch nods, his colour returning and breaths slowing.

'I'm not afraid,' he shouts back at me, shaking his head as much as the noose allows. 'I'm not afraid!'

I nod. The crowd applauds his courage. He smiles at their cheers, closing his eyes for a second.

The executioner nods for the cart driver to pull away. The mob roar as the men begin thrashing and gasping for air. Two more and Halfinch will drop. I mouth *I love you* to him, but I don't know if he sees me. His eyes are locked on mine.

'*Vis et armis!*' I yell, fist in the air, tears in my eyes.

'*Vis et armis!*' he shouts back, just as the cart goes from under him. I watch as his small body falls towards the ground, never reaching it.

I sob as I go to grab his legs, but I feel hands around me. Jimmy is holding me back, preventing me from reaching Halfinch. 'What are you doing? Let me go!'

'Let Red do it!' Jimmy shouts.

I look at Halfinch's terrified, strangled face and know I wouldn't have done it. Perhaps couldn't. Big Red reaches the boy, knowing what he has to do. He wraps himself around the boy's tiny legs and pulls down with all his might.

CHAPTER 33

B Y THE TIME I reach The Black Hog, most of the seats are taken, people are standing in corners, and the air is filled with conversation about the day gone by. John is racing back and forth behind the bar refilling tankards, delivering food from the kitchen and taking more orders. I weave between the crowd towards the bar and on to my usual stool, which John knows to keep for me. I nod my head as John places a gin in front of me.

It's been over a week since Halfinch's death. And I've spent it either here in the tavern drinking, or sleeping – back at the twopence house. Days merge into night, night into day, and I try my best not to feel anything in between. I want to die. Death would be less painful than what I feel. I'm certain of it. My body has healed from the attack, but my heart hasn't. The loss is too strong, the void too deep. No amount of gin seems to fill it, no matter how hard I try.

'Come fight with me,' urges Jimmy, for the umpteenth time, leaning against the bar next to where I sit.

I shake my head, not bothering to look at him.

'We all miss Halfinch,' says Sophie, coming to stand on the other side of me. I press my eyes shut, willing them to leave me to drink away my sorrow in peace.

'You promised him,' Jimmy says, pointing at me.

I slam my tankard down. 'He's not going to know now, is he?'

Jimmy's face softens. 'Maybe not, but you will.'

'Just because he's gone doesn't mean he's not here,' Sophie adds.

I glare at her. 'It's exactly what it means, Sophie.' I gesture at John to refill my tankard. He does so without question. I like that about him.

Sophie sighs and pushes the tankard away from me, towards Jimmy, who takes it and puts it out of my reach. 'He loved you. And you loved him. He's gone, but you're here. The love you have for him is still there, within you, is it not? Just because you can't see him, or hear him ... doesn't mean you can't feel him, right?' Sophie presses her hand against my chest, over my heart. 'Here,' she says.

I grab hold of her hand and cling to it while rubbing my eyes with my other hand. 'I just want it to stop,' I weep. 'This ... this ache! I want it to stop. I can't—'

Sophie wraps her arms around me and hugs me. Letting me cry. Damn you, Sophie, this is what I was trying to avoid. Feeling this – this torture, it's agony.

'I know, me too. But that's how we know we love. Because it wouldn't hurt so much, if we didn't.'

I spot Jimmy standing outside a house on Brook Street off Holborn Hill, a big smile plastered on his face. He secured two rooms out of a block of four in Clerkenwell. I rent one room on the first level, and Jimmy rents the room opposite. It is a step up from my small room in Marylebone, and worlds apart from the twopence rooms or St Giles rookery.

It is getting to the end of summer and the days are already beginning to shorten. But today is a bright, crisp day. Full of opportunity. A chance to look ahead, rather than dwell on the past. My heart still aches at the loss of Halfinch – in truth, I don't think the pain will ever subside and I'm not sure I want it to. Sophie reminding me of what that pain represents propels me forward. Gives me purpose.

The shift from the Boarded House to Jimmy's amphitheatre near Sadler's Wells was not without its challenges. First, Jimmy doesn't own it. Second, because it's a new venture, it means we have to spend more time advertising to draw an audience. The place is laid out in gardens, and hosts more evening concerts than prize-fighting. Its low reputation isn't helped by its isolated location deep in the fields at the north end of Clerkenwell, requiring link boys to light people to and from London.

Sophie is living with Big Red near Covent Garden. When I ask her about it, she blushes. Still. And still her response amazes me. She constantly asks when I'm fighting next, not wanting to miss it. I tell her my typical response, which is 'soon'. I can't be more specific because Jimmy is taking care of the organising. He's been chasing down possible opponents and bartering with promoters and trainers. I'm not sure he thought it would be so difficult to arrange fights – James always made it seem so easy, always having a supply of fighters ready and willing to step up on the stage for a contest.

The days leading up to my first fight at Sadler's Wells amphitheatre are uneventful. Jimmy spends his time promoting the fights and in particular the bout featuring myself, which follows a new structure for me – I'm no longer engaging in pure bare-knuckle boxing, but will be competing in a three-round fight, the first two using weapons and then finishing with fists. The first round utilises the short dagger, and is won by whoever draws blood from their opponent three times. The second, with the cudgel, is won by breaking heads three times. However, the third round will only be won when one of the fighters is knocked down, no longer standing. It is as much a fight of endurance as skill – a new challenge for my fighting abilities. But my body has healed from Vincent Love's assault, and my training at Figg's has served me well for the new three-round structure. Jimmy and I need the money to make the theatre a successful rival against Figg's Boarded House.

Now that the day of my first fight for Jimmy has arrived, any fears I had about earnings evaporate as soon as I see the line of people waiting to enter the venue.

The amphitheatre is located off Islington Road. Its horse-shoe-shaped seating area allows for a great number of spectators, all ranks of Londoners. The stage itself is sturdy, floored with heavy wooden planks.

It is the most bizarre thing, but before, when I fought in St Giles, I felt no fear, no pain. There was never any question about my ability to win a fight. I'd beat the woman in front of me or be beaten myself because I wanted to survive. Now, I actually look forward to fighting, the feeling I get when I ascend the stage, the noise, the smell of blood and sweat – all of it. My name and reputation as a fighter brings something else. Pride. The location may have changed but what is expected of me is constant. Soon I'll enter the stage, fight and win. People come to watch my skill. People come to be entertained. People come to see me win. Not just to win, but to dominate in the fashion I've become known for. Jimmy tells me he'll introduce me as the 'London City Championess' – leaving no doubt as to my role on this stage. The people of London come to love me for it.

I have a drink of small beer while I wait for the fight to be called. My mind wanders to Halfinch, but I push those thoughts out of my mind as quickly as they enter, choosing to think of Alice enjoying her life up north. Magistrate Trelawny issued an order to speak to her about her husband's death, but she wrote a letter stating that she had no information about it because she wasn't in the city when it happened. Hopefully, they have turned their attention elsewhere.

I can't dwell on that last thought for long. The crowds are in their seats and are waiting for the entertainment to begin. Jimmy has secured two other fights to open the night's entertainment. The first is between himself and a man called Alex Biggins. I'd never heard of him. Jimmy wins easily. The second is a bout between two younger men, who can't be older than seventeen.

Jimmy has changed into a dress shirt to announce my fight. I can see him through the cracks in the curtains. His voice bellows over the crowd, hushing them.

'LADIES AND GENTLEMEN, ARE YOU READY FOR THE NEXT FIGHT?' His question is answered by a huge roar. He invites my opponent up first, a woman unknown to me and to the crowd, who boo her when she ascends the stage.

'AND NOW, LONDON, PLEASE WELCOME TO THE STAGE THE CITY CHAMPIONESS, ELIZABETH WILKINSON!

The noise is so deafening it almost throws me off balance. I bounce up the stairs to the stage, out into the open, and manoeuvre across the wooden floor to meet Jimmy and my opponent. For the first time, I come face to face with my challenger. The woman is huge – not in height but in girth. *All right. Not what I expected.*

I win easily. Too easily. At certain points, I almost feel like the crowd is bored. I manage to salvage things a bit in the third round when I break the woman down, her fists dropping to her sides before her body collapses to the floor. The thud hitting the deck is all I need to secure my victory. I won.

The crowd jumps up and down, cheering my success. My right eye is swollen shut – my opponent landed a lucky punch – so I squint through my left eye at the woman, still sprawled on the stage. Jimmy comes to my side and holds my arm up. It's only when he drops it and the noise from the crowd abates that the commotion starts.

'Is that it?' a woman in the audience yells. She has fair skin and dark hair that matches my own. She is a tall woman, as tall as me, and is accompanied by two equally dark-haired men.

'This is Elizabeth Wilkinson?' she shouts again as she makes her way down the stairs between the sectioned seats. She has a profound Irish accent. 'The famous City Championess? I've challenged you, Elizabeth. Why haven't you accepted?' the woman asks. She stops in front of the stage. Jimmy is still standing by my side.

'Bloody Irish,' I mumble under my breath, and I take a few steps towards the edge of the stage so I can get a better look at the woman who is slighting me.

'You must be Mary Welch,' I state. It isn't a question, I know who she is. I've heard of her. I know the name. Heard of her pugilism success across the sea. A worthy opponent, it would seem.

'I am, and you've not accepted my challenge. They say you are the best. You are unbeatable, the great *Championess*!' Mary looks me up and down. 'I'd say they're full of shite. The lot of them.'

'*I* never *received* your challenge, Mary. As for my title, you'll find out soon enough,' I reply, jumping off the stage to face Mary on her level. Jimmy follows closely behind me.

Mary grunts, casting her eyes around at the crowd. 'Well, *Championess*' – she spits the last word, full of sarcasm – 'you know what happens now?'

I grin. 'My answer.'

CHAPTER 34

'ELIZABETH! ARE YOU in there? Open up!'

I shout at him to come in, without leaving the bed. He looks around at the empty gin bottle. 'Christ.'

I don't stir.

'Are you going to get up?' He pulls back the curtain blocking the daylight from my room, the day from my mind. I hear Jimmy leave and, a few minutes later, return. I feel a shock of cold before I can react. Jimmy pours a bucket of freezing water over me. In a moment, I am jolted from slightly asleep and fragile to fully awake and definitely ill from drink.

'Jimmy! You bastard!'

Jimmy laughs and takes a seat on the edge of my now soaking bed. He places the empty bucket on the floor and throws a drape over his shoulder. I stand and go to punch him, but he grabs my wrist and holds me still. He doesn't fight me, he doesn't retaliate. He just pauses, holding me, and looks at me. The sound of a bird chirping outside, of a door closing somewhere in the building, makes the silence in the room unbearable. His intense stare holds me captive for a moment; his slight smile makes me uncomfortable. I gulp and then grab at my white blouse, which I realise is stuck to my skin, exposing every blemish, every scar, every freckle I have. Jimmy studies my wet, half-naked body with interest.

'Get out!'

'Oh, relax! I've seen worse!' He winks, tossing the drape at me.

'Go!' I shout again, holding up the material to cover my body. Jimmy rolls his eyes and turns his back to me. 'I have good news—'

'I don't care what you have!' I yell. 'I want you out of my room!'

'All right, but it really is good news ...' His voice trails off as he quietly closes the door after himself.

I finish dressing and sigh deeply. Adrenaline subsided and my sleepiness gone. I glance at the door and frown. I didn't hear Jimmy walk away. My mouth widens into a grin. I open the door and see him standing not an inch away from it, about to knock a second time.

'What's the good news?' I ask, cocking my head to the side.

He returns my smile. 'Use that anger that's fuelling you against your next opponent. Mary Welch – it's done.'

'At Mr. Stokes's Amphitheatre, in Islington Road, near Sadler's Wells, on Monday next, being the 3rd of September, will be performed a trial of skill by the following Championesses.

CHALLENGE - *Whereas I Mary Welch, from the Kingdom of Ireland, being taught, and knowing the noble science of defence, and thought to be the only female of this kind in Europe, understanding there is one in this Kingdom, who has exercised on the public stage do hereby invite her to meet me, and exercise the usual weapons practised on the stage, at her own amphitheatre, doubting not, but to let her and the worthy spectators see, that my judgment and courage is beyond hers.*

ANSWER - *I Elizabeth Stokes, of the famous City of London, being well known by the name of the Invincible City Championess for my abilities and judgment in the above said science; having never engaged with any of my own sex but I always came off with victory and applause, shall make no apology for accepting the challenge of this Irish Heroine, not doubting but to maintain the reputation I have hitherto established, and show my country, that the contest of its honour, is not ill entrusted in the present battle with their Championess, Elizabeth Stokes.*

Note, The doors will be opened at two, and the Championesses mount at four. N.B. They fight in close jackets, short petticoats, coming just below the knee, Holland drawers, white stockings, and pumps.'

Jimmy is in the middle of changing when I barge in. 'Elizabeth Stokes?' I ask, tossing the *British Gazetteer* onto the bed.

'Come in, Elizabeth,' Jimmy says sarcastically. He picks up the paper. 'Let me explain ...'

'Yes, you do that!' I shout, standing in the doorway with my hands on my hips.

Jimmy faces me, picking up the paper. 'After you left the Boarded House, and since you came here, with me ... people began to talk, the rumours started.' He looks down at the paper in his hand. 'Rumours have big teeth. I didn't want you bit. I thought it would mean less offence if it *appeared* you and I are married. It changes nothing.'

'It changes everything. My name is my reputation.'

'Your fighting skills are your reputation, Elizabeth. And as long as you continue to win you will be known as the City Championess, regardless of whether you are "Elizabeth Wilkinson" or "Elizabeth Stokes" on the advertisement.'

'If it doesn't matter then why change it?'

Jimmy sighs. 'You mean, besides creating some distance between you and your murdering criminal of a husband, Robert? All right, on the stage, you are the Championess. But on the streets, you will be taunted and shamed. And we all know what happens when you are insulted, especially if you've been drinking.' Jimmy rolls his eyes, tossing the paper back on the bed. 'Which, let's face it, is most days now. Don't think I haven't noticed.'

I stand firm. 'Next time, ask first when you make a decision that involves me,' I say, pointing towards my chest with my thumb. I then turn and leave Jimmy to put his shirt on.

James has been busy since we parted ways. He put himself back in the ring only to lose to Ned Sutton, an old rival. So for him to lose me and then his next fight wasn't the best pairing of events to transpire. That doesn't stop him though. He's a successful fighter and an even better promoter. So in another attempt to pull crowds back to his new amphitheatre, he arranges a trial of skill between four masters to fight at his venue: Joseph Hamlin and Thomas Philips versus Ned Sutton and George Bell.

And for the first time, I find myself intrigued by a bout I'm not fighting in.

Big Red lets out a long, deep belch. I breathe in the gut-rotten air and gag.

'Zounds, Red, what did you eat today? Smells like something died.' I waft the air in front of me. Big Red releases a deep rumble from his chest. I meet him at The Black Hog after he asked me to. John slams down a plate full of meat and potatoes in front of Big Red, who begins shovelling it into his mouth, barely chewing before swallowing the pieces of meat.

I grimace at the sight as food and juices dribble down his beard. 'Sophie not feeding you at home?' I ask, turning up my nose. Sophie always gave me a hard time about my poor eating habits. I dread to think what she would say about this display.

He grunts.

'What do you want?' I ask, impatient. I'm keen to get a seat at the Boarded House to watch the four masters bout.

Big Red looks at me. 'We have a problem.' He speaks with his mouth full, more pieces of food falling out.

I pause, uncertain of how to take this revelation. 'We?'

Big Red lifts one shoulder in a shrug. 'You, and your former employer, Mrs Piddington.'

Oh. 'What kind of problem?'

Big Red wipes his hands on a napkin. 'Magistrate Trelawny.'

'What about him?' I ask, not really sure I want to hear the answer.

CHAPTER 35

ACK AT THE house, I'm still stewing over my discussion with Big Red about Magistrate Trelawny when I hear banging and cursing coming from Jimmy's room. I leap up and burst in to help, only to find Jimmy holding a chair up over his head. I take a quick look about and see no one else there.

'Jimmy? What are you doing?' I see the fury in his eyes. I'm not used to that look, not from him anyway. If they could burn, his eyes would singe holes all over my body.

'Mary Welch, she can't fight on Monday.' Jimmy slams the chair onto the floor and it smashes. He had purposefully declined challenges from other women who wanted to fight me so that I would be injury-free for my bout with Mary Welch.

I close the door behind me and lean back against it. 'What happened?'

'She's ill. At least, that is what she is claiming.'

'So you thought you'd break furniture?'

Jimmy laughs. 'Yes! I thought it would make me feel better!' He picks up a bowl and flings it against the wall, smashing it into pieces. 'Figg will jump at the chance to host another fight, swooping in to take our business.'

I sigh. 'We'll rearrange for another date.'

I pull open the door, but pause, thinking of Jimmy. His passion and steadfast dedication. *Zounds.* This isn't good. We need that prize money. I close the door again. Jimmy stops throwing things for now, and watches me closely.

'So increase the stakes,' I say. 'How can we entice a bigger crowd? Give them something different?'

Jimmy, intrigued, waits for me to say more. We both stand in silence. Finally, it's Jimmy who volunteers an idea. 'What if *we* fight as a couple?'

I glower at him. 'What do you mean?'

Jimmy's anger turns to wonder, his eyes wide with realisation at what he is thinking. 'We challenge Mary Welch and another man to a joint fight. We can each fight in turn. I'll fight the man, then you fight Mary. We'll use the same format as before – short dagger, cudgel then fists. What do you think? Surely that will excite the masses!' His smile takes up most of his face, his excitement fills the room.

It takes some convincing, but eventually I agree. Now I just need to see the magistrate. Not a conversation I am eager to have.

'By God, I think I love you even more, Elizabeth Wilkinson,' Jimmy says, beaming.

'I thought it's Elizabeth Stokes?' I toss back over my shoulder playfully as I leave.

He laughs. 'We could make it official, if you want to.'

Jimmy anticipated it.

The next day, James announces his rematch against Ned Sutton, having lost to him the first time. It's scheduled for the night I should have fought Mary Welch. James is seizing the moment to capitalise on the cancelled fight. Jimmy is still touchy about it, but

I don't care. I'm not interested in Figg or his reputation, or the pissing contest between him and Jimmy.

Instead, I am heading to see the magistrate. The man who has accused me of murder. A man who I am quite certain does not like me. Convincing him that Alice had nothing to do with her husband's death – a lie – and that she wasn't here when he died – another lie – is going to be difficult. Especially as I understand from Big Red that he is pressuring Mr and Mrs Piddington. He didn't say how, but I'll find out from the Mistress herself. That will be my next stop.

I am shown into Magistrate Trelawny's office and I'm surprised to see there the Piddingtons' apprentice, Benjamin, blocking my view of the householder. Constable Clayton is also there, standing off to one side. Benjamin finishes speaking to Magistrate Trelawny and leaves after being excused, without acknowledging me. The magistrate begins sorting through various papers piled on his desk, picking up a few to read over the contents.

'Good day, Mrs Wilkinson' – he pauses momentarily – 'or is it Mrs Stokes?' Magistrate Trelawny queries, raising his gaze to meet mine. So he follows the fight announcements. Interesting.

I nod at him. 'Alice didn't kill her husband.'

The magistrate freezes. 'I don't understand,' he states, dropping the papers to the desk to give his full attention to me.

'Just what I said. Alice didn't kill her husband. I know you are investigating his death—'

'His murder, Elizabeth. I'm investigating his murder,' he corrects me. The fact that he uses my first name doesn't go unnoticed by me. I shift on my feet, trying to think of what I want to say, where to start, but the magistrate isn't in a patient mood today. 'I have a coachman who gave testimony that Mrs Alice Griffin only left London the morning of the Thursday. We can't be sure when Mr Griffin died, but it was around that same time, and there is no way of knowing whether she left before or after his ... demise.' He considers me for a moment before continuing. 'The Piddingtons' apprentice, Benjamin Halliday, who you just saw leave, informed us that he overheard you, Mrs Piddington and Mrs Griffin discussing murdering husbands one day at work. More specifically, that you thought it was a clever idea to chop him up and post his head on London Bridge ...' He cocks an eyebrow and purses his lips as his voice trails off, before standing to walk around and lean against his desk in front of me. I'm speechless. I didn't think Benjamin heard us that day. He always seemed so engrossed in his work.

'One of you killed him, or all of you did it together. When Alice gets here, I am certain we'll find the truth. I've already summoned Mr and Mrs Piddington to come and give a statement. I was about to send Constable Clayton here to come and get you, but ... it seems someone else has been passing information your way.' He crosses his arms, tapping a finger against his chin. 'You know, it's a shame about the Piddingtons' shop and all the robberies they've had. Must be causing devastation to their business.'

I frown. How does he know about that? And there's been more than one? Feeling bold, I ask him, 'And are you looking into those robberies?'

His mouth forms a slow smile. 'Yes, I have made a few enquiries into that.'

There's a loud knock at the door before Jimmy enters. 'Good morning ... all,' he says, looking around my room and seeing Sophie. 'I come bearing good news!'

'Please share, we could do with some good news,' I reply, glancing at Sophie, who is now leaning over, her hands clasped in her lap.

'Mary Welch has found a partner for the joint fight – a Mr Robert Barker. And we have a date for the fight!' Jimmy says, pumping the air with both fists. His excitement is contagious. I just wish I could share in his delight, but unfortunately, his news is overcast with the looming cloud that is Magistrate Trelawny.

Life, it seems, does not care for plans. It happens on its own, whether one wants it to or not.

'We Robert Barker and Mary Welch, from Ireland, having often contaminated our swords in the abdominous corporations of such antagonists as have had the insolence to dispute our skill, do find ourselves once more necessitated to challenge, defy, and invite Mr Stokes and his bold Amazonian virago to meet us on the stage, where we hope to give satisfaction to the honourable Lord of our nation who has laid a wager of twenty guineas on our heads. They that give the most cuts to have the whole money.'

CHAPTER 36

MONDAY NIGHT. *FIGHT night.*

The boisterous noise of the crowd brings me back to the amphitheatre. We expect a full house tonight. The winnings to be significant. But that is just icing on the cake. I want to win not because of the reward but to protect the reputation I've built. And because it might be the last bout I get to fight. My name is known across the country for having a reputation as unbeatable. When people speak about me in the streets it's about my fighting capability, my ability to dominate in the ring, not my statuesque height or gangly limbs.

I look down at my hands. They've helped me through so much over the years. The same hands that could stitch a bone casing and detailed pattern into a stay. If only my life had somehow started differently, not at the orphanage, not at Sir Frederick Stockton's estate, not at the rookery with Robert. But then I think of Halfinch, the boy who gave me a reason to live. I wouldn't have met him if I hadn't endured it all. Is it selfish of me to be content at my lot, knowing I got to meet him? Probably. Knowing that he died because of me? Definitely.

'It's time,' Jimmy calls for me. I nod once and peek out at the crowd.

Full house.

There's thunderous applause mixed with heckling and booing. Mary Welch and Robert Barker must have taken the stage. A man's voice cuts across the noise, introducing Jimmy and me. Jimmy walks out first and people cheer, but when I appear closely behind him they rise from their seats and the applause becomes deafening.

Mary Welch is pacing. Her partner, Robert, a stalky man with thick black hair, stands still, popping his knuckles. The noise is like a pot whistling, boiling over, grating on my ears. Jimmy smiles broadly and walks across the front of the stage holding his arms up and egging the crowd on, encouraging them to scream louder. I watch my partner with pride.

The announcer asks us to take our positions. I pick up a dagger and toss it in the air to get a sense of its weight. I scan the crowd and see Sophie near the front with Betty, who is still fat. To my surprise, Big Red is also there.

I smile at Sophie and wink, before returning my attention to my opponent – Mary Welch, the Irish championess who has challenged and insulted me on more than one occasion. I've been looking forward to fighting her. I've waited a long time for this moment to arrive and all of a sudden it's here. The mallet falls to signal the start.

Smack!

Mary steps forward and bobs her head from side to side, her footwork light and quick, impeccably trained. We dance around each other for a few minutes. I'm first to draw blood with my dagger, and the audience responds with a whoop. I nip her a second time on the left arm and again the fans roar.

Then I miss my next few shots and, in a rush of over-confidence, lose my footing. Mary takes advantage, stepping in and gashing my side.

'Ahhh!' I wince, jumping away from Mary's blade. There is a collective intake of breath and the crowd urge me to finish the round.

'*Go on!*'

'*One more!*'

'*Finish this one, Elizabeth!*'

Feinting to the left, ducking to the right, I manoeuvre around the stage with ease and confidence. As Mary launches at me, I block the advance and land the third and final cut on her left thigh. Our first round is over. Mary casts me a scathing look and spits on the floor.

I leave the stage and behind the curtain Jimmy tends to my wound, bandaging my side. 'Mary's injuries are far worse, you did well.' We exchange a quick look of encouragement and then Jimmy leaves to face Robert.

Jimmy and Robert's round goes by in a similar fashion. Jimmy manages the first two tags, with Robert getting one cut in, but Jimmy finishes the round quickly after.

Next is the cudgel, my least favourite of the three rounds. I'm pleased Jimmy and I continued practising with weapons after leaving Figg's gym. Mary is clearly more comfortable with the cudgel. She manages to hit me first on the shoulder and then once more on my side where I was already cut, causing the wound to bleed more, staining my white blouse. I take a moment to catch my breath before launching an attack: I club Mary on the back twice. We're all square. The next to score wins this round. We both take our time, dancing around the stage, taking a step closer before jumping back, trying to throw the other off guard. In the end, I crack the side of Mary's head and draw blood when she misses me with an attempted swing. Mary throws her cudgel on the ground and the crowd meet her temper with laughter.

My side is stinging, the blood dripping down my skirt. I press a hand over it to ease the pain. Jimmy isn't performing well in his round. He misses several shots and leaves himself exposed when trying to regain his balance. Barker taps Jimmy on his back once, twice and then a third time after the longest round so far.

The Londoners let Jimmy know he is disappointing them. He grimaces at me as he sits down. Mary has already stepped into the middle of the stage, waiting for me to join her for the final round. Our real bout is set to start, the one with fists. There are no coins in this fight. We're going to stand and trade punches until one of us isn't standing any more.

I take my bloodstained hand from the wound on my side. I push myself off the wooden bench and walk to the middle to meet my adversary. I don't flinch when Mary raises her arms in front of her. I wait for the mallet to fall to signal the third and final round.

Smack!

There is a feeling-out process, cautious circling to get the measure of each other. When the mallet sounded, the action started, exciting the crowd for this thrilling encounter.

Mary hops from one foot to the other, ducking her head in and out and away from me, keeping enough distance between us so I can't reach her. Mary knows if I make contact with a blow from my right then the fight will surely be over before it even has a chance to get started, and she needs time to suss out my movements and her reach.

I throw a couple of quick punches with my left and bounce back to create space between us. Mary follows me everywhere I go. Like a baby suckling its mother, she smothers my movements around the stage.

I try a combination, two jabs with my left and then a right, but miss. Mary counters with some jabs of her own, catching my right cheek with a glancing blow. My head snaps back but I shake it off.

We mirror each other for a few minutes; one tries something and the other retaliates. Mary manages to strike me again on the right cheek with a quick left and I stumble backwards, taking my time to straighten. Mary quickly follows me, reaching out to grab me around the neck, but I see it coming. I side-step and punch Mary in the stomach, knocking the air from her lungs. As Mary doubles over, I hit her twice more before Mary spins around away from me. My turn to chase. This is my chance.

The crowd can sense the end and they all stand up to cheer me on.

'*Finish her!*'

Mary holds up her hands but I brush them away and punch Mary again and again and again. Finally, Mary's legs give way. Robert rushes on to the stage and shields her from further blows. Our fight is over.

I won.

I instinctively look over at Jimmy, who is standing and clapping along with the crowd. He meets my eyes, smiles at me and fist-punches the air. Sophie is jumping up.

Jimmy is at my side, then holds up my arm in victory. I let out an almighty bellow in celebration.

Jimmy beats Robert in a much quicker time. It is clear that Robert hadn't fought many serious fighters before. I watch Jimmy pick his opponent apart. James would have finished Robert in a matter of seconds. At the thought of James, a chill runs down my spine. *Are you here? Are you watching?* I hope he is. I proved him wrong.

After their defeat, Robert and Mary leave the stage swiftly, scurrying off before the Londoners can give them a piece of their minds. Jimmy and I stand side by side, enjoying the victory for a few minutes. Jimmy reaches for my hand. I look down at our clasped hands and, for once, I don't pull away.

'You did it,' he says, looking into my eyes.

I hold his gaze. 'We did.'

For the first time in my fighting career, I don't go out to celebrate. I plan on staying in and visiting Mrs Piddington in the morning. A wash is all the excitement this night is going to offer. Or so I thought.

Knock, knock.

I pick myself up off the bed and slowly make my way to the door. It is Jimmy, his hands behind his back.

'Good victory tonight,' he says. 'May I come in?'

I turn to the side, giving him enough space to enter, but not enough that he can't pass without brushing against my arm. He stops in front of me when we touch and looks at me. I close the door and clear my throat. 'You too.'

'You're not out celebrating?'

I shake my head. 'I don't feel up to it.'

'You'll have an even bigger entourage now.' He looks at me coyly.
I laugh at his joke. 'Not really.'

'I saw them, cheering you on, how they responded to you when
you came out tonight. You must have felt it, there on the stage.
You're a hero to them.'

'Do you know what people love more than a hero? A hero's fall.
That's why they come to see me fight. They can't wait for the day I
fail.' I roll my shoulder back and wince.

Jimmy reaches out to me. 'Is it bad?' His voice is full of genuine
concern. 'How is the cut doing?' He leaves and returns with
supplies: hot water, herbs and some fresh bandages. He sits down
in the chair and beckons me to stand in front of him. 'Raise your
arms,' he instructs. I do as I'm told, for once. I don't flinch at his
touch, quite the opposite. I notice how comfortable I am around
him.

He pulls up the loose piece of fabric, unpeeling the bloody linen,
and inspects my wound. I have to hold my shirt up so he can wrap
a clean bandage around my torso to keep the gash clean. 'It looks
shallow. You'll have a scar, but no long-lasting damage.'

When he's finished, we stay as we are for a few awkward
moments. Him seated, eyes level with my hips. Me, standing
between his legs, looking down at the top of his head. He coughs
and pushes the chair back to create room for me to step away.
Creating distance.

'Right, well, I will leave you to rest.' He picks up the bowl and
dirty rags. I haven't moved. Taking my silence as a sign, he turns
for the door.

CHAPTER 37

BANG. BANG. BANG.

We look at the door simultaneously. Jimmy answers.

'Big Red?' he says, but it's more a question.

'Where's Elizabeth?' the voice grunts.

Jimmy stands back, allowing the large man to enter. Big Red sighs. 'Alice Griffin has arrived in London,' he announces.

My interest is piqued. 'Already?'

Big Red nods. 'The magistrate plans on questioning her and the Piddingtons today. Thought you'd want to know.'

I freeze, my limbs suffering from the shock of hearing the words uttered by Big Red. I press my eyes shut, trying to comprehend what he is telling me. 'When?'

Big Red looks at Jimmy and then back at me. 'Piddingtons are there already. Alice is being brought to his house now.'

Jimmy's confusion is evident on his face. 'What's this about?'

I grab my coat and fly past him. He is at my heel. 'Elizabeth?'

I pause at the top of the stairs and turn to face Big Red. 'Why are you helping me? And how do you know all of this?' I ask, my eyes narrowing on the big man who always seemed indifferent towards me.

Big Red breathes in deeply. 'My loyalties have changed. I'm tired of doing his bidding. He's greedy and always changing the terms,' he explains, although without making clear who *he* is. Shaking his head, Big Red rubs his beard. '*Corrupt cunt.*'

'But you know who did,' I hear the magistrate state, before seeing him.

Knock. Knock.

Constable Clayton answers the door, giving me a tight-lipped smile. Not to my surprise, Mr and Mrs Piddington are here already, but not Alice herself.

'Ah! Mrs Stokes, right on time. I trusted Albert to deliver the message to you. Always so diligent, that man,' Magistrate Trelawny states, not bothering to hide his amusement. 'Mr and Mrs Piddington, please wait outside while I speak to Mrs Stokes. You too, constable.'

What? My mind reels at the revelation. The Piddingtons shuffle outside and Constable Clayton closes the door firmly behind them. My eyes flick side to side, trying to make sense of everything. 'Big Red ... He ... But Halfinch ... he works for you?' I can't seem to make my words come out clearly.

The magistrate's grin widens. 'Of course he does. You don't get to my position without joining forces with some lowly sorts ... and some higher placed ones. My connections go much further than you imagine, Elizabeth.' His lips remain curled. 'Take Vincent Love, for instance. You don't honestly think he was able to run a brothel in my ward and not pay me handsomely to turn a blind eye, do you? Of course, I didn't anticipate the boy's actions. That was ... *unfortunate.* But I couldn't let it go unpunished. My other ... *partners* wouldn't trust me, if I did.'

Unfortunate? Partners? Air escapes me and I can no longer breathe. 'Wh-Why? Why the boy? Why not some other poor sod whose life is meaningless! There are hundreds, if not thousands, you could have pinned Vincent's murder on! London is filled with evil, vile, worthless individuals! You could have taken your pick!' My voice booms within his office as I don't even try to hide my fury.

'Why? James Figg, of course. He saw the boy shoot Vincent. He followed your new husband, curious, I believe, about your relationship. He suspected Mr Stokes of trying to convince you to leave him to set up a rival amphitheatre. Needless to say, he wasn't happy about it. Felt you both ... ungrateful.'

My fists clench, my muscles tense and my chest heaves as I look at this pompous, *corrupt* man sitting across from me. Figg. He did this ... I gasp. *Corrupt.* Big Red said it himself. He also knew? He allowed this to happen? To Halfinch? I'll kill him. I'll kill them both. Right after I kill the magistrate. My life be damned. It is anyway. Always has been. I start towards him, my intentions on full display as I approach.

'Constable!' Magistrate Trelawny summons the lawman standing outside. He enters as I reach for the magistrate, yanking him from his chair. Arms circle around me and I am pulled back before I can take a swing at the wig-wearing criminal. Mr Piddington is also there trying to restrain my arms, but they are failing. I'm kicking and shouting, determined to break free, when I feel a whack across the back of my head. I fall to the floor, woozy from the blow. I blink as I brace myself against the rug, preventing myself from falling face first.

'What is this? What happened?' Constable Clayton barks – I think at me, but then I realise he is looking at the magistrate, who is straightening his wig and attire after my assault.

'Take her, she doesn't need to be here when Alice arrives and is arrested for murdering her husband. The Piddingtons have given me all I need to see her burn.'

I enter King's Coffee House in a trance. I have no idea how I got here. Big Red is in his usual seat at the bar. I pull his shoulder back and punch him, connecting with his jaw. His head snaps back. 'Oi!' he shouts, startled from my assault, and he spins off his chair, one hand holding his chin, the other raised up to halt my advance. 'What was that for?'

'You work for him!' I spit out, stepping forward again.

He drops his hand and exhales deeply, not defending himself against my next strike to his face, which hits his nose. He stumbles back and I hit him again, this time in his gut. He folds over, clutching his stomach.

'All right, enough!' he shouts. I stop, waiting to hear his explanation.

'I'll tell you what you want to know. I'm-I'm not happy with how this has all turned out ...' His voice breaks off, and I see it. The darkness under his red eyes, blotches all over his skin – mottled like stained paper. I know that look. The look that comes from trying to lose yourself and your mind at the bottom of a tankard. He's been punishing himself, just like I have.

I sigh, lifting my swollen hand to my face. After a moment, I pull out a stool and sink on to it. 'You'd think with the number of clientele this place churns through that they could afford to keep it in better state,' I remark, nodding towards the curling wallpaper behind the bar.

Big Red copies me, picking up his stool, which had been knocked over. He grunts, still rubbing his nose, which has turned a bright red, matching his cheeks. 'Not like The Black Hog tavern is any better.'

'Hmph,' I grumble. 'True. But at least they try to hide it with hanging pictures. Gin,' I order and the bartender, after seeing Big Red nod, stalks away to get my drink.

I look at Big Red, who raises his eyebrows at me. 'Should you be drinking?'

'No, should you?' I retort.

'No.'

The bartender returns and slides my drink my way. I give him money and raise the tankard slowly, relishing the smell of booze as I hold it to my mouth. I take a long gulp, closing my eyes, basking in the sensation of the cool liquid burning my throat as it trickles down to my belly.

I take a deep breath before refocusing my attention on Big Red, who's frowning at me. 'I'm sorry about your friend.'

I don't respond. There's nothing to say to that. We finish our drinks in silence and after we're done, Big Red stands.

I look back at him. 'You said you'd tell me what I want to know.'

He nods. 'And I will.'

'Now?'

He nods again, places his cap on his head and buttons his jacket. 'Follow me, Championess. I need to show you something.'

CHAPTER 38

ALICE SITS ON the floor of her cell in Newgate, her legs stretched out, her back resting against the wall. She smiles when she sees me.

I'm surprised at how calm Alice looks, her hands resting in her lap. She'd never seemed so comfortable in all the days of me knowing her. She almost looks ... relieved. Like a different woman.

'How did you know I was here?'

I cock my head to the side as if to say, *how could I not know?* By the next morning, the news of Alice's arrest over the brutal murder of her husband was all over London. There's been little other talk either in the coffee houses or in the gin shops and taverns around Covent Garden. And nothing Big Red has shown or told me can change her fate now.

'Have you spoken to Mrs Piddington?' I ask, knowing the answer already. The Mistress won't be able to look at Alice. Not after what they did. What they said to the magistrate. I close my eyes. *Stupid woman.* I'm referring to myself, not Mrs Piddington. I should never have allowed her to talk me out of reporting the death to the night watch. We could have avoided Trelawny, I should have spoken to Constable Boyle. He had access to the other magistrate. What was his name? Mildrum? I can't recall it now, but he might have helped. Might have been more impartial, less crooked. Maybe.

Alice shakes her head. 'She hasn't come to see me yet. I knew you'd come though,' she says, her voice soft as always, just like her. 'It's nice to see you, Elizabeth. I missed you. Your presence makes me feel strong. Like I can handle anything, even a painful death.'

Hearing Alice say she missed me was like a dagger to the stomach – excruciatingly gut-wrenching. I didn't think there was anything left to break after Halfinch died. But it seems the love I feel isn't just for him, it's for Alice, too. I dare say if anything happened to Sophie, I'd feel the same harrowing heartache. My mind drifts to Jimmy, worried how much heart space he's taken too. After spending so many years in the shadows cast by hate, who knew my heart was so big? Love so strong I have enough for not just one but a few people. I shake my head and sigh, as I lower myself to sit on the floor of the room, facing Alice through her cell. 'Did I ever tell you about the first time I hit someone?'

Once inside the Old Bailey, Alice's handcuffs and fetters are removed and she's taken into the courtroom.

Cases are tried in batches, with juries hearing half a dozen trials before retiring to consider their verdicts. There are over fifty prisoners defending themselves at trial over the next three days, but only one matters to me: Alice Griffin. The court, having heard the report of the conviction from the Old Bailey sessions, require little more than evidence of identification. The Keeper of Newgate provided that. The rest is merely formalities. I'm about to curse Mrs Piddington for her cowardice when she suddenly enters and joins me on the pew, awaiting Alice's case.

'Didn't think you'd have the audacity to show yourself,' I state, not looking at her when I spit the words out. They taste like vinegar.

'I didn't either,' Mrs Piddington replies eventually. 'We didn't say anything to incriminate Alice, just so you know. My husband merely confirmed the last time he saw her ... Seems that was enough for the Magistrate.' She looks downtrodden. 'I never knew that day I first met him would be the undoing of me.'

I feel a twang of sympathy for my old employer. A kindred feeling of utter exhaustion. We continue to sit, side-by-side, in silence.

The court building is open on one side to the weather; the upper floors are held up by Doric columns. A wall has been left out to increase the supply of fresh air, so that prisoners suffering from gaol fever don't infect others in court. I notice the herbs and scented flowers sprinkled around the courtroom, undoubtedly to mask the smell of the unwashed prisoners. There is a bench for judges at the far end, and, on both sides, partitioned spaces for jurors and balconies for court officers and privileged observers. Other spectators crowd into the yard. I spy Magistrate Trelawny among the aldermen, busy talking with one another. My body tenses. He's scanning the spectators as he does; he rests his eyes on me when he sees me, and smirks.

Arrogant bastard. Just you wait.

We sit on the far side of the courtroom from the court officers. No bloodied clothes for me today, no gin either, but a simple brown dress, a busted lip and one black eye still half closed from my fight against Mary Welch. My victory, and name, are known to all of London now, yet I came here to show support for Alice.

Shortly after the arrival of the Lord Mayor and Chief Magistrate, Sir Gerard Conyers, Alice's case is called. She makes a speech in her defence, which isn't a denial but rather a plea for mercy. She is asked why she killed her husband, choosing to stab him in the back rather than leaving to reside with family. She does her best to explain the abuse she suffered at the hands of her husband, saying she had been beaten and tortured by him one too many times. She deeply regrets his death, but couldn't handle any more pain. It simply became too much. She doesn't even remember killing him.

The memory of finding Henry Griffin's bloodied corpse on the floor of Alice's kitchen usurps the scene unfolding before me. There is outrage in the court. The despicable fashion in which Henry Griffin's body was found clearly does not sit well with the court officials, let alone the jurors, especially the knife in his back.

Alice's trial lasts less than an hour. The jury retire at the end of the day to consider their verdicts for the cases heard and when it comes to Alice, she is found guilty. The judgment is decided the next day by the Chief Magistrate. Mrs Piddington faints when the judgment is read out: 'Alice Griffin is to be drawn on a Hurdle, to the place of execution, and there to be burnt.'

It is the worse punishment that could have been given. I clasp my hands over my ears to silence the yelling in my head. I can't make it up the stairs to my room before my legs give in and my body begins heaving, throwing up whatever contents are in my stomach. The pain I feel is too much, much worse than any beating I'd suffered, and yet all too familiar since Halfinch died. It seems since his death my chest has been ripped open and I am unable to control any feeling I have – tears flow too easily now. Alice's fate could have been mine, if I had given in to the desire to kill Robert like I had always wanted. Craved.

Two arms encircle me and I care not if they are friend or foe. The anger I feel has finally pushed me over the edge and my body is capable of giving nothing more. A voice hushes me, a body rocks mine. It is over thirty minutes before I calm down enough to recognise the man sitting behind me on the stairs: Jimmy. I should have known by his smell – the slight woody tint, mixed with ale. A smell I've come to associate with comfort. I need this – someone to hold me. And Jimmy is always there.

His gentle voice whispers in my ear. 'I hate seeing you in pain. By the grace of God, I would take all of your suffering and make it my own.'

The streets are thronged with Londoners and outsiders alike, and all the windows are filled with faces eager to see the woman to be executed today. Even roof tiles are removed, creating a canopy of heads bursting from buildings overlooking the streets from Newgate to Tyburn. There are no hangings today, but there is to be death, a gruesome one, for the spectators.

I've watched hangings. I've seen death. But watching someone burn is something entirely different. Gruesome. I push my way through the crowds towards Tyburn and wait. In all directions, everyone from the man of leisure to the most ragged urchin is out to witness the spectacle. I spot a group of gentlemen laughing and drinking brandy, the tipple from France. It's popular among those who can afford it, but that doesn't include the likes of me. I stand with the masses and their lifeline is gin. I need a few drinks to get me through this day. I have to be here for Alice; I'm not sure whether Mrs Piddington will be able to stomach today. She collapsed after the sentencing alone. I duck into a gin shop and buy a bottle. A pot isn't enough.

It isn't long before I hear a roar, signalling the arrival of Alice. She's tied to a wattle fence panel, dragging along behind a horse, towards Tyburn. Her eyes are wide, full of fear and red from crying. She is begging for forgiveness, pleading for mercy. I squeeze my eyes shut and drop my head, fighting back my own tears at the sight of the desperate woman. I shake my head and drink a large gulp of gin, and then another. *The Tyburn Tree.* I didn't want to ever come back here after Halfinch's execution. But I can't abandon Alice now.

At Tyburn, Alice is secured to a stake, set in the ground a few yards from the gallows. An iron chain is wrapped around her body and a cord is put round her neck and passed through a hole bored in the stake. I watch as the executioner takes hold of the cord and stalks back behind Alice.

I push my way to the front, waving my arms, trying to get Alice's attention. But Alice is staring fixedly at someone else.

Mrs Piddington.

I'm relieved to see her, for once. I start pushing and shoving my way through the crowd to get to her. Mrs Piddington scarcely has time to notice me before I join her side, resting a hand on her shoulder. Mrs Piddington doesn't look at me, but clutches hold of my hand, rubbing the back of it with her thumb. She's shaking, sniffling back despair. 'Dear Lord, Elizabeth, how can this happen?'

My mute concession is apparent by the embrace I wrap around my former employer, my first impressions of and long-held disdain for the woman forgotten.

During our discussion, two cartloads of faggots have been piled around Alice and a signal is given to light the fire. The flames begin to devour the bundles of dry brushwood and Alice starts to cry out. 'Please! Oh God, have mercy! Please, please pull the rope!'

Alice begs the hangman to strangle her before the fire can reach her, but as he takes the end of the cord and starts pulling, the flames blow in his direction, forcing him to drop the rope.

'No!' I yell. Mrs Piddington is sobbing and the people's excitement turns to horror at the sound of Alice's screams. People think they're ready to watch someone die, but a hanging is much, much different to watching someone burn alive. I frantically look around and spot a large piece of wood. I pick it up and throw it as hard as I can at Alice. Mrs Piddington tries to stop me, grabbing at my arms. 'What are you doing?' she cries, sobbing so loudly it enhances my torment.

I push her off. 'Help me! Find something to knock her out with!' Mrs Piddington, confused at first, shakes her head. I look up at Alice, who is still screaming in agony and trying to squirm away from the burning faggots, but to no avail.

'Come on! Quick!' I shout again. This time, it works. Mrs Piddington picks up a stone and launches it at Alice's head. And then another person follows suit. In the end, the hangman himself throws a large piece of wood at Alice's head, breaking her skull, and Alice shrieks no more.

I watch, panting, as the fierce fire engulfs her body.

CHAPTER 39

IT IS OVER an hour before Alice's body is reduced to ashes. Jimmy helps me home and sits on the bed next to me, handing me a bottle of gin. He takes a swig and grimaces. 'Christ, that's disgusting.'

A second later, a knock comes at the door.

'It's open.'

Jimmy and I watch as Sophie and Big Red enter. Sophie takes the chair and Big Red takes his usual position leaning against the wall behind her. We all stay like that for a while, in silence, letting grief and pain and every other emotion wash over us until the gin is finished. I toss the empty bottle at a basket in the corner, missing; it bounces but doesn't break.

Jimmy jokes, 'It's a good thing your fights involve hitting people up close because your aim is terrible.'

I let a small grin spread across my face. Big Red and Sophie guffaw at his remark. I struggle to stand up, but make it to the table, where another gin bottle rests. 'Alice's death ... God, what kind of world allows that kind of ... She – she must have felt such ...' My voice fails me.

Jimmy remains seated. 'We know.'

London is lost. Its creator abandoned it long ago, together with all its inhabitants. Even God knows it's beyond saving. He tried to erase London in its entirety several times, first with the plague and then with the great fires. But, like me, I decide, this city is not going to be defeated. It takes the bad, uses it and returns stronger.

I turn to face Big Red. 'I'm ready. Let's go.'

Big Red, Mrs Piddington and I stand outside the derelict building, waiting for Constable Boyle and Magistrate Mildrum. Big Red, Mrs Piddington, Sophie and I all went to see Constable Boyle together. Told him he couldn't speak to Constable Clayton for fear he was loyal to Magistrate Trelawny. Constable Boyle assured us he wasn't, but after much persuading he reluctantly agreed to our request to bring the magistrate from the next ward over to meet us here.

The sign carved above the door is now illegible, but Big Red told me it's an old warehouse previously used to store crates that come off the ships. But as I now know, it stores stolen goods for Magistrate Trelawny. With a great number of highwaymen, pickpockets, housebreakers, shoplifters and other thieves, he used them, playing London's criminals off against one another and the authorities in a web of conspiracy and cunning, to account with him for their robberies. He'd then conceal their booty, after persuading the owners to set rewards for their retrieval – a main source of his profitable wealth. It seems only fitting that he now be arrested for receiving stolen goods.

I look at Mrs Piddington, then at Big Red, who watches the magistrate, constable and a few beadles look around the stacks of items.

'And you say Magistrate Charles Trelawny is responsible?' Magistrate Mildrum asks, shocked at what lies before him. Big

Red gives a curt nod. Mrs Piddington also confirms after spotting several items missing from her shop. Horrified, she spins to face Big Red. 'Why didn't you speak up before?'

Big Red lifts his shoulders to ears, casts his eyes downward and thrusts his hands into his pockets, as if an answer can be pulled from deep inside his trousers. 'Didn't think anyone would listen...' His eyes rise to meet mine, 'Until Elizabeth.'

I stare at Big Red. There is nothing to be said. He and I have been over this before. There are so many things we both could have done – no, should have done differently. Things we should have said. But courage is a strange thing: you only realise you have it when you put yourself in a position to need it. It's easy to lie to yourself, to tell yourself that you don't want to hurt others... but more often than not, the reality is that we don't want to bear the consequences of our choices. The lies we tell — or in this case, the truths we didn't voice – don't protect others, they protect ourselves.

'My God ...' Constable Boyle utters, horrified that a magistrate could be so conniving and be responsible for sending so many people to the gallows. Mrs Piddington shakes her head and exits the warehouse.

'I never liked that man,' Magistrate Mildrum states, his eyes still focused on the door Mrs Piddington fled through. I follow his gaze.

'Not many do,' I whisper.

EPILOGUE

BIG RED SAVED me the day Halfinch died. Even if it damned him forever, he ended Halfinch's suffering quickly. He also helped secure the arrest of Magistrate Trelawny, who was sentenced to death shortly thereafter, and for that I am eternally grateful. Several witnesses chose to stand at his trial to give evidence against him, including my old employer, Sarah Piddington.

As Charles Trelawny was transported to the Tree, a huge, hostile crowd showed up to watch him hang, pelting him with rotten fruit and eggs and howling for his blood when the executioner took his time hanging him.

I chose not to attend his death. Instead, Jimmy, Big Red, Sophie, Betty, Sarah and I sat in The Black Hog having a drink, and spoke of Halfinch and Alice. Sharing stories and reminiscing of brighter days.

Life didn't become routine immediately. It took years for me, for all of us, to reconcile ourselves to the loss of Stephen Hatfield, or Halfinch as he had been so affectionately known to those who knew him well enough, and then Alice. I became the best female fighter in London but failed to save not one but two friends. Years passed but the emptiness remains. The useless questions remained too. What would have happened if I had not joined Figg's Boarded House? Would Halfinch still be alive if I hadn't asked him to live with me? There are so many variations of how things could have turned out. Self-reflection can be useful, but it can also be hurtful, often at the same time. Utterly pointless too. Nothing can be undone. The past has passed, as Alice once told me.

I look across at Jimmy like I do every morning as he drinks his coffee – which I enjoy much more than tea – and reads the daily paper. He's taught me how to manage my money and we opened our training gym for children at Sadler's Wells, teaching them the arts of self-defence. I wish Halfinch could have seen it, could have experienced it, yet I know that somehow he is still part of it. Jimmy handles the management while I run most of the training. Jimmy never loses his temper with me, though I've tested him on more than one occasion. I still wonder sometimes how such a man exists, especially one who sees me as a person, before the fighter. I can dish out a beating on a stage, but nothing can protect you from the hurt and turmoil that accompanies the death of a loved one. It's the unseen injuries that cause the most damage, the deepest scars.

And yet, despite my many flaws, Jimmy has stuck around. He stood by my side through those dark days after Halfinch's death, and then Alice's. Not letting me flirt too long with the darkness of gin that threatened to pull me under, always pulling me back before I fell over the ledge. And there were many, many dark days. Many ledges. Jimmy is always there, constantly proving me wrong whenever I think I've pushed him away once and for all. He comes back to me, ever faithful.

We bought a house a few months after Alice's death. And married shortly thereafter, making my name official. Jimmy gave me time to grieve first. I appreciated that space.

We live a quiet life. Our home is small but it is just the two of us for now. There is a small front room and a kitchen on the ground floor, with two bedrooms on the first floor. Coffee replaced gin. Soft-spoken words are exchanged, rather than insults and challenges. The best part is waking in the same bed next to the same man every day.

Sophie and Big Red are happy. We see them as often as we are able, but we live different lives. Sophie cooks and cares for their son, Stephen. She's a natural mother. I have a strong feeling that it won't be long before another baby is on the way.

Apparently, Constable Boyle told Jimmy of Halfinch's request of me to hasten his death. They'd agreed I couldn't live with that guilt. Jimmy volunteered, but in the end it had been Big Red who did the unbearable. My appreciation for that remains unspoken.

Jimmy throws me a look across the kitchen table and then quickly stands, taking the paper with him. He normally leaves the paper for me to read while he finishes his coffee and breakfast, so his sudden movement puts me on guard. It has been so long since I felt the hot rush of blood flood my veins and rapid heartbeats in my chest.

'What it is?' I ask him.

'You've been challenged.'

He slaps the paper on to the ledge near the sink, finishes his coffee and turns to face me. He watches me to see how I react to the news. I don't, because I don't believe it. It's been years since I last fought in a boxing bout; no one was stupid enough to challenge me after my brutal defeat of Mary Welch. We fought a rematch with weapons again after Alice died. I knew Halfinch would have wanted me to and I dedicated my victory to him. And I'm never the one to back away from a fight, especially not with that Irish wench. I never actually retired, I just stopped going to the fights. The challenges stopped. At least, until today.

And yet Jimmy appears deadly serious.

'Who?'

He takes a deep breath and places his hands on his hips.

'Ann Field,' he answers, 'of Stoke-Newington.'

I shrug, not recognising the name, which says all I need to know. The woman is either desperate or has a death wish. But even as I think it, I know there is more to this than just the challenge itself. I can tell by the way Jimmy holds my gaze. He is concerned, and that isn't like him. A few years ago, I never would have rejected a challenge, but if Jimmy feels so strongly about me fighting again then I don't have to. We have our own life together now, and I've proven my ability to Jimmy, to London, to my young friend Halfinch and, most importantly, myself. All those years I fought for survival, then for love and then for me.

Jimmy comes to my side and crouches down beside me. 'I know you, Elizabeth. You're a fighter, the *Championess* ...' His eyes light up. 'You'll accept this challenge. And you'll win. It's who you are. It's who you've always been.' He isn't telling me what to do. His words pique my interest. Why is he so sure I'll want to fight? I don't know who Ann Field is nor do I care that she wants to fight me. Jimmy sighs. 'Elizabeth, Ann Field is one of *his* fighters. *He* claims she's the best fighter he's ever trained.'

Ah. I don't have to ask who Jimmy is talking about. *Figg.*

He's right. I am going to accept this challenge. And I'll beat Ann Field into the ground. There will be no doubt as to who the best female prize fighter is.

CHALLENGE - Whereas I, Ann Field of Stoke-Newington, ass-driver, well known for my abilities in boxing in my own defence wherever it happened in my way, do fairly invite Mrs. Stokes, styled the European Championess, to a trial of the best skill in boxing, for 10 pounds, fair rise and fall; and question not but to give her such proofs of my fall; and question not but to give her such proofs of my judgment that shall oblige her to acknowledge me Championess of the Stage, to the entire satisfaction of all my friends.

ANSWER - I, Elizabeth Stokes, of the City of London, have not fought in this way since I fought the famous boxing-woman of Billingsgate 29 minutes, and gained a complete victory (which is six years ago); but as the famous Stoke-Newington ass-woman dares me to fight her for the 10 pounds, I do assure her I will not fail meeting her for the said sum, and doubt not that the blows which I shall present her with, will be more difficult for her to digest than she ever gave her asses!

I feel only pride, passion, fury.

I might not be a regular in the prize-fighting world any more, but that doesn't seem to matter. My reputation is known and the public still long for entertainment. They've not forgotten me. As I enter the stage at Sadler's Wells, the crowd roars. It seems bigger than I remember, or perhaps I'm just appreciating it for the first time.

I look at the woman who challenged me. Ann Field's hair is stapled to her scalp, blouse tied tightly to her upper body, her skirt swaying to follow the dance of her legs. She holds her fists in front of her, ready for battle.

I search the stands and find my mark. James Figg stands with his arms crossed. His eyes are dark as they stare down his crooked nose back at me.

The crowd is cheering and it brings me back to my opponent. The faces in the crowd are mostly unfamiliar but they clearly know me, if not personally then by reputation. I find Sophie's face. She isn't concerned for my safety. She sits with Big Red who holds their son, Stephen. While she chants with the rest of the audience – 'Elizabeth! Elizabeth!' – Big Red does not. Ever the silent bear of a man that he is.

It's a bittersweet realisation, to be back here, without Halfinch, without Alice.

I open my hands and look at the centre of my palms. I think of my friends and roll my fingers into tight fists. I recall the last words Halfinch shouted out before his death: 'by force and arms'. This woman is going to fall. I nod to my challenger.

Elizabeth Wilkinson-Stokes, London City Championess, is back on the stage.

I feel the sweat trickle down the side of my face, the vibrations from the audience pulsing through my limbs as I wait for it to begin.

Ding!

The bell chime echoes in my ears. The sweet sound I am so accustomed to. I take one last look around the cheering audience, using their chants to fuel me. With a deep breath I move forward, fists raised.

Here we go.

THE END

Acknowledgements

It takes a patient and supportive team to help a writer realise their dream of publishing a finished novel, and I am so grateful for all of the wonderful people in my life who helped me achieve mine.

Special thanks go out to:

My girls, Eloise and Mia, my world – everything I do is in the hope of giving you a better life and being a positive role model for you both. Mummy loves you so much.

My husband, who always has my back and is my pillar of strength in times of need – your support and encouragement mean more than you know. I love you.

My dad, Frank, the first man I ever loved, who told me about Elizabeth Wilkinson-Stokes and has been such a positive influence in my life, and is the ultimate story-teller.

My mum, Miriam, my fiercest supporter, who read countless drafts for me and encouraged me to follow my dream of writing.

My big bro, who is always there for me and taught me the importance of creating art for oneself rather than others. He also created a kick-ass website for me too!

Kiana Palombo, and the Whitefox Publishing team, for their support and guidance on this publishing journey. Special shout out to Kiana who had the pleasure of holding me to account and responding to my numerous questions and emails! You're the best lady.

Jenni Davis, editor extraordinaire, who helped copy-edit my writing, and with whom I enjoyed full-blown conversations all through comment boxes in my manuscript. She challenged me, corrected me and was a great support in finalising my story edits. Love your work and words.

Donna Hillyer, who proofread my story and helped pick up errors, typos and inconsistencies the rest of us missed!

Emma Ewbank, who prepared the cover design, putting up with my indecision but ultimately brought my vision to life.

Jamie Whyte, for creating a beautiful map of London during 1720 for readers.

Monica Chakraverty, and the Cornerstones Team, for their help in the structural edit and encouraging me to finish the damn book! Monica, my time with you was one of the best and most enlightening times in my book-writing life! You are an amazing woman.

My readers – I'm so humbled you picked up my book. I hope you enjoyed it. From the bottom of my heart, from one book lover to another, thank you. #justkeepreading

www.ingramcontent.com/pod-product-compliance
Ingram Content Group UK Ltd.
Pitfield, Milton Keynes, MK11 3LW, UK
UKHW030643040325
4842UKWH00027B/165

9 781916 797604